A COUNTERFEIT BETROTHAL

SCOUTS OF THE GEORGIA FRONTIER
BOOK ONE

DENISE WEIMER

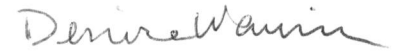

Copyright © 2023 by Denise Weimer

All rights reserved. No portion of this book may be reproduced or transmitted in any form or by any means - photocopied, shared electronically, scanned, stored in a retrieval system, or other - without the express permission of the publisher. Exceptions will be made for brief quotations used in critical reviews or articles promoting this work.

The characters and events in this fictional work are the product of the author's imagination. Any resemblance to actual people, living or dead, is coincidental.

Unless otherwise indicated, all Scripture quotations are taken from the Holy Bible, Kings James Version.

Cover design by Evelyne Labelle at Carpe Librum Book Design.
www.carpelibrumbookdesign.com

ISBN-13: 978-1-942265-81-8

CHAPTER 1

Late November 1813
Jackson County, Georgia

The unmistakable tang of smoke in the air stiffened Jared Lockridge's spine as he urged his big red roan down the ridge that cradled the Apalachee River. Not just a little, either, as one would expect from a chimney or even a campfire. Drawing back on the reins, he scanned the treetops. There, to the north—a sooty fingerprint against the purpling twilight sky gave evidence of trouble.

He'd already steeled himself against overnighting at his brother's nearby cabin, stuffing his growling stomach on his brother Noble's new wife's cornbread. The report he bore should be carried straightaway to his commander at Fort Daniel. In counties to the south, there'd been two attacks in early November by Creek Indians allied to the British. Those incidents verified Major Terrell's intelligence from Indian Agent Benjamin Hawkins—the Red Stick Creeks had indeed been recruiting in the Upper Creek towns and could soon be pressing all the way up the Jackson Line. The line Jared was paid to scout.

Could the fire be more evidence of Creek war parties? This far north? He couldn't ignore the possibility—or that of a settler in need of assistance.

Jared kneed his stallion toward the smoke. Within minutes, he caught sight of flames dancing between the trees. In the center of a clearing, a cabin was burning. Instinct begged him to charge up to the homestead in case anyone needed rescuing, but wisdom whispered caution.

He dismounted and tethered Chestnut to a low-hanging branch, palming his loaded Springfield. He approached the house slowly, at a crouch. Who lived here? If memory served, a feisty Scot named Andrews. Jared had only seen the man once or twice, in the Hog Mountain settlement that surrounded the fort, and his off-putting manner had called for distance. Andrews had appeared amply able to protect himself.

At the tree line, Jared froze. The settler's massive frame lay sprawled face down before his front porch, unmoving, a Brown Bess inches from his fingers. An arrow projected from his back. Indians, then. No sight of them around the cabin, the front of which was engulfed in flame.

There was no barn, but a movement between woodshed and corncrib caught his eye. A taller figure pulling on a shorter one. A woman.

"Stop!" Jared ran toward the struggle and skidded to a stop in the clearing, seeking a line of sight. Just as he shouldered his musket, the man—in a buckskin hunting shirt and leggings, his long, dark hair flying loose—sprinted for the forest.

The shot from Jared's musket rang out, but the intruder had already blended into the shadows.

Breath coming fast, gaze darting for evidence of other assailants, Jared ran to the woman—or she might be a girl, she was so small. She had sunk almost to her knees, her weight against the woodshed.

"Are you all right?"

"Y-yes."

"Anyone in the house?"

A rapid shake of her head.

He dropped to one knee and reached for another powder cartridge on his belt. "Are there more? More Indians?"

Her answer came, tremulous, strangled. "I ... I don't know. I only saw the one."

Weapon reloaded, Jared stood. "Stay here. I'll check."

Dark eyes met his, enlarged in a pale oval face, and she nodded.

Moving into the fringe of trees, Jared circled the perimeter. No sign of anyone, or even of the recent presence of horses. He made his way into the yard, the heat of the fire warming his side as he knelt to press a finger to Andrews's throat.

The young woman came forward, shoulders slumped, wringing her hands. "Is he...?"

"He's gone, ma'am." He rose as she neared. "Are you a relation?"

"I am...I was...his wife." She stared at Andrews a moment, no expression on her face. Not shock. Not grief. Not even anger. Then she dropped her head. Were her lips moving? Had the evening's events unhinged her?

Bending to pick up the Brown Bess, Jared swallowed. "I'm sorry for your loss. I'm also afraid it's too late to save your cabin."

"I don't wish to save it." The hardness in her reply drew him up short.

"Is there anything inside you want?"

She turned to him, her voice small and uncertain now, clasping her hands before her. "A small chest on the trestle. And my clothes, on pegs by the back door."

He nodded. "Let's see what can be done."

She followed him around to the back of the rough-built cabin—not nearly so nice as Noble's, the bark not cleaved from the outside logs. "You mustn't endanger yourself."

"I'll be quick." When Jared glanced back, her uneven gait drew a concerned query from him, along with a touch to her arm. "Are you hurt?" He nodded toward her feet.

She pressed her skirt down and lowered her chin. "I'm fine."

Her manner smacked of deception. Jared narrowed his gaze on her. What was she hiding? "There is nothing else I should seek?" Had Andrews really brought a young bride here to live in such a hardscrabble fashion?

"I have nothing of value, Mr...."

"Lockridge. Jared Lockridge."

"Mr. Lockridge." Still she kept her eyes down. "But my clothing and my herb box are needful, if you please."

"Then I will do my best to fetch them." He handed her both muskets and bolted up the steps to the rear entrance.

Barred, of course. He drew his tomahawk and chopped until he could get a hand inside to lift the latch. Cinders flurried down and flames whooshed and crackled as the door sprang open. Fire consumed the front half of the cabin. The wood-thatched roof could cave at any moment. Trapping a deep breath in his chest, he lunged for the box she'd described on the trestle, then gathered an armful of garments on his way back out. In the dirt clearing well back from the fire, he knelt and deposited the items at her feet.

"Thank you." The woman placed the guns beside him and reached for a woolen cloak.

Jared rose as she swung the garment around her, and he swallowed hard. For her linen dress hung on her frame as loosely as it might on a stick scarecrow, and her collar bones protruded as she secured the clasp of the cloak. As small-boned as she was, she was older than he'd originally thought, perhaps two or three years his senior.

"What's your name?" And...was that a bruise on her cheek?

A tremendous crash came from behind him as the roof fell, flames shooting toward the dusky sky like some bonfire in a war camp. The woman stared at the inferno a moment, her lips pressed together. In the orange light, she looked other-worldly. Rather than cringing or wailing as most women might, she switched her disheveled dark-brown braid over her back and lifted her chin. At last, she met his eyes.

"Esther Venable Andrews. Andrews no longer."

The pronouncement raised half a dozen questions he couldn't voice. One had to be asked. "Mrs. Andrews, have you any kin nearby?"

Her throat worked. "I have no one. My father, Thomas Venable, is dead. He was James Killian's partner at the trading post."

"Thomas Venable...indeed, I remember the man. He was still there when my brother, Noble, and I first arrived here last spring." But barely, for his stained kerchief had been ever at hand to staunch the unsightly effects of his frequent coughing. He must've died of consumption. "We went in to stock up on supplies. But I don't recall seeing you."

"I was there, working on the account books in the back. I often helped the men in that way." The piercing howl of a wolf from the far ridge made Mrs. Andrews start—more reaction than she'd given to anything thus far.

He placed a hand on her elbow, but she jerked back. "We should bury him." He spoke gently.

She blinked. "With what? The only tool left is the ax on the stump." She gestured to the other side of the woodshed.

Night devoured the twilight by the second. "The fire should keep the predators at bay tonight. You can come home with me for now, and I'll return at dawn to see to the task."

She stepped back as if he'd slapped her. "I cannot go with you, sir."

He spread out his hand. "You propose to stay here?" When tears filled her eyes, he gentled his tone. "Perhaps you know your neighbors?"

Mrs. Andrews shook her head. "Liam, my husband, did, but I did not." She covered her mouth as the desperation of her situation seemed to finally hit her. "Oh, what shall I do?"

Jared took a half step forward. "You'll let my sister-in-law see to your needs. I share a cabin with my brother and his bride a short ride from here."

Her gaze swung to him. "You have a horse?"

He jerked his chin toward the woods. "Tethered just over there. I realize the events of this night have been traumatic, Mrs. Andrews, but it seems you must trust me. No harm will befall you on my watch. We'll sort everything out at the cabin with Noble and Tabitha."

Their names appeared to give them substance and thus to calm her. She rolled her clothing around her wooden box, tucked it under her arm, and nodded.

Silence claimed Esther Venable Andrews as Jared bore her home, plans of reporting to the fort relegated to the morrow. The woman did not once look back. She sat as erect as a small person could while straddling such a large, moving horse. Jared tried to give her as much space as possible, merely bracing her with his arms. She gripped the front of the saddle and stared straight ahead. Even the small, scampering sounds of the forest and the wind rustling through drying leaves did not induce her to peer at either side of the three-foot-wide trail.

Questions rose and stuck in his throat, burning as he held them back. What had happened in the minutes leading up to his arrival? Clearly, the Indian had shot her husband, likely when Andrews threatened him with his musket from the porch. But how had Mrs. Andrews gotten outside? How had the fire started? And why had the Indian not harmed her—or dragged her off with him into the night, even after Jared arrived? Why had the Indian been alone? The widow's posture told him now was not the time to ask. Perhaps Mrs. Andrews would respond to his sister-in-law's soft voice, the warmth of a hearth fire, and a cup of tea.

Jared took it upon himself to tell her about his family in hopes that such knowledge would ease her. He made his voice soft, conversational.

"Noble is two years older than I and has already taken a bride. He went back to Augusta to wed her this winter past. He married above his station with Tabitha, for sure and certain." He gave a brief chuckle. "I'm not sure she finds the frontier to her liking, but she is learning. Being teachable is half the battle out here...that and having good neighbors. We share a simple cabin now, a little bigger than yours was, but Noble promised her that one day, he will build her a fine house. Not quite so fine as Elisha Winn's, perhaps, but something like it. With fancy moldings and double chimneys, not of creek stone but quarried by John Hill. Have you seen Winn's house? Half a mile from the river, south of here."

The barest shake of her head provided him answer.

He scanned the openings in the trees. "We share four-hundred acres as a start here, bounty land granted our father for his service in the War for Independence."

At the small sound she made—one of admiration?—Jared clamped his mouth shut. He planned to build his own cabin next year, if the war with the Creeks allowed. It was why he scouted for General Frederick Beall and Major John Dabney Terrell, why he'd chosen to enlist officially, to become "first class" when the federal government had called up the state militias. He would earn a reputation he could build a future on. Unlike his father. But he'd not tell a stranger that failure and shame, not glory, had driven them here.

∽

The heat from the man behind her caused chills to travel down Esther's body. Only that uncomfortable awareness kept her brain from shutting down, for she did so want to lapse into a daze, to find an end to her churning thoughts.

This Jared Lockridge's family was above hers, even above her mother's kin from Augusta—that much was evident from his speech, his manners, his plans for his future. And from the house he brought her to—of local logs, true, but with the bark planed off, two shuttered windows, and large enough to hold an extra room inside. Several sturdy outbuildings clustered around the cabin, the cluck of chickens and bark of a dog sounding a greeting.

Jared spoke again as they entered the clearing. "I usually hail them, so don't be alarmed." He raised his hand to his mouth. "Halloo, the house!"

She still jumped but likewise marveled at his thoughtfulness in warning her.

The door flung open, and figures framed in firelight spilled out, including a massive canine whose bark made Esther's heart pound.

"Duchess, heel," the man said, and the dog sat at his feet.

"Is she safe?" Esther whispered to Jared.

A deep chuckle broke from his chest. "Not at all safe, but she will be to you if you heed my instruction."

Heeding instruction...that she was good at. Jared swung down, then offered her his hand. She stared at him a moment, shoved her bundle into his arms, and scrambled down from the roan stallion on her own. Heeding instruction did not mean he had to touch her. When her lame foot—the malady that had caused her mother's death in childbed, according to her father

—turned under her, he caught her, and she jerked upright, folding her cloak about her.

"Brother, good to see you after your long scout. You bring us a guest." The man came forward, his dark-haired wife trailing him with her hand on her middle, but the dog remained on the porch. At a rumble from its chest, Esther's feet locked in place.

Returning her clothing to her arms, Jared bent his head closer to hers. He smelled of pine, smoke, and horse. "Duchess will welcome you if she sees you're one of us. But you must do your best to appear unafraid. Here, take my arm."

One of them? What a strange thought. She was not one of anything or anyone, never had been. But under the watchful eyes of the canine, Esther slid the tips of her fingers into the crook of the elbow Jared offered. He led his horse forward with his other hand.

"This is Mrs. Esther Venable Andrews. She has need of our hospitality. I found her cabin burning and her husband shot by a native downriver."

His words evoked a flash of memories, too unbelievable to be true—the Indian's hand on her mouth stifling her cry, his whispered warning, Liam calling from the porch as he set the lantern at his feet.

A gasp came from the woman, jerking Esther back to the present, and she hurried forward to lay her delicate hand on Esther's arm. "Oh, you poor dear. Of course, you must stay, take some nourishment, and rest."

"Thank you. I am sorry to impose. I...had no place else to go." She couldn't look at the woman, who even in this dim light appeared perfect. Like a china doll Esther had once seen in their competitor's—Moore's—trading post.

"I am Tabitha Lockridge, and this is my husband, Noble. You are most welcome here."

"I'll take your horse, Jared. You see Mrs. Andrews inside." Noble stepped forward and reached for the roan's reins. He was

9

an inch or two shorter than his younger brother, though still tall. Almost six feet, she'd guess. As much as Esther would have preferred Tabitha to show her in, the massive, bay-colored mastiff with her black-masked face made her tighten her grip on Jared's elbow as they ascended to the porch. He bent to pet the beast. Esther's knees jellied, but Duchess's thick tail thumped out a rhythm on the boards beneath her.

Sparing a quick glance at Esther, the dog darted around them to follow her master to the stable.

Releasing a shaky breath, Esther dropped her hand to her side.

Jared winked at her. "She'll get used to you."

His gesture, so familiar, so relaxed, had the opposite effect than what he'd intended. Everything in Esther tightened up. How had she ended up at this man's home? The very man who, when she'd first seen him at the trading post, had made her yearn for some say in her own future? Instead, with her father on his deathbed, she'd been forced to choose between his lecherous, aged partner and the settler who'd deceived her into thinking he'd care for her.

Such a man, with the laugh lines beside his mouth and his golden hair glinting in the cabin's firelight, could be nothing but trouble. If Liam and his false kindness had fooled her, what hidden dangers did Jared Lockridge's charming exterior conceal?

CHAPTER 2

The place at the table where Tabitha bid Esther sit offered a good view of the lady of the house as she adjusted the iron arm holding the kettle and a Dutch oven over the fire. The flickering light danced over Tabitha's rosy cheeks, bright eyes, and gently rounded form. She was indeed perfect. What was more, she was pregnant. A firm mound under the waist of her skirt beneath her linsey-woolsey short gown proclaimed her state without a doubt.

Esther turned her face away.

While this was hardly a fancy home, comfort and care surrounded the occupants as warmly as an embrace. Not only was the trestle at which she sat finely made, sanded, and polished, but nearby, a substantial work station rested below open shelving, and, amazingly, a ladder-back chair and a rocker had been placed before the hearth. They'd had only rough benches at the cabin Liam had built. A ladder led to a loft, while a wall separated another room. A hutch against that wall displayed pewter and pearlware dishes in a blue floral pattern Esther had never seen before. And the puncheon floor...why, a body could walk barefoot across it and encounter nary a speck of dirt.

After propping the muskets against the wall, Jared laid his floppy-brimmed hat on the table, then lifted the straps of his powder horn and hunting pouch from across his torso. As he strung them over the ladder-backed chair, Tabitha addressed him.

"Take the rocker, Jared." She lifted a carved wooden box down from a shelf. "Noble won't mind."

"I admit, I've been many days in the saddle. Perhaps I will, just for the moment."

Tabitha looked up from shaving tea from the block she'd brought out of the box. "You made the piece, after all."

This farmer had crafted such an intricate chair? Esther couldn't hide a flash of surprise. She'd assumed he was a farmer with his many acres, yet what had he been doing riding north along the river at twilight? And on what he claimed had been a long journey? Despite the light color of his hair—cropped just below his ears and scattering his jaw with a fine bristle—he looked more like a native in his fringed linen hunting shirt, buckskin leggings, and moccasins.

He eased himself into the rocker. His broad-shouldered body filled it, and he extended his long legs toward the flames with a sigh. The gap between tunic and leggings exposed muscular thighs.

Esther looked away.

Curved wood squeaked as Jared rocked gently. "Have you any cornbread, Tabitha?"

She sent him an indulgent smile. "I do, and squirrel stew besides. It's already heating."

Jared's sudden cough covered a laugh. Why would that be funny? Esther looked between them, but Tabitha's brows drew together. Some amusement at Tabitha's expense, then?

Tabitha glared at Jared before pointedly asking Esther, "Will you take some stew, Mrs. Andrews?"

As empty as they were, her innards churned at the notion of partaking of meat. "Thank you, but no. Although I'm sure it is delicious." She hastened to add this last in support of her hostess. How many times had Liam criticized the meals she'd labored over for hours at a hot hearth?

"Some cornbread, then." Tabitha hurried forward with golden squares nestling inside a folded-back cloth.

Jared urged Esther when she hesitated. "Best cornbread in Jackson County."

She took a piece into the palm of her hand, thanking her hostess.

"I will bring your tea straightaway to wash it down." Tabitha turned to her brother-in-law with the larger remaining slice.

He received it with an appreciative assessment. "Needs no tea."

"You'd prefer something stronger, perhaps?"

Jared shook his head and bit into the bread, speaking around his first mouthful. "Moist enough as is." At least the man was complimentary of the bread.

Tabitha chuckled. "Owed to an alarming excess of lard."

Esther nibbled the corner of her serving. As the rich texture melted on her tongue, her stomach rumbled, and she finished the cornbread in a few quick bites. She looked up to find Jared watching her. Her face heated, but Tabitha reaching for pearlware cups in the hutch claimed her notice.

Esther raised her voice to carry across the room. "Oh, please, don't trouble yourself on my account." That these fine people would serve her as though she were a distinguished guest made her want to sink between the floorboards.

"Nonsense. I always take my tea in these. A woman must have her comforts in this wilderness, after all."

Esther ducked her head. The dishes she'd shared with Liam

had been buckeye, and he'd been right proud of those. But a memory flashed of Aunt Temperance in Washington, entrusting her five-year-old niece with a real china cup for the first time. She'd felt so special that day.

Tabitha snipped cane sugar from a cone into the bottom of three cups. Esther didn't dare protest although she couldn't imagine such regular indulgences.

Jared leaned his head back and rocked. Perhaps he would stay like that, not looking at her. She much preferred it. That she owed her rescue to such a fine gentleman—to any man—galled her. But the crackling of the fire relaxed her, and despite herself, her heart warmed with gratitude as Tabitha set a cup in front of her on the table.

She'd just raised it to her lips for a tentative sip when the front door flew open. A growl sent her cup clanging back onto her saucer. She whirled around to find Noble smacking Duchess's broad head. The growling desisted, but the damage was done. A trickle of tea appeared on Esther's saucer.

"Oh no!" She had chipped the base of the teacup, and a hairline crack spread up the side. "I'm sorry, so sorry."

"It's of no account." Tabitha rushed for another cup.

"Please, not the fine ones." Esther tucked her hands in her lap. "I fear I shake too much."

"Oh, you poor dear. Of course, you do. I should have thought of that."

Esther's brow furrowed. Her hostess would take the blame upon herself rather than spearing her with the disgusted glare she deserved? She'd never met a woman so young and lovely and yet so compassionate. That she might be in the company of a true lady made her stomach knot all the more.

Tabitha selected a tin cup and hurried to her side. She deftly transferred the hot liquid, then took up her damaged pearlware. Liam had always said Esther had no need of fine things. Here was proof.

"I am so sorry." Esther sought to meet the other woman's eyes. Hopefully, Tabitha sensed the sincerity of her regret.

Tabitha laid a hand on her shoulder. "Please, speak no more of it."

Noble took a seat in the ladder-back chair, and the mastiff curled at his feet.

Esther tried not to tense as he looked at her. "Perhaps, Mrs. Andrews, you can tell us what happened before my brother arrived at your home."

She nodded, wrapping her hands around her cup. Maybe the warmth would still their trembling. "I went out to get wood, and when I looked up, the Indian Mr. Lockridge saw stood before me."

Noble cocked his head. "Was he arrayed for battle?"

What did he mean?

Noble must've seen the question in her expression, for he added, "Feathers? War paint?"

"His face was not painted, though I got only the barest glimpse of him. When I cried out, he put his hand over my mouth and pulled me against him." She shuddered. She could still smell the sweat and bear grease, feel the hardness of the man's lean, muscled body.

Jared sat up straighter. "You hadn't seen him before?"

"Not that I recall. There were many Indians who came into my father's post. I did not deal with them close up, so they all looked much alike to me. Although...there were incidents when I felt I was being watched. Even that afternoon." That she'd gathered herbs at the river which divided their land from Cherokee Territory had sparked Liam's ire. He'd never wanted her to go out of sight of the cabin. When she'd told him of a suspicious bird call, he'd taken it as justification for his strict rules. Maybe his demands held some validity, if not genuine concern. Had the same brave been lying in wait? "I thought it might have been my father's

15

old partner, who had wished to wed me, but now I am not so sure."

Jared frowned at her, expression so intense that a chill shivered down her back. Then his gaze flicked over to meet Noble's, and he provided explanation as Tabitha handed him a bowl of stew. "Mrs. Andrews's father was Thomas Venable."

"That would make James Killian the man you feared." Noble pinched the high, thin bridge of his nose. "Understandable. Shall we merely say that his reputation goes before him?"

Jared made a sound of disgust low in his throat but did not look up from his stew.

Esther dipped her head, grateful she need not explain this one thing, at least.

Noble drummed his fingers on his leg. "Then what happened? Did the native try to take you away?"

"He...spoke."

Tabitha turned to her with wide eyes. "What did he say?"

"*I-gi-do.*"

Jared narrowed his gaze upon her. "Sister? That's Cherokee."

"Yes. I picked up enough when I worked at the post to understand him."

"Why would he call you *sister*?" Tabitha asked. "Was that all?"

She swallowed, recalling the next words. *U-yo-i u-ye-hi...bad husband.* But she couldn't bring herself to voice that. The Indian had been watching her, no doubt. He had probably spied her crying at the woodshed, even before today. Had he witnessed Liam's cruelty?

"Mrs. Andrews?" Jared prompted softly.

She licked her lips. "My husband must've heard my cry, for he came onto the porch with his gun and called for me. The man holding me tried to draw me away. He whispered to me —*u-tli-s-da.*"

Tabitha's mouth hung open. "What is that?"

"*Hurry.*" Jared hung his hands on his knees. "He wanted you to go with him. And yet he drew no weapon?"

"I felt no knife. But Liam saw us, and he raised his musket. The Indian moved so fast, all I felt was a *whoosh* beside me as he loosed his arrow." Finally, her story was complete. The telling had been draining. She gulped her tea, failing to appreciate its fine taste. Holding the cup hadn't helped either. Her hands shook harder. She thumped the beverage back onto the table. Thankfully, no pearlware to break this time.

Tabitha slid onto the bench beside her and placed a hand on her back. How long since she had felt the gentle, comforting touch of another woman? After Aunt Temperance, there had been only Ahyoka...She Brought Happiness, when she'd first rubbed herbal salve onto Esther's callused, twisted foot. The memory brought tears to her eyes. Then, the woman had showed Esther how to locate the herbs and make her own potion, and there had been no more gentle massages.

Tabitha took her reaction for grief, and she faced the men with a frown. "Must we question her so? She just lost her husband."

Jared released a sigh. "I am sorry, Mrs. Andrews, but I must grasp what happened so that I can take an accurate report back to Fort Daniel."

"Fort Daniel?"

"My brother is a scout under Major Terrell." Noble petted Dutchess's massive shoulder. "He keeps a watch on the Jackson Line."

So that was why he'd been riding northward along the border. Stirred up by the Shawnee prophet, Tecumseh, most of the Creek Indians had allied themselves with the British, which was once again at war with the United States after the English navy continued to impress American citizens into service in their conflict with Napoleon's France. Hog Mountain lay at the crossroads of three civilizations. While Cherokee Territory lay to the northwest, Creek war parties raided swiftly and silently from the southwest.

"I usually work with a partner, but he fell ill and had to return early," Jared added. "And Noble is due at the fort in a few days as well for his ten-day guard duty. But I'm sure you are aware of all that, seeing as how most men in the area volunteer." Although he'd never seen Liam Andrews at Fort Daniel.

"Liam did not serve in the militia." In fact, her husband had never involved himself in much besides his own hunting, fishing, and trapping. And drinking, of course. "I suppose because he was rather near-sighted." It was his excuse when he missed game, anyway.

Jared's gaze narrowed. "Did the Indian leave the mark on your face when you tried to get away?"

Her fingers flittered to her cheekbone, and her face heated. She had forgotten about the blow Liam had rendered when she returned from foraging by the river earlier that afternoon. It must be nice and purple now. Not for the first time, she'd had to choose between finding something to eat and receiving a beating for her supposed defiance. "Oh, no. That was my fault." And according to Liam, it had been.

Jared continued to frown, but his eyes were skeptical rather than angry. As though he could read her thoughts. She shifted on the bench, dropping her gaze.

Noble rose and reached for a pipe on the mantel. He opened a small leather pouch and tapped tobacco into the bowl. "And the fire...how did it start?"

"When Liam came out to check on me, he'd carried a lantern onto the porch and set it at his feet. He stumbled when he fell, and it overturned. It's been so dry, the flames spread quickly." Seeking something to do with her hands, Esther raised her cup but found she could only manage the barest sip of the now-tepid tea. The family's well-meant questions churned up the bitter dregs of her recent past.

"Only one more thing for now, that we may determine a course of action," Jared said as his brother lit his pipe.

Esther gave a brief nod.

"Your father...did he leave you any provision? Any way to travel to family, perhaps?"

She plucked at a loose thread on her sleeve. "I don't doubt that my father intended any grandchildren to inherit his half of the trading post, but as there were none born yet, he died without stating his intentions. When my husband tried to claim ownership, Killian's sons chased him away at gunpoint." That was the day she knew exactly why Liam had married her. He no longer tried to hide his true intentions after that—nor his disgust for her.

Tabitha rubbed her back. "I have a bit of coin set by. 'Twould be no harm in dipping into it to send you back to relatives."

"You are too kind." Esther blinked back tears. "But I have none to go to...at least, who would have me."

The woman made a sound of gentle reproach. "Surely, that is not true."

"My father was a widower. My mother died in childbed." Esther spilled her sad history with her gaze trained on the table before her. She couldn't bear the pity in Tabitha's eyes...and certainly not the dismay in the men's. But it was needful they grasp this part of her situation. "My mother's father had been a merchant in Augusta. His son, my uncle, moved his family to Washington, Georgia, to open a store. He and my aunt raised me until I was five, when my father sent for me. He was establishing a permanent post at Hog Mountain then."

Tabitha nodded, tucking a stray strand of hair behind her ear.

"Shortly after, my uncle and two of the children sickened

and died of fever. My aunt took her remaining children back to her family in Savannah." And with her, any hope of care or intervention for Esther.

"And your grandfather?" Jared's question and the thickness of his voice drew a glance from Esther.

"Dead also. So you see, I have no family. Tomorrow I will walk into the settlement and see if there might be work for me at the Hog Mountain House."

Jared sipped his tea. "You won't walk. You will ride—with me. After we go to the fort."

Her eyes widened. "For what purpose?" Indeed, what could be worth attracting the snickers and gawping of the rough men overflowing the stockade?

"To tell my commander what transpired on your property. Taken together with the two Creek attacks in Clark and Morgan counties, it may be of note." Frowning into the flames on the hearth, Jared tapped his finger on his teacup, which looked delicate in his wide, long-fingered hand. "You said the man spoke in Cherokee?"

"Yes." The fact that his voice had been persuasive rather than fierce somehow made her all the more afraid. A tremble went through her.

"So now we have Cherokee as well as Creek warriors abducting women?" Jared shook his head, his brow knit.

Those abductions had offered another ready excuse for Liam to keep her close to the cabin.

Noble pulled his pipe from his lips. "It makes no sense. In September, when the Tennessee militia rallied under Andrew Jackson, the Cherokee council volunteered five to seven hundred warriors. Their chief, The Ridge, has already taken his mounted men to Creek Territory. They fight with us."

"Do they all?" Jared's gaze cut to his brother. "It was not so long ago their braves were scalping white settlers."

Tabitha shuddered. "Now we must fear not only the Creeks,

but the Cherokees too?" Hog Mountain's location near the north-south dividing line between the two tribes meant that both had easy access to the settlement.

Noble released a puff of smoke, which made Esther stifle a gag, reminding her of Liam. "Could it be possible a Creek warrior was speaking the Cherokee language?"

"I have never known them to be deceptive." Jared rose and placed his empty cup on the table. With a hand on his lower back, he stretched.

"Eh? And how many Creek warriors have you parlayed with, my brother?" Noble raised an eyebrow.

"Guess you have a point there." Jared chuckled and headed for the ladder that led to the loft. "We will let the commander make of it what he will." He turned back to Noble. "But first, at dawn, you and I must hie back to the Andrews place to take care of some business."

Esther averted her eyes from the meaningful look he gave his brother. At the thought of Liam lying out there in the cold and dark all night, with the tygers—as the locals here called the panthers—and the wolves, she should be horrified. Grieved. But shame swallowed the seed of relief, that emotion she would not—could not—let herself feel. Especially in front of this loving family.

"Very well." Noble tamped ashes from his pipe into the hearth. "Mrs. Andrews, if you can't find a situation, you are welcome to come back here until your path be clear."

Did Esther imagine it, or did Jared pause—ever so briefly—as he climbed the ladder to the loft? "Oh, no, I couldn't."

Tabitha's hand on her arm stopped her protest. "I would so enjoy the company of another woman."

Even one such as herself? No, it was she who would find female companionship a balm.

The rosy lips turned up. "Just say you will keep it in mind."

"I will keep it in mind." Esther said the words her hostess at least pretended she wanted to hear. Tabitha was too much a lady to show it if she felt put out. Besides, Esther hadn't the strength left to argue. With her stomach finally settling and the warm fire licking her face, she wanted nothing more than to lie down by the hearth, wrap her cloak about her, and fall asleep. If only that hairy monster weren't sprawled in the spot she craved. But Esther rose as Tabitha retreated to her work station with dishes. "Let me help you."

"No, indeed. But if you wish to wash before bed, you may go into our bedroom. You will find water, soap, and a fresh cloth in the wash stand."

Esther bowed her head. She must look a fright, her hair disheveled, her face smudged with dirt and soot, not to mention that awful bruise. "I thank you."

Tabitha tilted her chin. "Take that tallow candle in the holder from the hutch."

She did and passed into the adjoining chamber. Her heart squeezed at the cozy scene. Different colors of linen, wool, and even a fine, printed cotton gown hung on pegs on the wall. Another ladder-back chair sat in the corner, and a quilt graced a four-poster bed. The posts were short rather than tall and canopied, but still, to find such comfort on the frontier!

She located the water in an earthenware pitcher. Lifting a small chunk of soap to her nose, she gasped. A creamy English blend with a hint of lavender. Esther searched for a bar of lye, but finding none, dampened the woven cloth and used the barest amount of the floral soap on her face, hands, and neck. Heavenly. Tears sprang to her eyes. What was the matter with her? The events of the day had undammed all the tender emotions experience had taught her to vigilantly guard.

She jerked her braid loose and combed her fingers through her long thick tresses, never daring to use the bone comb on the stand. She mustn't let these luxuries and kindnesses affect her. They would not last.

When she returned to the main room, Tabitha had disappeared, Noble rocked in his chair with Duchess at his feet, and Jared glanced up from lighting a pine knot on the hearth. An expression of shock flitted across his features before he quickly looked away. Esther froze. What was the matter? Oh. She'd left her hair down. How could she have been so careless? She gathered her long locks and drew them to one side, ducking her head. Lacking any ties, she should have made another braid.

He had laid a quilt by the hearth. She cleared her throat. "Thank you for the blanket."

He stood, brushing off his hands. "It is not for you. I will sleep here tonight. You will stay in the loft."

A knot the size of the twisted chunk of pine that now burned on the hearth formed in her throat. "In your bed?" The question barely made it out.

He hid a smile. "I will be here, so it matters not whose bed it is."

"But it does. I would never ask that of you."

"You aren't asking. I'm offering." A grin crooked up one corner of Jared's mouth. "Unless you wish to sleep with the dog."

"Oh..." Esther's gaze darted to Duchess as she raised her dark, droopy muzzle, and words failed her.

Tabitha returned from the porch, holding the now-empty Dutch oven and a wooden spoon. A rush of cold wind joined her until she closed the door behind her. "Mrs. Andrews, I would not sleep tonight if my lady guest lay on the hard floor."

A lady? She had never been called such. She managed a breathy response. "Esther."

The woman turned from bolting the latch, brows raised. "I'm sorry, what was that?"

She cleared her throat again and spoke just loud enough that she hoped only Tabitha would hear. "My name is Esther." Despite her efforts at subtlety, the men stared at her.

"And I am Tabitha." She came forward to squeeze Esther's arm. "You should find everything you need in the loft, but if not, just call down."

Esther nodded though she had no intention of doing so. She'd make do with whatever she found. She crossed to the table, where she deposited the candle and gathered her sole bundle of belongings, Tabitha's eyes on her. This was probably the first time she'd noticed Esther's uneven gait. But Esther couldn't explain one more thing tonight. She limped to the ladder, then stopped. Her ankles, and maybe more, would be visible as she went up. Liam would slap her for exposing herself to another man in such a fashion. She glanced over her shoulder. Noble was rocking, reading from a big book, but Jared was watching.

"Good night, Mrs. Andrews." He offered a smile and a nod, ungodly handsome in the soft golden light. Her innards twisted into a tight, painful knot, then guilt washed over her. How could she think any man handsome? Especially one who stood gawking while she prepared to climb a ladder?

The next minute, her confusion intensified, for Jared turned his back, leaning in a would-be casual manner against the mantel. Esther scampered—fast as a hare but awkward, more like one with an injury—up the rungs and into a dark living space beyond. Enough firelight flickered into the upper reaches to show that the loft held a trunk, which served as a table with an unlit taper, an empty chamber pot, and a low bunk with another quilt.

Her legs collapsed when her calves touched the wooden bedframe. The straw in the mattress crinkled. Esther raised the edge of the quilt and sniffed it. Not sour, like the covers she'd been forced to share with Liam, but spicy, like the man who'd held her on his horse this night.

She unfolded her cloak from the bundle, wrapped it around her, and lay down in a tight ball. Far away in the night, the cry of a wolf pierced the virgin forest. For a moment, Esther held her breath, then released it in a slow sigh. Only the charity of these people kept her from being out with the beasts. Yet she knew better than to find false comfort in that fact. The treachery that wore a smiling face often proved most dangerous of all.

CHAPTER 3

Forty-year-old Major John Dabney Terrell leaned across the rough table that served as his desk and affixed his gaze on Jared. "Let me be sure I have the facts straight. You are telling me that in the last week, eleven people have been killed by Red Sticks just south of our county line?"

"Yes, sir." Jared rested his palms on the knees of his buckskin leggings. His commander had bid them sit after Jared introduced Mrs. Andrews and indicated that she would take part in his report. "The main attack occurred on the sixth of November in Morgan County."

Terrell tapped a long, square-nailed finger against the paper before him. "And that was the one that injured the justice of the peace, Lewis Brantley."

"And claimed the lives of his wife and son, as well as the others...plus a young woman and an old man at the Snow settlement, who fought back. They lived near Brushy Fork Creek, Clark County, closer to the southern tip of Jackson."

Jared glanced at the widow Andrews, sitting next to him, but her chair was drawn a bit farther back into the shadows that fell beyond the reach of the tallow candles guttering and dripping in hurricane lamps on the major's desk. Despite the crisp air they'd partaken of on their ride that morning, she'd turned pale. He had hesitated to bring her into the officer's house where no privacy could shield her from his grisly tale, but he couldn't consider leaving her at the mercy of the men packed into the fort either. Many more men than he'd ever seen here at one time. The recently ordered reconstruction of the old seventy-five-foot-square stockade neared completion, requiring incessant activity, but there appeared to be extra militiamen and horses about as well.

"And these attacks were simultaneous?" Terrell dipped a quill in his inkpot and scratched out some notes.

"Almost exactly so. The settlers believe the Indians forded the Apalachee River at High Shoals, split their party, and executed the two ambushes."

"The most important question is, did they leave the same way?"

"As I saw no sign of them as I returned north, it seems likely." Jared shifted. "Besides, they took captives." He kept his eyes on the major, but how would Mrs. Andrews react to news of the abductions? Especially when she might have found herself in a far different situation at this very moment?

Terrell paused in his writing, looked up, and raised an eyebrow. "From the Snow settlement?"

Jared nodded. "Ephraim Snow's wife and daughter. The man was bedeviled to track them west, all the way past the Chattahoochee River, even though they lost their sign as near as the local creek. Ephraim's younger brother, Enoch, was away, serving in the militia, when the attack occurred. The old man who died was their father. But Ephraim had the support of his cousin—the one whose bride was killed." He paused and rubbed his temple, then shook his head. "I disremember his name. It was all the local men could do to keep Ephraim and this cousin of his from piking off. They were still nettled at their neighbors some days later, when I came through, for not joining them in a rescue party."

Terrell pursed his thin lips. "It would have been a lost cause. Once the Creek warriors boarded canoes on the Chattahoochee, they could have disembarked at any number of places."

"Exactly what I told them, though they were loath to hear." He'd thought the Snows might spend their wrath on him before he could betake himself north.

Terrell made a few more scratches with his quill. "Just the same, I will dispatch a report to Governor Early. He may wish to alert the local militia and perhaps send guns and ammunition to the area." The major tilted his narrow chin toward Esther, who sat up straight in response. "And this young woman? You said when you entered she had a tale to tell also."

"She does, sir, and from our county, just south of my place on the Apalachee." Jared gave Mrs. Andrews an encouraging smile, but she remained frozen—all but her one index finger which fretted with the edge of her woolen cloak.

Major Terrell waited a moment. "Mrs. Andrews, is it?"

She nodded, but her big brown eyes rounded on the officer, and her delicate throat worked as if she choked on her words.

Terrell, a family man and a faithful Baptist like Jared's kin, offered a slight smile and a gentle tone. "Simply tell me what occurred the night Private Lockridge came upon your homestead, ma'am. I see that you've endured a great shock, but I can assure you, I have no intentions of leaping over my desk or dragging you off to jail or anything else alarming."

The teasing twinkle in his eye elicited an unexpected response—a barely audible giggle. Jared hid his surprise as Mrs. Andrews's shoulders relaxed. She repeated the story she'd given the night prior. He listened closely, but she made no alteration of fact. The major asked the same questions that Jared and Noble had.

When she finished, Terrell leaned back in his chair and folded his fingers over his lean torso. "Given the fact that your attacker sought to persuade rather than force, and that we've received no reports of Cherokees disloyal to the United States, I don't think this was a Cherokee bent on war."

"Then what, sir?" Jared furrowed his brow.

The major focused on Mrs. Andrews again. "I see two potential explanations. Either the native was Creek speaking Cherokee because a white settler would find it the more familiar of the two dialects, or this Cherokee would have you as his wife."

Mrs. Andrews's gasp indicated that she'd no more considered this possibility than Jared had.

"It's not impossible." Jared slowly straightened. "Like other tribes, the Cherokees are still known to replace lost family members with captives, even though I doubt they'd do so by force when we are at peace with them."

"Perhaps he hoped Mrs. Andrews needed only a little persuading." The commander chuckled as mottled color crept upward from the widow's collar.

She began indignantly, "I assure you, sir—"

He waved aside her protest. "No aspersions intended upon your character, Mrs. Andrews. But either way, you can't be too careful in the coming days. I have received more reports than these of women taken from along our borders. Have you a safe place to go?"

"She does." Jared touched her elbow, urging her to stand with him. No need to multiply the woman's humiliation by forcing her to detail her destitute condition. Even if the commander offered a military escort—which she would certainly refuse—she'd already stated she had nowhere to go. "If you don't have further questions, I will see that Mrs. Andrews is situated."

Terrell rose behind his desk. "No further questions. The

information you brought has been invaluable, Private Lockridge. I will report it all posthaste."

"Very well. What are my orders, sir? Shall I make another pass down the line?"

"You may make one more, but new spies are being recruited as we speak. They will report to the new commander, Major Tandy Key, Major General Daniel's aid-de-camp. He has just arrived with a company of militia from the 25th Regiment. Two other drafts of fresh soldiers will follow."

"I hope this doesn't mean..." Jared hesitated to finish the sentence. He'd come to respect Major Terrell. Was the man being replaced? Finally, he settled on a question. "Will you remain in the area?"

Terrell rubbed the back of his neck and looked away as he answered. "For now. But shall we just say my business ventures here have not all gone as hoped? I have land to the west. Perhaps once this Creek business is settled, my fortunes will prove better there."

"You will be missed, sir."

"Thank you, but you will find Major Key worthy of respect. And he will find you of value as well. You have kept our borders safe whilst we rebuilt this old fort. Report back by December second, but after that, you may enjoy the season of Christmas with your family."

The breath eased out of Jared's lungs. His father had taught him the ways of a scout—much of the useful things he'd absorbed during the Revolution about being a tracker and a skilled shot—but his grandfather had taught him the ways of a woodworker, and that was what called to him. The peace he found drawing out the grain, chiseling a design, even sharpening his tools on the grindstone, compared to nothing else. It had been too long since he'd created something both beautiful and functional.

"Thank you, sir. And my brother? He is due to report tomorrow for his ten-day guard stint."

"He may do so, but then he, too, can entrust our borders to fresh eyes. Stay at the ready, though. We may have need of you both in the new year."

Jared saluted, and Major Terrell returned the gesture. Then he bowed to Mrs. Andrews.

"Ma'am, my condolences for your losses. I pray the coming year may be kind to you."

She offered a faint smile. "As you are kind, sir."

Rough as she had lived, someone had taught this woman manners. She even lifted her chin before following Jared to the door with that odd, rolling gait of hers.

Outside, she blinked in the bright sun, and her eyes darted about the stockade yard, from the volunteers hammering away at the commissary next door to the blacksmith swinging his anvil across the way.

Men in linen and buckskin stopped to stare.

Jared stepped to the side she seemed to have a shortened leg—perhaps he could make a platform for her shoe to compensate for that—and offered his arm. She hesitated only a moment before tucking her hand in his elbow, her fingers digging in a bit. Did the ogling of men make her that uncomfortable, or was her reaction due to uncertainty over her future?

He placed a smile on his face. "Where to?"

"Hog Mountain House, if you please." Her lips pressed together as though she regretted her own request.

As they set out through the east-facing gate beside the blockhouse and turned north toward the settlement, Jared's mind swung back to that morning, a conversation he'd overheard as he returned from burying Mr. Andrews. He'd been washing up on the porch, Noble tending their horses, when Tabitha's voice had carried outside—a voice thick with unease.

"Now you see why I'd be so thankful if you could stay."

When he'd entered a few moments later, Tabitha had dashed her sleeve over her eyes as though she'd been crying. He'd asked Mrs. Andrews when they'd first set out if all was well with his sister-in-law, but she'd replied primly that Mrs. Lockridge's condition of either mind or body was not for her to report on. And that had verified his suspicions. Something was amiss with Tabitha's pregnancy.

Should he tell Noble? But tell him what?

The scent of freshly hewn logs still hung about the new Hog Mountain House. Jared escorted Mrs. Andrews inside, but she paused just over the threshold, staring into the tavern room where several burly men downed spirits from pewter tankards.

He tilted his head toward hers. "The owner here is William Foote, but perhaps you would like to speak to Mrs. Foote?"

She nodded.

Jared crossed to the counter to make his request, and the barkeep sent a boy scampering upstairs while they waited in the foyer. "The place seems neat and clean," he said, but he couldn't imagine Esther Andrews working here. They would have to offer her living quarters, and even if an upstanding family ran the inn, many of the men frequenting it would be anything but. How could he leave her here? How would she manage with no protector?

And why was he thinking of her as Esther now? He let his arm cradling the widow's hand fall to his side, partly out of exasperation with himself and partly because a linsey-woolsey skirt appeared on the narrow stairs.

An ample woman came into view, a basket of linens on her hip. "Good morning, sir." She raked Jared with a gaze as warm and sugary as hot cross buns fresh out of the oven. "I am Mrs. Foote. Are you the one asking after me?"

Esther stepped forward. "I was."

A corner of Mrs. Foote's mouth dented as she surveyed Esther. "And who might you be?"

A COUNTERFEIT BETROTHAL

"Mrs. Andrews." A hand to her chest, she spoke in a voice so low Jared could barely hear her over the conversation and clanking of utensils from the other room. "I am a recent widow and find myself—"

"Eh?" Mrs. Foote cupped her free hand behind her ear. "You'll have to talk louder than that if you want to make your requests known around here, my sweet."

Esther pressed her hands together, her knuckles whitening. She raised her voice. "I find myself without prospects, ma'am. I wondered if you might...might need any help." A flush, then a flash of hope, skittered across her pale features.

Jared's heart twisted. Watching a woman who was already humbled plead for her most basic needs skewered him as sharply as any Indian's arrow.

"Ach, you mean for wages?" Mrs. Foote shoved a lank strand of faded golden hair behind her ear as she rocked on her heels. "That's what my two daughters are for. Don't have need for anyone else."

"Of course. I understand."

Esther's downcast face must have spurred some pity in the innkeeper's prow of a bosom, for her demeanor softened. "You might check across the street. Old Killian's ailin', and I daresay he could stand some help with his books...iffen you can stand *him*."

Jared stiffened. Send this defenseless woman into the paws of a greedy and lecherous man who—ailing or not—would doubtless use her ill? Jared would just as soon run the gauntlet in a Creek war town.

But Esther responded with her prior meekness. "Oh. Well. Thank you." Her lashes fluttered, but she did not raise her eyes.

Mrs. Foote planted her hand on her hip, her now-indignant gaze swinging to Jared. "Tried to charge me twice for cedar piggins, he did. *Santalanks*, the Indians call him. And indeed, they gave him his just dues. Last week when trade was brisk, he

33

kept giving them firewater for furs. Suddenly, he goes back to his storeroom and finds only three furs remain." She burst out laughing, flinging out her arm. "They'd cut a hole through his rear wall and taken them right back!"

Jared couldn't resist a chuckle.

Even Esther pressed her hand to her lips to stifle a smile. Lowering it, she asked, "Do you mind me asking what ails him?"

The matron harrumphed. "Consumption, they say...same thing what took his partner."

Esther's eyes rounded. "I see."

Shifting her laundry, Mrs. Foote tilted her head. "You look a bit like that girl who used to live over there. Venable's daughter. Esther, wasn't it?"

"Yes, it-it's Esther. Although it's Andrews now." Her pale cheeks reddened again. "I didn't think you recognized me."

"Well, I hardly did, for all you stayed hid. More like a shadow than a girl. Married that no-account Liam Andrews, did you? He was always in here drinking and, often as not, fighting. My husband had to throw him out more'n a few times."

Jared darted a glance at Esther. Was this true? Had her husband been of no better stock than the man she'd wed to avoid?

Esther held the matron's gaze. "That doesn't surprise me. But he was killed yesterday."

Mrs. Foote's mouth popped open. "You don't say!"

The lure of potential gossip, not benevolence, warmed the woman's demeanor. She wasn't going to give Esther a job. But she would spread her business through Hog Mountain and well beyond. Jared drew Esther's hand through his arm and took a step toward the door. "We thank you for your time, Mrs. Foote. We won't detain you further."

She hurried after them. "Well, now, it's sorry I am that I

haven't employment to offer, given the circumstances. Check back again. Warm weather brings more guests."

Esther glanced back. "Thank you, Mrs. Foote."

They stepped outside, and Jared closed the door behind them. He let out a huff of a breath. Waited a moment. "I can't believe she didn't follow us onto the porch to demand the details of your husband's demise."

"At least she was kind about it."

Kind? Jared looked askance at Esther, but she had focused on the ramshackle trading post across the rutted street, where she had spent much of her youth.

His chest tightened, then a sense of vindication burned in, and he couldn't refrain from stating his thoughts. "'Whatsoever a man soweth, that shall he also reap.'" He turned to her, expecting agreement, but she stared at the building with what was surely not... He sought the tone he used when Duchess wanted to go tearing off through the brush. "No. You will not go over there. You won't subject yourself to that treatment again."

Her hand fluttered to the side of her face. "What other choice do I have? Moore's store?" She glanced down the street.

"I will take you there but not to seek hire. He has a partner, William Maltbie, and employees. Male employees."

"Then why should I go there?" Glistening, doe-like eyes lifted to meet his.

Even his sweetheart back in Augusta, Keturah Caldwell, in the innocence of her sixteenth year, had not stirred his protective instinct in the manner of this dispossessed widow. Keturah's optimistic view of the world and of herself—a product of the sheltering and adoration she'd received from her family—lent her a reckless strength, charming for its naïveté. But if Esther Venable had ever grasped such a confidence, it had long ago been stripped from her.

Jared sighed. "You shall acquire the sundry items a woman finds needful."

"Sundry..." She frowned.

He held his hand out, ticking off items with his fingers. "Comb, hair pins, soap..."

Esther stepped to the back of the porch as two lanky youths in coonskin caps burst out the front door and scuttled down the street. She folded her hands under her chin and drew a tremulous breath. "Mr. Lockridge, it is impressive a man would even think of that, but need I remind you, I have no money?" She spread her hand, and a plain silver band on her fourth finger winked in the afternoon light. It seemed to catch her eye. "But I do have—"

"Your wedding ring?" He let out a little gust of disbelief.

She slid it off and studied it. "It was used as such, but before that, it belonged to my mother."

He blocked her from view of the street while trying not to loom over her. "Then you have double the reason not to pawn it." Didn't she? Or had he been right about Liam Andrews, that she was willing to part with the symbol of her attachment to him the very day after his death?

Her attention flashed to him before refocusing on the piece of jewelry. She seemed to speak as much to herself as to him. "True, it is the only thing I have of my mother's, but wouldn't it be worth parting with to buy passage to Savannah? I must do something."

"Savannah?" Where had that notion come from?

"Remember, I said my aunt returned there? She is my relation by marriage, but Aunt Temperance was kind to me when I stayed with her and my uncle. She treated me like one of her own. She might take me in until I could find a position for myself."

"But what if she can't? Who will escort you on such a long journey? And with winter closing in?" Jared snapped his mouth shut rather belatedly, after the questions spilled out.

Loyal to a fault, that was him. Even to any injured animal

that happened across his path. Noble had always laughed at him for bringing home birds with broken wings and hares whose legs had been caught in a trap. Esther reminded him of those creatures. "There is no need to make a rash decision today. Return with me, and let us discuss it with my brother and his wife."

She tilted her head. "And what new idea might they offer?"

He shrugged. "You heard the major. Noble and I both will be gone for ten days hence. I daresay my brother would ask you to stay with his wife, at least through then. Perhaps longer."

Her face contorted. "Thank you, but I can't count on that."

"And I can't leave you here with no resources. Let us make a plan. But first, let us stop at Moore's. Consider it an advance."

Esther twisted her lips to one side. She had a wide mouth, pale pink and clearly molded. With any firmness, it might make her look confident, that mouth. "How far along is Mrs. Lockridge?"

Jared lowered his chin, studying her. Not *when is the baby due*, but *how far along is she*? His earlier fears solidified. "A little more than five months, I reckon."

She frowned hard, then she nodded. "I will go back with you to discuss it."

Jared allowed his full smile to break forth, and her gaze darted away as though he'd suggested something obscene. Indeed, perhaps he *should* feel guilty rather than being so self-righteous. For he had just offered to take a vulnerable young woman into his home when, to honor his previous promises, he should be doing everything possible to fasten his attention elsewhere. So why did he feel such relief that she had agreed?

CHAPTER 4

*E*sther couldn't suppress a moan of relief as she slid down into the small tin tub in front of the fireplace.

Tabitha giggled from her bedroom and called out, "How is it?"

"I lack the words." She tucked her legs against her chest, and her knees stuck up like two little islands. The bath temperature was lukewarm at best—the product of river water the men had hauled in before they left, which Tabitha had heated over the fire—but it eased the ever-present ache in her twisted foot, ankle, and calf. And when she took up Tabitha's generously lent lavender soap and began to scrub the grime of the past weeks—not to mention the smell of smoke—from her skin, she could have cried. "I can't recall the last time I had a real bath. Probably my wedding day. Liam believed the river worked just fine for washing, and he never owned a hip bath."

Tabitha came to stand in her doorway, Duchess following and plunking down in the threshold. The men had left her for their protection, although Esther would have preferred otherwise. "I would never have married such a brute." When Esther ducked her head, Tabitha held her hand out. "I am sorry. You had no choice. Well, him or that awful slug at the trading post."

Water dripped from Esther's chin. "The slug would have been better." Slugs were disgusting, but you needn't constantly fear an attack from them.

Tabitha approached, and Esther scrambled to hide herself. Tabitha sat on the far side of the table. Thankfully, the dog remained at the door to the other room. "Tell me true, Esther, now that the men are gone. Was it Andrews who left the mark on your face?"

She touched the still-tender flesh over her cheekbone. What was the use in lying now? A dead man needed no excuses. She nodded.

"I knew it." Her hostess's voice firmed and fired. "Bloody coward got what he deserved with that Indian arrow."

Despite her admission, she couldn't let Tabitha believe Andrews had been a complete monster. The instances of kindness from him—glimpsed just often enough to feed her hope—had showed her that a good man lay beneath the hardened exterior. Or had once. From what he'd said, he'd received even less love in his life than she had. "You mustn't say such things of the dead. And had he not been provoked—"

"How, pray tell, did a gentle soul like yourself provoke him?"

Esther picked a sliver of soap from beneath her fingernail. "Well, if you haven't noticed, I'm clumsy and slow."

"You are neither of those. I did not want to ask, but I assume one leg is shorter than the other?" The young Mrs. Lockridge rested her chin in her hand.

"That, and my foot is malformed. Has been from birth. It points inward and downward, the toes curling toward the big toe, and the arch higher than should be." She demonstrated with her hand.

"Clubfoot, then."

Esther nodded, though she hated the word. "In Washington, a physician used stretching tape and splinted it, but because my treatment did not start until I was five months old, it was too late to fix it entirely."

"You poor thing."

Esther did her best not to cringe at the expression she'd heard her whole life.

Tabitha spoke again softly. "Does it pain you?"

"Not terribly. I get calluses and infections easily, though, and a bad ache in my ankle sometimes." Tentatively, keeping her elbows close to her sides, she began to soap her damp hair. "I have found many things that can help—infusions of black cohosh root, tulip tree bark, the summer fruit of the elderberry, not to mention prickly ash bark and other herbs for swelling." She stopped herself from naming them. While her hostess wouldn't be likely to smack her as Liam when she rattled off her "plant fiddle-faddle," she might grow impatient.

But Tabitha gasped. "How do you know all that?"

"A kind Cherokee healer who often came to the trading post when I was a child, Ahyoka, taught me how to make poultices for the rheumatism that sometimes plagues me. She taught me many things."

"Would you teach *me*?"

Esther's heart leapt. "Of course. It would be my pleasure." No one had shown interest in her botanical knowledge before —well, until they were practically dying for want of it.

She would not limit her help to household chores, even though chores were all that were required of her. Not if something she knew might benefit the Lockridges.

Noble had asked her to stay the winter to help his wife, who —at Esther's urging yesterday morn—had finally confessed to him about the occasional bleeding she'd experienced. Noble had even offered to pay her, in addition to purchasing the "sundry" items Jared had her pick out in town—without the sacrifice of her wedding ring. She had insisted on room and board only but had eventually agreed to take money for passage east come spring.

She had slept well last night even in Jared's bed, simply for having the coming months decided. She wouldn't think past the next ten days to when she had to share this house with two unfamiliar men.

Tabitha drummed her fingers on the table. "Seems to me your husband knew about your lameness when he took you to wife. And yet he used it as an excuse to abuse you?"

She did not want to talk about this, not now, perhaps not ever. "Among other things."

Tabitha frowned. "What other things?"

But Esther clamped her lips together. She had soaped her hair and sat waiting for a private moment to rinse it. Tabitha seemed to know better than to offer to help. She rose, smoothing her skirt over her belly, and headed back toward her bedroom. "I am sorry. I am of a curious nature and do tend to pry. Will you forgive me?"

Esther's mouth fell open. "There is nothing to forgive." In fact, guilt had tangled in her gut the moment she refused to answer her hostess's question.

"I won't press you to talk about anything you don't want to, but I am here should you change your mind." She peeked over her shoulder. "I will finish my carding while you finish your bath. Then Duchess and I will show you around."

The mastiff raised her head, her wrinkled jowls sagged in something of a smile, and her tail beat against the floor. As submissive as she might appear when of a good temper, she possessed massive teeth.

Esther shuddered. "Does that beast not make you the least bit nervous?"

Tabitha laughed. "She did at first, but she is fiercely loyal to her family. She would never hurt us. And you are family now." Pausing at her bedroom door, she glanced back at Esther's shocked expression. "It's true. I heard Jared giving Duchess a talking-to before he left."

Her lips parted. "What did he say?"

"That she should guard you as well as she guards me, or she will have him to explain to."

Esther gave a disbelieving scoff. "He said as much as that, and she understood it all?"

"Indeed." Tabitha patted Duchess's head. "Don't be fooled by her drooling. She is very wise. But for now, she knows she needs to give you some space so you can get used to her. Just as you must get used to all of us."

The understanding smile her hostess offered curled its way around Esther's heart like steam around a warm mug of coffee, staying with her as she lowered her head scalp-first into the water. She could almost believe she belonged here, but she mustn't fool herself. She was a charity case, just as her father implied she might always be. She could almost hear his voice, teasing and whip-thin at the same time. *Earn your way, girl.* He'd first said it when he'd sat her down with a ledger, and many times since. And that was what she'd do here. She'd not give the Lockridges a moment to regret taking her in.

She dried off with a linen towel, enjoying its weft against her clean skin, and dressed quickly—linen chemise, stockings, petticoat, and her brown-burgundy gown in a light wool, since Tabitha indicated they might spend much of the day outdoors. A brisk, late-autumn wind whipped the house, although they'd left the shutters closed to preserve the warmth of the fire for her bath. That plus the snug chinking and the way the half-dovetailed notches ensured the logs squared as tight as possible meant no drafts swirled through the cabin.

She went to one of the windows and opened it a crack, peeking out while brushing her hair with her new comb. The stable, its dimensions the same sixteen-by-twenty as those of the original house, stood in front of a big oak that shed a storm of russet leaves eddying about the outbuildings. Chickens clucked from their roost high up inside the shed, and golden ears and neatly squared logs filled the corncrib and woodshed. In every way, this farm proclaimed forethought and provision, while her recent home had displayed only lack.

Tabitha returned with Duchess, a shawl about her shoulders and a basket on her arm. "Come, let us go meet our nanny goat and billy goat."

"I should do something with my hair." Esther hobbled over to the bench and reached for her moccasins. She waited for Tabitha to close the window before putting them on. As kind as the young wife might seem, Esther was not ready to show her lame foot.

"Leave it down to dry. We will only go to the barn and the springhouse."

"Ah, you have a springhouse?" Another thing Liam had lacked, which had meant they'd had to boil all their drinking water drawn from the river.

"Yes, there is a nice spring on the hill that leads down to the river, just past the clearing."

If she could have pictured her dream of a place to live, this would have been it. And to think, it had been less than a half dozen miles away all the time.

The stable held further surprises. The moment they stepped inside, Esther was more taken by the tang of wood in the air than the bleating of the goats from their stall.

Tabitha added a scoop of dried corn from a bucket to the animals' hay feed. She pointed out a black-and-white billy with two horns, then a smaller brown-and-white nanny. "These are Simon and Daisy. They had a baby this summer. We sold it but continue to milk Daisy."

Esther had paused at a tall workbench under a shuttered window, lightly touching the tool chest atop it. A hand-cranked grindstone sat in the corner, a long, arched piece of wood propped next to it with a design partly chiseled out. Wood shavings provided a fragrant carpet for the dirt floor.

"I see you've found Jared's workshop, such as it is." Tabitha came over and opened the window. "He gets pretty good light here when he has time to work." She gestured toward the project nearby. "That is going to be a headboard for our bed, mine and Noble's, started back in the summer." She gave a wry chuckle. "Before Jared was called away for all the scouting."

"He made this?" Esther examined the boards that had been skillfully planed and joined, running her finger through the still-rough openings in the vine design.

"Indeed. His grandfather on his mother's side was an expert cabinetmaker in Augusta before the Revolution. He passed on as many of his skills as he could to Jared before he died."

"Were these his tools?" Esther indicated the large oak box, its sides still mostly adorned in flecking black paint.

"They were." Tabitha unclasped the lid and opened it.

It was not the veneered, multi-drawered, professionally crafted chest of a wealthy man such as Esther might have expected. A saw was secured inside the lid, while several compartments contained tools she had never seen. Despite the variety, many appeared homemade. It almost felt as if she were looking at something too personal without Jared's permission. There might be a story here, but it was not one she should be privy to.

Tabitha closed the lid with a thump that betrayed none of Esther's reverence. "Perhaps we shall get our headboard for Christmas now that the men will be home soon." With a wink, she turned toward the door. "Now to the springhouse. How would you like butternut squash for dinner with our Johnny cakes?"

"That sounds fine."

Esther followed her in the direction of the river. The dog, who had waited outside the stable, trailed at a distance. In a rocky cleft between two hills, a small stone room with a tight-fitting framed door offered just enough space for one person at a time to duck inside. Esther peeked in. A trickle of water emerged from the ground, channeled through a rock trough, and disappeared under the wall. From there, it made its way out of the springhouse and over an abundance of rocks and marshy areas toward the river. And along the trough were crocks of cream and butter, eggs, and the remnants of the season's goodness—apples, pumpkins, squash, and sweet potatoes. Esther exclaimed over the bounty.

"I also dried some beans and fruit with the help of one of my neighbors, but I am not much of a housewife." Tabitha's face fell. "My greatest fear is disappointing my husband."

"I am sure that could never be the case."

Tabitha shrugged. "Back in Augusta, my father had servants that did this sort of work. The food we put away goes so fast, Esther, I worry it won't be enough."

Esther stepped back as Tabitha selected a squash, placed it in her basket, and secured the door. Guilt slid over her, sticky and hot. Her presence added to this family's burden. All the more reason she must be productive. "I can show you how to forage to supplement your meals. Would you like to explore around the house a bit?"

Tabitha's face brightened. "I would, indeed. I detest being closed up inside all day."

A compliment pushed its way past Esther's reserve. "You will do fine here, Tabitha. You have no need to worry."

"Oh? Why is that?"

"Because you are willing to learn."

"I must learn. Next year, my best friend, Keturah, is coming west, and I must be ready to teach her." A laugh burbled from her throat. "If you think *I* was coddled..."

"I don't think that." No. Tabitha had been raised well, as she herself might have been had she remained with Aunt Temperance. Perhaps they could learn from each other. But she would never presume to suggest such a thing. She would merely watch and listen, that what she absorbed might aid her transition into Savannah life. "We can start right here." Her eagerness spilled into her tone as she gestured toward the rocky glen. "There are plants you can find near a spring or a creek that cannot be found elsewhere."

Tabitha clasped her basket tight. "Oh, you make it sound like a treasure hunt."

Esther's chest warmed. "That is just the way I see it." As no one else had seemed to since Ahyoka. She picked her way down the slope, then lowered herself to her knees, folding her shriveled leg to one side. "Look, Tabitha, yarrow. Its leaves are beneficial to stop bleeding. We won't collect anything from it now, but it is good to know it is here if we need it." For after a delivery, perchance, though she would not say as much to Tabitha. From her seated position, she pointed out triple-tipped leaves nearby. "And yellow root. A find, indeed!"

"What does it do?"

She climbed to her feet while Tabitha examined the plant. "The fresh root is soothing to a sore or burn. Shall we walk the perimeter of the clearing? It will be helpful to know what else is at hand."

She needed to replenish her herb box, and there might be varieties she could still dry for winter, but she didn't want to tire the expectant mother. Perhaps tomorrow she would plunge deeper into the forest and on to the river. She eyed the waist-high mastiff huffing along behind them. Hm. Would it take more courage to venture out with or without the dog?

Even their short foray revealed a wealth of nature's offerings —bugleweed with its underground tubers nestled just below the earth, beechnuts in their prickly husks beneath coppery leaves, and best of all, blue-black sparkleberries on a small tree.

She and Tabitha cradled the berries in large but drying mulberry leaves inside the basket.

Esther pulled a branch down and collected the fruit in her other hand. "It's always easy to find a sparkleberry tree this time of year because the leaves stay green into early winter."

"Mm. Sweet. Almost as good as blueberries." Tabitha nibbled a couple of berries, then grinned and stuck her tongue out. "Is my tongue blue?"

The unexpectedly childlike gesture—along with an accompanying warmth that hinted this might be what having a friend was like—made laughter bubble from Esther's chest. But it died on her lips at a movement past Tabitha's shoulder. The breath froze in her throat, for she was sure she had seen a shoulder, moving behind a poplar trunk as wide as a man was tall.

She got a wheezing command out—"Tabitha, run!"—just as Duchess tore into the forest barking fiercely as she ran toward the river.

CHAPTER 5

The gunshot came from the cabin of Ned Bledsoe just as Jared prepared to make camp near the Jackson-Clark line. He drew his musket from the homemade sling on his back and kneed Chestnut forward. Alertness fired his veins, gobbling up the fatigue of his first long day of riding back on patrol.

As he broke into the clearing that held the cabin and a few outbuildings, the gray-haired settler ran away from him for a path wending west through the trees, his musket in hand. Horse hooves pounded toward the river. Chickens bawked and fluttered in the overhead branches, sheep bleated from a pen, and a child wailed from inside the house.

Jared pulled up reins as the man got off another wild shot. "Bledsoe! Who was it?"

"Injuns! Two of 'em, painted for war. They tried to steal my sheep."

Jared turned Chestnut's head for the river path. "Mount up and follow."

"Can't. My son's got the horse on militia duty."

Jared waved his hand and called over his shoulder, "I'm on them."

Chestnut thundered down the narrow trail. A dark form—the rear rider?—came into sight around a bend, but twilight played havoc with the shadows, and branches slapped Jared's face. One shot and two opponents. This was why scouts usually patrolled double. And what wouldn't he give for a rifle instead of his musket? Despite the slower reloading time, he'd be far more accurate firing from horseback.

Water splashing ahead attested to the raiders crossing the Apalachee. By the time Jared reached the bank, they were to the other side. Just as Bledsoe had said, their naked torsos gleamed with red and black paint, and feathers dangled in long, dark hair. Both rode unsaddled ponies.

Red Sticks. Had to be. "Stop!" He drew Chestnut to an abrupt halt and leveled his musket, sighting on the rear rider.

The Indian swiveled and fired his own weapon—a rifle. The sound made Chestnut flinch, and Jared's finger tightened on the trigger, sending the shot awry.

"Blast!" A bullet tore past his left shoulder, igniting his flesh with a searing trail of fire. Blood seeped through his hunting shirt where his arm joined his torso.

They were getting away, yet he had no choice but to deal with the wound. He angled Chestnut behind a tree and swung to the ground. He felt in his bandolier bag for the tiny leather pouch that contained crushed geranium root. Gritting his teeth, he tore the hole in his hunting tunic wider, held it open, and sprinkled the powder on his flesh. He exhaled and stowed the bag. That should staunch the bleeding for a time...a trick he'd learned from a Cherokee who frequented the fort.

Locating another paper cartridge rolled with eighty grains of black powder, he loaded the muzzle. A glance showed the far bank was now clear. In less than a minute, he was back in the saddle, but chances of catching up to his quarry were slim.

Jared urged his stallion down into the river. The slow-moving current offered no challenge for the massive roan, but the icy water closing around Jared's legs snatched his breath. Half expecting one of the men to lay in ambush, he flattened himself against his mount's neck. But no further shots rang out.

Both he and his horse came up the other side shedding liquid in sheets.

A few hundred yards farther and the trail split three ways—north, south, and west. Jared muttered under his breath and slid off Chestnut for a better look at the ground in the failing light. Recent, unshod hoof prints continued north and south. Of the two, the northerly one posed the most danger, for its traveler could cross back into Jackson.

He remounted and set a course parallel to the river, gaze sweeping in a continuous arc and weapon at the ready. Heavy shadows settled beneath the trees, night's frigid breath fanning Jared's neck, and warm dampness trickled down his arm. The flesh wound might be deep enough to require stitches.

The trail played out at a small creek that fed into the Apalachee. As a thin moon rose, he endured the river's cold embrace once again and made for the main path that would lead him home.

~

The flare of burning pine knots illuminated Jared's entry into the clearing about the cabin. It was early in the season for such a precaution against nightly predators. Had the women encountered some foul beast? And though it was the middle of the night, thick spirals of smoke curled from the chimney, and light slanted out as one of the shutters cracked open. It glinted off the muzzle of a musket while a gruff voice demanded, "Who goes there?"

Alarm raced through him as he dismounted. "It's Jared!" All

he needed was to be targeted again. Doubtful his luck would hold for the accuracy of the second shot.

The door sprang open, and Tabitha rushed from the porch. Before he could brace himself, she flung her arms around his neck, nearly setting him off-balance. "Oh, thank God."

Duchess ran out, wagging her whole body and licking his hands, while Esther appeared in the doorway, clutching her musket.

He drew back from his sister-in-law's stranglehold. "What happened here?"

"We were out gathering herbs this afternoon when—" The grip she moved to his shoulders elicited a stifled cry from Jared. "Oh! What..." She raised her fingers to study them as they came away damp with his blood. "You're hurt!"

"A flesh wound, that is all." He set her gently away and wrapped Chestnut's reins around his hand. "Are you in danger?"

"Esther saw someone in the woods, but we can tell you about it when you come inside." She turned toward the house and raised her voice. "Esther, Jared is bleeding."

With a gasp, their guest loped over. As she drew near, Duchess ran a circle around her, her body brushing right up against Esther's skirts. Esther did not react.

Jared flicked his fingers toward the dog. "What strange magic is this? I thought I had a tale to tell, but it would seem I am to be upstaged."

Esther did not seem to hear him. Her soft fingers fluttered like moths around his wound a moment, then she spoke in a firm voice. "Tabitha, I will go to the spring to gather the yarrow we saw earlier."

"But—"

"I will take the gun...and the dog." With a glance at the mastiff, Esther added, "Come, Duchess."

Jared gave his head a brisk shake as his canine trotted off at

51

Esther's side, just as if she'd always been there. Tabitha tugged his uninjured arm, but he gestured her toward the house. "I must see to my horse first."

Once Chestnut had been fed and given a hasty brush-down, Jared crossed to the cabin. He entered to find Tabitha working over the hearth while Esther stood at the table in a rust-colored dress, her herb box open before her. Her unbound hair, so thick it resembled a cape about her slender shoulders, glinted with a whole range of hues and highlights. Her manner possessed the same firmness she had exhibited when she'd gone to the spring. It flashed in her eyes now as she surveyed him.

"Come. Hurry." She indicated folded leaves in front of her. "They won't stay damp long."

What did she mean for him to do? Disrobe right here? But, of course, she did. Both women had been married, and she'd need the firelight to examine the wound.

Jared bolted the door, then lifted his accoutrements from his frame, hanging them near his musket. Approaching the table, he started to shrug his hunting tunic over his head. The burning of his upper arm made him reconsider. He eased the material back down to find Esther before him, her hand outstretched as if to assist him. But her eyes were round and her features frozen. He eased his head and his right arm free, then she reached for the left sleeve and gently tugged it from the injured limb. A sizeable bloodstain plastered his linen shirt to his arm.

"Sit." Esther nodded toward the bench nearest the fire.

As he lowered himself onto it, Tabitha paused in stirring some porridge to peek at him and grimace.

Esther's face had smoothed but paled. Due to his wound or his state of undress? The latter, it would seem, for while her eyes raked his chest as briefly as possible, they fastened on the gash in his shoulder with none of the same alarm. Thankfully, he had worn breeches today rather than leggings and breechclout.

She reached for a damp cloth and used it to gently wipe around the wound, patting when fresh blood trickled out. Whatever she'd put on the linen stung a bit, but in a cleansing way.

Tabitha ladled porridge into a wooden bowl. "Can you tell us what happened?"

"Two Red Sticks attempted to make off with livestock from Bledsoe's farm on the south border of the county. I tracked them, but..." A waterfall of Esther's hair fell in front of Jared's face, obscuring Tabitha's and bringing with it—*egads!*—the fresh scent of lavender. Without thinking, he reached to tuck it back over her shoulder. The strands slipped through his fingers like silk.

Esther levered to an upright stance, breath hissing in as though a snake had lunged at her. When his eyes widened, her face flooded with color...and remorse. "Sorry." She cuffed her hair behind her, looking about a bit frantically. "I should have secured it first." Her reaction hinted at fear, but what did she think he would do?

Jared softened his expression and said the first thing that came to mind. "No harm done, ma'am. It looks right fine as it is."

"W-what?" Esther snatched at a bit of twine Tabitha stepped over to offer her, quickly binding the heavy mass.

It resembled molasses in the firelight, although from the incredulous stare Tabitha shot him, he'd no call to voice that. Or even think it. He was pledged to another, and though she be far away at present, his word was his vow. Enduring. Unbreakable.

Not only was he not a free man, but Mrs. Andrews was a widow of under a week. Of course, she'd be mourning her husband and might mistake his reassurance for inappropriate flirtation. It galled him that his flesh could override his finer sensibilities so easily. Wasn't the Scripture full of instruction on how to protect and care for widows?

Jared tucked his chin. "I am sorry, ma'am. I overstepped in both action and word." Something in him sensed a deep void in the widow, a great need for kindness, though he could hardly say so. And it was probably his imagination, anyway. A misinterpretation of her grief. Just because Andrews had been given to tousling at the tavern didn't mean he hadn't cared for his wife.

Returning from the hutch with a spoon, Tabitha gently nodded her approval.

Esther hesitated as she turned from the table with a yarrow leaf in hand. Again, parted lips and fluttering lashes indicated her surprise. "Of course, you meant nothing inappropriate."

"No."

Standing as far from him as possible, Esther covered his wound with two damp leaves, then secured them with a strip of linen. "You should lean back and keep still, Mr. Lockridge. We will let that set on the wound while I prepare a poultice."

Hope stirred. "Will I not need stitches?"

She answered with a brief shake of her head. "I fear that you will, but after the poultice is applied."

"More's the pity, but I thank you for tending me."

"I am thankful I can help. And that you were close to home." Esther's lips clamped down again, as if there had been something mortifying about that last sentence.

"Indeed." He leaned his right arm against the table. "May I eat my porridge while I wait, or must my sister-in-law feed me?"

Tabitha made a blowing sound. "Right."

Esther angled away as she began sprinkling various powders from her box into a small wooden bowl. "You may feed yourself if you are careful."

"And you were saying," Tabitha reminded him, "you were tracking Red Sticks."

Jared downed one bite before answering. "To the river. One of them fired a split second before I did, and you see the result. I had to dismount to cover the cut with geranium root—"

"That is *not* a cut," Esther muttered under her breath. When he glanced at her, her face softened with a grudging admiration. "But the geranium was wise."

"Thank you." He met her gaze until she looked away. "I reloaded, remounted, and we forded the river, but not far on the other side, the trail split two ways. I followed the northbound sign until I lost it at a creek as night fell."

"So you think one of them came this way?" Tabitha's voice rose to a high pitch.

"I don't believe there is cause for alarm. They merely intended to throw me off. He would circle back to join his companion." Jared applied himself to his porridge, then to the corn cake she set before him. As he bent forward, another trickle of blood seeped from beneath the yarrow.

In an instant, Esther was at his side, wiping the drip.

"Thank you again." He smiled at her, but she kept her lashes down.

"You are welcome, Mr. Lockridge."

"Well, we had our own visitor." Tabitha stood with her hands on her hips.

He fixed his attention on her. "You said you saw someone in the woods?"

"While we were picking sparkleberries." Jared didn't even know what sparkleberries were, but his sister-in-law now did, apparently. She tucked the edges of her lips up into a grim expression. "Esther glimpsed movement off toward the river. We ran for the cabin, and Duchess went on the attack."

"Did I miss a corpse in the clearing?" While Duchess might well have dragged any kill back to the house, his words were ill-advised, for Esther stopped her mixing and made a small choking sound. He held his hand out. "Forgive me." Was there no end to his insensitivity?

She shook her head, limping around him to the hearth. "No need." She took up the kettle and brought it back to add water to her poultice.

"No...quarry, but she did bring back this." Tabitha marched over and flattened a bloody strip of buckskin on the table before him.

His cornbread lost some of its appeal. How could he in good conscience leave the womenfolk untended to go scout elsewhere if they were in danger here?

Jared's question was for Esther. "Do you believe it was the same man as before?"

She returned to the fire and hooked the kettle on the crane, out of the flames this time. She did not meet his gaze as she replied. "I only caught a glimpse of his shoulder, but my instinct tells me it is most likely."

Tabitha circled her hand in the air. "What does this man want?"

"I believe he wants Esther." As Jared's words fell like thick stones in a pond, the widow's face went red from the neck up. But he continued speaking, his tone measured. Wary as he wished her to be, he should not incite panic. "He may have come to check on her, to see how she was being treated here."

"That's crazy." She mixed her concoction with more intensity than necessary.

"Is it? Could he not have killed both of you with an arrow or a musket ball long before you saw him today?"

Her throat worked. "He could have."

"Well, then?"

"No." Her hair rolled back and forth between her shoulder blades. "No one ever..." She drew a breath. "Why would he...?"

Why couldn't she finish a sentence? "Do you find it that

preposterous that, for whatever reason, an Indian man might have taken it upon himself to be your protector?"

By her expression, she did find it preposterous. "I don't need a protector now, as hopefully Duchess convinced him. Tabitha, have you a needle and sinew?"

His brother's wife nodded but seemed disinclined to fetch them, preferring to stand and watch until Esther reminded her the needle should be heated over the flame. As she disappeared into her bedroom, Esther slid onto the bench beside him and unwound the linen. She waited to peel back the leaves until Tabitha returned and knelt before the hearth. Then she used the cloth from earlier to scoop up a generous amount of the poultice.

She leaned close, then paused, her eyes seeking his. "This may sting a bit."

For whatever reason, he found himself wanting to keep her there. "What is it?"

"Ground alum, ginger, and plantain." Her creased brow almost seemed to beg permission. "I am sorry if it causes you discomfort."

Jared offered her a reassuring smile, though he clenched his hands in his lap. "No need to fret on my account. Do your worst, Widow Andrews."

A flash of alarm crossed her face when he spoke the name, then she blinked and set to her task. She clasped her lower lip between her teeth—fine, straight teeth. The breath from her nose fanned his collarbone, raising gooseflesh despite the crackling fire. Jared averted his eyes, but when they focused on a frowning Tabitha, he returned his attention to Esther. Easier to study her face than her handiwork. At the warmth of her so near and the soft lavender fragrance wafting from her skin, his pulse picked up a notch.

Her gaze skittered to where it beat in his neck for a fraction of a second. Then she sat back. "There. Have you any brandy, Tabitha?"

His sister-in-law nodded. "Noble has some set by for toddies."

But before she could go in search of it, Jared spoke up. "No!" Esther stiffened at his abrupt tone. Her concerned frown prompted him to explain. "I don't countenance the use of spirits except for medicine...or the occasional syllabub." He offered this last with a sheepish smile.

Esther tilted her head. "This is medicine, is it not?"

"I'll be fine without it."

She drew a breath, and her face softened into acceptance touched with something firmer. Admiration, perhaps? She glanced across the room. "Then just the needle and thread, Tabitha?"

Noble's wife laid the requested items atop some linen on the table. "Would you like me to do it?" She looked between them, but her glance faltered when she affixed it on Jared's wound.

He pushed down a chuckle. "How many men have you sewn up, sister?" Now was not a time for misplaced jealousy over Keturah to assert itself.

She pursed her lips. "None, as well you know."

He studied Esther as she prepared the sinew. "And you, Mrs. Andrews?"

A soft laugh escaped her throat. "Oh, at least a dozen. When I worked at the trading post, it seemed brawls or accidents happened every few weeks." Esther glanced up with a flash of understanding, her expression and tone becoming ingratiating again. "But, of course, I will step aside if you wish, Tabitha."

Jared put his hand on her arm. "Please, don't."

The humor coupled with earnestness in his tone appeared to satisfy her, but Tabitha turned away. "I will fetch you a fresh shirt."

"Thank you," he called after her. "Your willingness to try is admirable." No need to vex his sister-in-law going into a long winter.

And Esther? He would be going into a long winter with her too. One without the distractions of scouting absences, at least for a while. Was Tabitha wise to be concerned? He couldn't blame her. She thought of the widow's vulnerability. And, no doubt, she thought of her best friend, miles away. But what if Esther became a dear friend as well? Well, that was all she could ever be.

Pressing one hand against his shoulder, Esther raised her other with the needle, but it shook in her grip. She lowered it, drew an unsteady breath, and adjusted herself on the bench.

Jared spoke in a low voice. "It's all right. You'll do just fine. It's thankful I am that you are here. Else I would have faced sewing up my own shoulder." He gave a teasing nod toward Tabatha in the other room.

When Esther's eyes shot open wide, Jared allowed a soft chuckle. If only she might acknowledge his attempt at humor with at least a small smile, a hint that kindness and healing might ease her toward joy. Instead, her face flushed, and she applied herself to her task with her jaw clamped tight. If he had to guess, something more than her husband's death had hardened this woman.

He sat stiff but silent while she stitched his wound and tied off the thread. Then, as she dabbed ointment over the stitches, he watched her, trying himself—his reaction to her—by refusing to look away. Thick brown lashes swept over chocolate-colored eyes no longer encircled by shadows. Esther bit her full bottom lip as she worked. Their proximity, their mingled breath, the popping of the fire, the absence of Tabitha —who must wish to avoid witnessing the mending of his wound more than she wished to chaperone—created an intimate elixir more potent than the strongest whiskey, warming him to his bones.

Jared turned his head and closed his eyes, and crisp, refreshing logic flowed back into his thoughts. He'd passed too much of the past year on the frontier, scaling ridges with none for company but Chestnut. After all, there was little enough to recommend Esther Venable Andrews. Her figure was as slight as a girl's, but a woman who had already lived too long looked back from the depths of her eyes. And had he ever met one more deserving of pity?

No. Tabitha could rest easy. Jared's mysterious pull toward the woman they had taken in was aught but compassion.

CHAPTER 6

The reek of melted deer suet lingered in the cabin, but more potent in Esther's mind was the memory of Jared's presence. Despite the stench from their candle-making, she could breathe now that he was gone. She reached overhead, doubling wick strings over the middle of a candle rod hanging from a rack and twisting the ends while attempting to untwist her own snarled thoughts. What was it about the man that addled her so?

His teasing, for one. The only teasing a man had ever given her had been mean-spirited. But Jared's was light, warm, as though he was including her in a delicious secret. Then there had been moments of...awareness, such as when he'd divested of his shirt for her to tend his wound. His chiseled physique had in no way resembled Liam's barrel chest and paunchy middle. Jared's strength had drawn her rather than repelled her. For a second, she had almost envisioned his muscular arms closing around her, but softly. Something told her he would never entrap or harm her.

When she'd been close to him night before last, she could've sworn they shared a strange connection. One that raised the fine hairs all over her body, followed immediately by a dousing of cold fear. Only pain of one sort or the other resulted from the awareness of a man. Best to stay out of sight. But his wound had made that impossible. She'd hardly been able to steel her shaking long enough to treat him. Had he really taken her quaking for uncertainty over her skills rather than discomfort at his nearness? No, the secrets of the living things of the forest and her ability to apply them was the one thing in which she held confidence.

To finish twisting the last of the wick strands called for her to stand right in the place she had when he'd swiped her hair behind her shoulder without thought—yet with apology. He'd not shamed her for tempting him with her careless failure to bind it. And stranger still, when she'd finally calmed herself enough to stitch his torn flesh, her pulse had slowed, her hands had steadied. She had felt *safe* next to him.

Esther peeked at the tallow in the pot—the rendering of suet heated since dawn and strained through a cheesecloth. Thankfully, Jared had helped her lift the heavy vessel before he left. Tabitha had sat at the table that afternoon in a sickly fugue, alternately staring into space and scratching looping script onto paper with her feather quill before going to lie down an hour ago. She'd insisted that Esther call her before she started dipping the wicks, as she'd never made candles herself before. Esther had done so when she lived with her father. Liam had seen no problem with sooty, smoky pine knots.

Esther knocked lightly on Tabitha's doorframe to let her know it was time.

"Coming." The young wife's weak response made Esther uneasy.

"Are you certain? I can manage alone." Her whole justification for being here, after all, was to help take care of Tabitha.

"No, I want to help. I must tell Keturah I've made my own candles. I will be right there."

Who was Keturah? The name rang faintly familiar. Perhaps the person Tabitha was writing the long letter to? Returning to the hearth, Esther passed by the table. In addition to Tabitha's half-finished missive, another paper filled with different feminine writing lay open, its signature bold and flourished. Esther paused to sound it out. "Ket-ur-ah Cald-well."

"That was the last letter I had from my best friend back in Augusta." Tabitha spoke from the door of her bedroom, fine strands trailing from her bun, her skin white against her dark hair.

Esther shuffled quickly away, but instead of the rebuke she expected, Tabitha waved her hand.

"You can read it. You might as well get to know her a bit, after all." Her tone sounded almost pleased.

Why would Esther need to form an acquaintance with a woman who lived in Augusta? She would never go there. "I promise, I would never read a letter meant for someone else. I only wondered what you were working on. Besides..." Face burning, Esther focused on stirring the tallow. "I can only read certain words."

Smoothing her hand over her abdomen, Tabitha approached. "I thought you said you helped your father with his books at the trading post."

"It was mainly numbers. I needed only to know names and to write out the items we carried or traded. For that matter, Father could hardly spell either." Esther leaned her stirring stick against the hearth and fetched a candle rod from the rack. "See here, I've prepared the wicks for the first dipping." The Lockridges had several rods that fit nicely over the cooling rack, which would allow for larger batches. "We'll immerse them quickly, then hang them to dry. Then we'll repeat the process over and over until the tapers are thick enough."

"So we should finish tonight?"

Esther gave a grim chuckle. "Tomorrow night, if we be blest."

Tabitha moaned. "That tallow pot hogs the hearth, and the smell makes me ill."

"I'm so sorry, Tabitha. I should have thought of that." Positioning the rod between the fireside chairs, Esther hurried to open a window. She knew aught of pregnancy personally. "From what I heard in the settlement, the noses of most expectant women grow less sensitive after their first few months."

Tabitha pressed the back of her hand to her temple. "If only I were like most expectant women."

"Truly, you don't have to help me."

"No, I wish to. I'm waiting to add it to this letter, see?" Tabitha held up her half-empty page. "I will record it after what I learned about tending a wound. Keturah finds such details of the frontier fascinating...and just as essential to preparing for her marriage as working on her hope chest."

"She is coming to the frontier?" Ah, yes. Now the memory returned. Tabitha had mentioned her friend shortly after Esther had first arrived.

Tabitha opened a drawer in the hutch and drew out a long narrow box. She turned back to Esther with a look of surprise. "Why, yes, had we not told you? She is Jared's betrothed."

Betrothed? Esther's hand fluttered to her throat. That sinking sensation between her chest and her stomach...it must be relief. For if Jared was engaged, she need have less concern of her own safety around him. "Why...that's wonderful."

"Truly? You think so?" Raising her eyebrows, Tabitha lifted the lid of the box and sniffed the contents. Immediately, her face relaxed, and a soft smile curved her lips. "Ah. Much better. If only we had enough bayberry candles to burn the whole winter." She came forward and held out the container to Esther.

Esther's eyes widened at the firm light-green tapers. Almost afraid to steal a whiff, she sniffed with hesitation. "I've only seen these a couple times at the trading post. What a luxury."

"Yes. We will burn them for Christmas and the New Year." Tabitha slid the lid back on the box and returned it to the hutch. Then she faced Esther with a quizzical expression. "What was I saying?"

"About your friend..."

"Yes. Keturah. Well, I am glad someone is pleased. Though they will hardly say so to me, Noble and Jared both secretly fear Keturah won't take well to the wilderness."

"Why is that?" Esther knew the answer, but Tabitha's glance sought prompting.

"She is from a good family, one even better off than mine. And she is beautiful. High-spirited. She could have anyone in the county. Even that troublemaker Shaw Ethridge. He is a lawyer, set to become the next justice of inferior court, but I've warned her he will only break her heart. He cares a bit too much for the ladies." Tabitha lifted her chin. "He won't turn her head. Keturah knows what kind of man Jared is. Hardworking, noble, and faithful. Due to the folly of his grandfather and father, he may start humbly, but with the money Keturah will bring to the union, he will be able to open his own cabinetmaking shop. He is already supplying Moore and Maltbie with ready-made pieces, and people are beginning to request his work. Or, at least, they *were* before all this trouble."

Esther swallowed a lump in her throat. Which thread to pull in the ball of information Tabitha had thrust at her? "I did not know that. That is wonderful." Had she said that same thing before? It *was* wonderful. "The talents of a man should not be consumed by the frontier but should expand with it."

She belonged with these people even less than she'd imagined. All three of them came from something special and had future prospects. But what had Tabitha meant, *the folly of his grandfather and father*?

That young woman smiled, faint surprise lifting her brows again. "I couldn't have said it better." She returned to the table, folding her hands. "Yes, Keturah will make certain of that very thing. She will help make Jared a success. I have no fear that living on the frontier will cow her. She has too much fighting spirit for that. Far more than I. Now, where were we?" Her gaze ran over the candle rod.

Esther plucked it from between the chairs. Better to focus on the task at hand than on a future she would not be part of. "How about if I do the first one, and you do the second?"

Tabitha clapped her hands, her enthusiasm restored. "And after we finish, you can help me relate the process to Keturah. Giving someone else the benefit of needful information makes the drudge-some task almost pleasant, does it not?"

Esther smiled. Pleasure mattered little in her experience, as long as the needs of those she served be satisfied. That had been her bargaining chip for survival. At least now, for a while, she might be surprised by a little kindness in return.

But she found it hard to train her thoughts to candle-making, even when Tabitha quickly retreated to her letter-writing. Rather than relying on descriptions, why wasn't Keturah laboring beside her servants at her own hearth this autumn eve? Then again, perhaps she was. Perhaps, as Tabitha indicated, the girl had given herself to preparation for frontier life. But could anything truly prepare one? Would Jared find himself saddled with a prim miss incapable of raising a family here with him? And a better question...why did such a possibility concern Esther?

~

*J*ared nodded to the sentry as Fort Daniel's gate closed behind him and Noble. He'd just made his report to the new major. Following his run-in with the three renegades, he'd found the Jackson Line quiet. Perhaps the close encounter had scared the troublemakers farther south. And hopefully, the increased number of spies from the fort would keep them there.

Noble leaned back in his saddle and cast a grin his direction. "How does it feel to get shed of that place?"

"All the better now that it's packed to the brim."

His brother guffawed, the sound attracting the stares of two buckskin-clad, turban-wearing Cherokees, headed into the post to trade furs. "What are you talking about? You spent the last ten days in the fresh air of the forest—"

"Eating pemmican and jerky without the benefit of a warm fire at night."

"And also without the stink and rowdiness of two dozen confined men."

"Soon to be even more, if what I heard from the officers was true." At the crossroads, Jared maneuvered Chestnut around a peddler bowed by his packs. He let Noble take point on the path leading south toward the river and home.

"What was that?" His brother adjusted his hat against the glare of the late-afternoon sun.

"They are keen to find a better way of moving goods for the army into Creek Territory. There is talk of expanding the existing path west to the village of Standing Peachtree, which would mean sending more troops to Fort Daniel."

"Peachtree...the friendly Creek village on the Chattahoochee?"

Jared nodded. Mixed-blood families farmed the bottomlands along the east-west dividing line between the Creek and Cherokee nations, all coming to trade at nearby Suwanee Old Town. "It would make a better entry point for shipping supplies by river than rafting them across from Fort Hawkins to Fort Mitchell so much farther south. They say the army in Creek Territory has requisitioned off the nearby Cherokee villages to the point that all will be starving this winter if we don't do something."

"Not *we*, my brother. *They*. We have done our duty, at least for now. All I want to think about are the comforts and hearth and home, although..." He cast Jared a wry backward glance. "I doubt you are anticipating sleeping on a pallet in front of the hearth."

Jared fought a depreciating smile. "I admit, I would rather have my comfortable bed in the loft, though I would never let on about that to the widow."

Noble wended his mount around a flaming oak tree. "You are more than thoughtful. And more than patient. I know you want your own place almost as much as we wish it for you, yet you spent these first two years building my cabin and barn, breaking ground, and tending crops with me, with naught but that trip after last year's harvest to visit your intended."

"It's what was necessary." The work...and the trip. While he had left Augusta with definite hopes about Keturah two springs ago, only during the winter visit had they confirmed their attachment and made their betrothal official.

"Your sacrifice will pay off." Noble grinned over his shoulder. "When your bride comes, you'll truly grasp the high premium on privacy." He winked before turning around.

"And we'll have my new home ready by then."

They'd already girdled trees on the adjacent hill along the river. With the help of neighbors, they'd make quick work of felling them and raising the cabin on the heels of winter's thaw. But there was no call to dwell on that. Spring was too many months distant to allow longing to give rise to impatience.

Jared tucked thoughts of Keturah away with her letters and

tried not to notice the last one had come in early autumn. Had his long absence made her start to question her promise to him? No. The pull between them had been almost irresistible, strong enough to withstand the miles and months. Letters often went astray in this wilderness.

In his need to deny his own flesh, however, he mustn't lose sight of his brother. Helping his bride adjust to frontier life while they shared a cabin with Jared had posed frequent challenges for Noble, especially in the early days. "Don't worry, I'll find plenty of occasions to absent myself to the barn. That is what I'm looking forward to. Although, I suppose I'll have to ask Mrs. Andrews if she enjoys watching woodwork." It was an escape he usually craved for himself. He couldn't imagine a stranger being present, feeling the need to pollute the soothing silence with talk.

Noble waved his hand, leather creaking as he adjusted his weight. "Don't worry on my account. Tabitha's condition is too delicate for me to make demands of her. But about the widow..."

"Yes?" He'd thought of her more times than he'd expected while completing his stint on the border. Whenever she'd popped into mind, he'd focused on his concern for how she and Tabitha were getting along and prayed for their harmony and safety.

What awaited them at today's homecoming? A warm and joyful welcome, or shock and sorrow? His middle stirred with unease at the memory of Esther's burning cabin. Every man feared such a sight.

Noble directed his horse to a wider opening between two massive pines, then he drew up his reins and waited for Jared to come alongside. His brows rode the crest above his deep-set eyes, and his lips formed a thin line. "I need to impart what Tabitha told me before I left. About Mrs. Andrews."

"What is that?" Jared cocked his head. "Is she having a hard time with the loss of her husband?"

Noble huffed. "Rather the opposite, I'm afraid. It seems Andrews was the cause of that bruise on her face when she first came to us."

Indignation poured like steel into Jared's spine, and he sat up straight, eyes narrowing at his brother. "He beat her?"

"Regularly."

Jared hissed a few unsavory names under his breath. What kind of man used brute force to intimidate a female he had pledged to protect—especially a small, lame, self-effacing young woman like Esther? The leaves on the trees ahead blurred into a fiery patchwork through the lens of his ire. Then everything came into focus. Her shrinking away from his nearness. Her constant apologizing. Her suspicious glances when he'd offered affirmation or levity. What he'd taken for lingering shock from the Indian attack, the fire, and the death of her husband had been fear...of him. Of all men. "It does cause a lot to make sense."

"Unfortunately." A wood chick with its scarlet plume and black-and-white wings lit on a branch high above Noble's head. It fussed at them a moment before flying off.

In his head, Jared's thoughts continued to screech. He almost regretted spending the effort it had required to put such a man in the cold, hard ground. And the Indian who had showed up at the cabin? Jared's instinct that the brave's presence was more protective than threatening gained credibility. He rubbed the bristle on his chin. "And her leg? Did her husband do that too?"

"No, she was born with a twisted foot and did not receive help for it in time to straighten it."

"Ah. I daresay it solicited much abuse throughout her life."

Noble raised his hat and scratched under the brim. "No doubt."

"Knowing all this, no wonder Tabitha seemed so protective."

"Yes. She wants us to give Mrs. Andrews a wide berth."

"I see." Jared cut his gaze to Noble. "Yet will she not take that as our displeasure that she's in our home? Already she is so subservient and beat down."

Noble drew his mouth up, considering. "Perhaps. We will walk a fine line, making her feel welcome yet not intimidated in any way." He looked back at Jared and spoke with firm emphasis. "Especially you."

He turned the reins over in his hands, staring at his calluses. "I will bear that in mind, but my conscience will demand that I balance any reserve with the fact that the woman is clearly starved for simple kindness."

"Let my bride offer that. You would do well to keep your mind on yours."

Jared watched his brother ride forward without comment, but a voice whispered in his head. *Not yet mine.*

CHAPTER 7

*E*sther stood outside the barn, biting the inside of her lip, her fingers curling and uncurling around the handle of her basket as soft scraping sounds came from the stable's interior. Tabitha had suggested she ask for Jared's help gathering any eggs the chickens had laid in the roosting boxes he'd built near the rafters. She'd rather locate the stool Tabitha used and check herself. But with her clumsiness, she was even more likely to topple off than Tabitha was in her unwieldy condition. And that would be far more embarrassing than just asking for help in the first place. Still, she disliked disturbing the man at his work.

She took a breath and pushed the door open.

At his work station, Jared raised some sort of plane from a board and scrambled to hide several pieces of wood with his body as he turned to face her, clasping the table on either side. His bright and innocent smile of greeting relaxed into a gusty sigh. "Ah, you are not Tabitha, after all."

"There is no need to hide the headboard." She ducked her chin and smiled. His attention always made her shy, even though she found him more approachable in his loose-sleeved linen shirt and fawn-colored breeches than garbed with the accoutrements of a scout. Except for the way the shirt hung open at his strong neck, where she'd noticed his pulse throb that day she'd treated his wound.

"Headboard?" He blinked a moment. "How did you know about that?"

"She showed it to me when she first introduced me to Simon and Daisy." Esther shuffled her moccasin in the dirt. "She is hoping you might finish it for Christmas."

He chuckled. "And that I will. Did she send you to inspect my progress?"

"To collect a couple of eggs for the stew. I told her about the recipe I use." The men had shot two fat squirrels on their trip home from Fort Daniel the afternoon before. When Jared's eyebrows flew up, Esther recalled the whispered exchange about squirrel stew the day of her arrival. She held her hand out before he could speak. "I assure you, I will debone the rodents."

His laugh broke forth but faded quickly, and he studied her with a seriousness that made her shift her stance. Suddenly, he jumped into motion. "Let me check for you."

She followed him to the roost across from the livestock stalls. "I'm afraid to hope. The hens have been molting."

At Jared's approach, the chickens squawked and fluttered to the rafters. He stood on tiptoes to pat the straw above his head. "They need their energy to make it through the winter."

Jared's big red stallion thrust his head over the door of his stall, blowing air from his nostrils.

Esther leapt back, stumbling over a pile of straw...directly into Jared as he turned. She cried out and latched onto his arm in an attempt to right herself, but her stupid foot gave way. His arm shot around her, and he held her against his chest while clasping a brown egg in his other hand. For a moment, his stubbled jaw rested on her temple, his breath fanning her forehead.

Horror filled her. She'd pitched herself into his arms. Would he think she'd done it on purpose? Or just that she was hopelessly clumsy? Either way, she looked a fool.

Somehow, he gently maneuvered her upright and away from the straw. He dropped the egg into her basket. "I'm afraid you'll have to make do with this one."

"And it's a mercy I did not break it." Such a loss would have been inexcusable. Tears blurred her vision as she glanced up at him. "Please, forgive me."

"It's just an egg, Esther." He laid his hand on her forearm, his voice gentle. "Do you not know your safety to be far more important?"

She blinked several times, the moisture clinging to her lashes. "You are too kind, sir."

A change came over his demeanor, his expression going blank, his posture going straight as he snatched his hand back. "You don't need to call me *sir*, but I should not have presumed to use your Christian name. It is you who I must ask to forgive me." He didn't even wait for her to respond but stalked back to his woodworking area.

Something that had begun to unfurl shriveled in Esther's chest. To her own astonishment, she followed him. "I know you only meant to speak kindly. In fact, I hadn't even noticed."

"I am glad I did not offend you." He offered a brusque smile before presenting his back as he sorted his boards. "I shan't do it again."

"I did not mind." The whispered words escaped of their own accord, a thought accidentally given breath. She studied the wood shavings at Jared's feet as she mulled over the impossibility of her statement. She was not afraid of him. Even in the face of his efforts to rebuff her, she was not afraid. A song began in her heart. Part of it was not dead.

He turned back and stared at her.

"What are you making?"

A COUNTERFEIT BETROTHAL

"Pardon me?" The question was incredulous but not rude.

She gained confidence. "If you are not making the headboard, what are you working on?"

"A cradle." Facing away again, he resumed the use of the plane.

She moved closer to peek. "Oh, Tabitha will be so happy. It looks quite a bit lighter than the headboard." When he didn't respond, she added, "Is it a different type of wood?" The scent created by warm sunshine on fresh-cut boards drew her, and she took a tiny step closer.

"The cradle will be white oak. The headboard, walnut."

She cocked her head, as intrigued by his use of the sentinels of the forest as the way she used leaves, roots, and berries. "Which is finer?"

The light from the window over his bench made his eyes as blue as the sky. This was the first she had noticed that. "Depends on what you seek. Walnut, like mahogany, lends itself to carving, to ornamental design. But oak...oak is sturdy."

"I want to be like the oak." Another thought that she'd had no intention of speaking. Why did this man's presence seem to solicit honesty? Losing control of her own tongue—now that flustered her. "Thank you for the egg." She headed for the door.

Jared's voice stopped her with her hand on the bolt. "Mrs. Andrews?"

"Yes?" What had determined him to remain formal with her? Of course. He wanted to make sure she knew his intentions were platonic, as though she would ever imagine anything else. But she would like to be his friend. Yes, that was what she wanted.

Jared raised the board he was working on and blew dust from it. "I didn't think you were ready for me to speak of this before, but when we buried your husband, we took a quick look through the rubble for anything that remained of value.

Nothing struck us, but it occurred to me, you might want to have a look. Just to make sure."

A dark shroud of dread dropped over her. She stared at the floor a moment. "I don't expect we had anything of value to salvage." And even if they had, she wouldn't want it. "But yes, I expect I should go, if only to make peace with the place."

He gave a grim nod. "Then we will ride over after breakfast."

~

The creak of leather and soft plodding of Chestnut's hooves broke the gentle rattle of the breeze through the brittle leaves. The sun warmed Esther's shoulders, as did the body of the man behind her. There was no way she'd have attempted to handle Noble's massive stallion, but this time, she wasn't terrified, riding in front of Jared. His silent, solid presence fortified her as they drew near her old home.

She only asked one thing when the horse's misstep caused her to bump into Jared. "How is your shoulder?"

"Almost healed. It barely gives me a twinge now."

"You were fortunate the musket ball did not pass a quarter of an inch to the inside."

"Indeed. It was not the first time I felt God's protection."

Yes. People like the Lockridges lived in a bubble of grace. She'd observed such favor before—but never applied to herself. She'd taken it as another proof that what her father and husband had said about her had been true. In the heavenly scheme of things, some people were simply of more value than others.

They rode into the clearing, and her eyes widened. What a scene of devastation. Besides the corncrib, woodshed, and the toppling stack of stones which had been their chimney, only a pile of blackened ash and some small bits of charred logs remained. Jared halted Chestnut where the front porch had stood, dismounted, and then helped her down.

He waited, holding the reins, as Esther made her way around the ruins. She bent once or twice to turn over a piece of wood, but no useful metal, nothing precious or solid remained. Fitting. And just as well, as she couldn't have explained to Jared why she left behind anything she might find. The very ash of the place smelled tainted.

Finally, he led Chestnut near and pointed beneath a massive hemlock. "Do you see that boulder? Next to that tree? That is where we buried him."

Steeling herself, Esther limped in that direction. They'd erected a small wooden cross, just two sticks lashed together with cordage and stuck in the earth. Memories flashed before her eyes, things she would never describe to the proper gentleman who trailed behind her. Things that shamed her to even think of in his presence. Nausea churned her stomach, and a new and horrible possibility stole her breath. She hadn't bled since the fire. What would she do if...

The mere notion turned her good leg to jelly, and Esther sank onto the boulder.

"Mrs. Andrews, are you—"

She flung her hand out. "Do not call me that. Please don't call me that ever again. And please, don't come closer."

He backed away and waited near the rubble.

In this place, she couldn't hold her head up. And if any seed of that monster had taken root inside her...

She knew of herbs that would eliminate it, of course. But could she do such a thing? Would that make her a monster like him?

Esther leaned over and vomited into the soft black earth. Then she folded her arms over her knees and wept. As she raised her face to wipe her eyes with her sleeve, the light snuffed out as though the moon moved over the sun. The beating of many wings filled Esther's ears just as the clearing filled with a moving cloud. It seemed to descend into the very trees. What was happening?

Fighting to calm his prancing stallion, Jared tugged Chestnut closer. "We have to go!"

She scrambled to her feet, and he handed her up and mounted behind her.

Cooing and flapping roared with the intensity of a hurricane. Feathers rained down around them. Esther focused on a nearby branch that sagged, then cracked, under the weight of maybe two dozen gray-and-white bodies. She couldn't believe her eyes. "Pigeons?"

Jared spurred Chestnut toward the path that led back to the Lockridge place. "Occasionally, a flock this big passes through. They decimate any area where they land. Let's hope they don't follow us home."

Home. Yes, this was no longer her home. Let them decimate whatever was left of it. She wanted every bit obliterated.

But what if there was a bit she couldn't obliterate? As Esther sagged in the saddle, Jared's arm came around her, supporting her, and tears eased from her eyes. His nearness no longer felt reassuring. It reminded her she was dirty. Ruined. Unfit for decent society.

Please, God, don't let it be. She hadn't thought of God in a long time. Aunt Temperance had taught her about Jesus, and in Washington as a small child, she had loved Him. But her father's coldness and Liam's abuse had long since driven away any notion that a gentle Savior might care for her. She could face any future but one where she had to raise the child of the man who had broken her. *If You are there, if You care at all, grant me this one request.*

*J*ared must have told his brother and sister-in-law while she was washing up at the spring that the visit to her old home place had been hard on her, for when she came into the cabin, everyone was especially kind. How could she bear it? They had no idea what a low, worthless being they embraced as one of their own. Only by working hard might she be allowed a temporary place. As long as she was useful.

But when she tried to cut the cornbread and serve the stew, Tabitha shooed her to the table and dished up the savory soup herself. Then she bragged on Esther when the men complimented the meal. "Esther showed me a new way of making it—a quarter pound of butter mixed with a bit of flour and cream to thicken it up. Just before serving it, you add the beaten egg yolk and a little parsley. Is it not divine?"

"Delicious." Noble raised his spoon in Esther's direction.

"Her industry in our absence has been amazing." Jared's gaze ran over the beams of the ceiling, where Esther had strung as many herbs to dry as she had been able to find this late in the season. He focused on her with a gentle smile. "You're going to need a bigger herb box."

She smiled back but ducked her head as Tabitha teased, "An herb *chest*."

Noble nudged his bride. "Mrs. Andrews is going to make a frontier woman of you yet, my love."

Tabitha stuck her tongue out at him, but Jared's eyes remained fastened on Esther. He cleared his throat and said softly, "Earlier today, our guest expressed the wish that we call her by her Christian name." He glanced at Noble. "Even you and I, brother."

Esther kept her lashes lowered, but she could feel the stares of everyone at the table.

Tabitha leaned toward her. "Is that your wish, Esther?"

"It is."

"Very well, then." Noble reached for his pewter tankard. "We shall honor the request and be pleased if you will do the same."

"You are all too kind to me, although..." She peeked in her host's direction.

He frowned. "Yes?"

Dare she say it? "If it does not seem ungrateful, as you are the head of the home, I would feel disrespectful calling you aught but Mr. Lockridge."

Noble's tankard thumped to the table. He glanced at Jared. Was he wondering what Esther would call his brother? Oh, please let him not ask it. Finally, at a tiny shake of Tabitha's head, he said, "If it pleases you. Although I hope by spring, you might find me approachable enough to call me Noble."

Esther pretended to scoop a bite of her soup. "Thank you."

She still couldn't eat, but she bluffed her way through the rest of the meal with tiny sips of broth and nibbles of crumbs. Then she insisted on taking a trencher of dishes to wash at the spring. Liam had sworn a corncob scrubbing to be more than sufficient, but the Lockridges' finer dinnerware deserved a thorough cleaning. Tabitha liked it to shine in her hutch.

While attending to her personal business near the springhouse, Esther discovered the linen strips she'd applied earlier beneath her chemise had been needed after all. She sat on the bank a moment, weak with relief. Was this happenstance, or an answer to prayer? Either way, she could think of the future again. *Thank you, God. Thank you.*

When she returned, Tabitha sat in the rocker, Noble in the ladder-back chair, and Jared on the bench facing the fire. He patted the space next to him.

"Come. Join us. Noble is going to begin our Advent reading."

Esther put the dishes away as quickly as she could. "Advent?"

Tabitha looked up from her knitting. "The holy days leading up to the birth of the Christ child. Did your father ever read to you from the Bible, Esther?"

"He never owned one, but my aunt and uncle did. I think...I think I remember them reading to me about baby Jesus, but so long ago." Drawn by a strong curiosity, Esther hurried over. She sat next to Jared and folded her cold, chapped hands in her lap. She'd put salve on them later.

Duchess got up from her place near Noble, padded over to nudge her for a still-hesitant pat, then sank with a heavy sigh at her feet.

"Well, look at that." Jared chuckled, tossing the dog's tail off the top of his boot.

Tabitha hid a laugh behind the scarf she was making. "You are officially adopted, Esther."

Heat licked up past the neckline of her woolen short-dress. As Noble opened the big book with its black leather cover upon his lap, a voice whispered in her head, an echo of Liam's but even more vindictive. *Worthless piece of trash. Lame witch.* Her breath came fast, but she forced herself to remain upright on the bench. Going back to that place had played with her mind.

"We will start with the prophecy in Isaiah 9 that foretold the birth of Jesus as a baby." Marking his place with his finger, Noble's deep voice rumbled forth. "'The people that walked in darkness have seen a great light: they that dwell in the land of the shadow of death, upon them hath the light shined.'"

That had been her, in darkness, and now, a light was shining. One she didn't even understand. The light of kindness to her.

"'For thou hast broken the yoke of his burden, and the staff of his shoulder, the rod of his oppressor...'"

The other voice competed for her attention. *You're lucky I put up with you. No one else would have you.* Esther's heart raced.

But no. Her yoke had been broken...and buried beside a boulder.

"'For unto us a child is born, unto us a son is given: and the government shall be upon his shoulder: and his name shall be called Wonderful, Counsellor, the mighty God, the everlasting Father, the Prince of Peace.'"

This was the Jesus Aunt Temperance had spoken of, for the words Noble read opened a floodgate of memories—happy, long-buried memories this time—and brought Esther the same sense of sweetness and safety she remembered from early childhood. Could it truly be God who had freed her, sending Jared at just the right time? Had the same God who came into the world at Christmas broken into her life to save her? To bring...peace?

Why now? The bitter accusations the Scriptures had silenced were back, snatching any seed of hope before it could sprout. If God loved her so much, why had He left her alone to suffer all those years? How could she know the future didn't hold worse? She might feel safe now, but one wrong word, one stupid mistake, and she could find herself out in the cold.

Esther's legs stiffened without her permission, springing her to a standing position. She stood there a moment with everyone looking at her, her chest rising and falling on rapid breaths. Trapped. Unable to speak, yet unable to quench the tears welling in her eyes.

A lie offered itself up. "I'm sorry. I think I forgot to close the goats' stall earlier." She snatched up the tallow stub burning in an earthenware holder and hobbled toward the door.

"I'll go with you." Tabitha's earnest offer trailed her.

But Esther shook her head. Sweet as she might seem now, Tabitha would be shed of her soon as she recovered from the birth of the babe—before Keturah could come. She'd left out that letter in the obvious hope Esther would read it and remember her disposable status. Esther glanced back. "No, please." That had come out almost panicked. She smoothed her tone. "No need to trouble yourself."

I am not worth it.

She swung the door closed behind her and plunged into the familiar cold of the night.

CHAPTER 8

*J*ared came to his feet as the door thudded behind Esther. He took a step, then hesitated. "She is not safe out there."

"Are you safe, working at your bench until all hours?" Noble rose also, but leisurely, and reached for his pipe on the mantel.

"That is different. I always have my gun. I am a man."

"And she is a woman. One who needs to be left well enough alone." Seeking his tobacco pouch, his brother sent him a warning look.

Jared balled his fists. "Something is wrong."

"She did seem distraught when you returned from her old cabin. Perhaps that was not a good idea." Tabitha laid her knitting in her lap and sighed. "I thought the Bible reading was helping, but then..."

"It started before that, this morning. A misunderstanding. It was my fault."

She pursed her lips. "Even so, Noble is right...you shouldn't be the one to comfort her. I should."

"I don't need to comfort her. I need to make sure she is all right. And I think she made clear she has no wish for your company." Mind made up, Jared strode to the door, where he plucked his overcoat and Esther's cloak from nearby pegs. It would be cold in the barn. Then he palmed his musket.

Tabitha flung her hand up. "She won't thank you for yours either."

"If that is the case, I will leave her the gun and return posthaste. Regardless, please don't follow me."

From the porch, Jared swept the clearing with his gaze, searching for movement, for light reflecting in eyes—something Esther in her hurry had surely not done. The single candle she'd fled with flickered around the edges of the stable's shuttered window. He jogged toward it. His footsteps would announce his arrival, but to help allay alarm, he gave a brief knock. He opened the door to find her slumped on a small stool. She turned her face away, swiping at the moisture streaking her cheeks that glistened in the weak light.

"You should always take a weapon when you leave the house at night. This is the time of year predators start to get bold." Jared leaned the musket next to the door. He stood there a moment, waiting. She did not acknowledge him, but she did not tell him to leave either. Pain radiated from every line of her body, like a palpable force. In response, something inside Jared ached.

He located another candle stub in an earthenware base and tilted it to the flame from the house. Another circle of light expanded—enough to see his tools. He opened his box and selected a chisel. Tonight was not for the noisy work of pounding out mortise-and-tenon joints. It was for the delicate work of carving. He drew the headboard closer, with its rough vine design approximated in the topmost arch, sat on his bench, and angled his tool into a groove.

Many minutes passed with just the sound of soft scraping

and the sighing of the wind. The animals had bedded down, the goats and horses in their stalls, even the chickens in their roost. Jared could have counted every one of those minutes, for during each, he feared and prayed. *Don't let my brother or Tabitha charge in here with the righteous intention of chaperoning.* Because he sensed Esther had something to say. Perhaps many things to say. But only silence would draw her, like the blade drew out the design in the wood.

She stared at the chest he'd left open. At last, she ventured in a low voice, "Tabitha said those were your grandfather's tools."

He kept his eyes on his task. "They were. What else did she tell you?"

"That he was a talented cabinetmaker in Augusta. But those tools look homemade, not what I expected for a man of means." She propped her chin on her fist and watched him.

"Many of them *are* homemade, either by him or me. Like these squares—of maple and walnut." Jared leaned over and lifted a couple of the ninety-degree angles from the top of the chest. "And the oak handle of this scribe, used for marking lines." He showed her the wooden portion that secured an awl blade. "A local blacksmith forged the metal, of course."

She nodded. "So he was not wealthy, your grandfather?"

"He was."

Jared returned to his carving. He'd no intention of sharing this part of his background with her, but might it not help him to relate to her? Did he want to relate to her? He looked up as Esther smoothed her skirt over her ankles, as though to cover the misshapen limb—or in preparation to rise. A sigh caved her chest.

And he drew in a breath.

"He was a Loyalist during the Revolution." When her wide eyes fastened on him, he went back to work. "Control of Savannah and Augusta swung like a pendulum between the two armies, and reprisals against those who supported the crown were oft-times fierce. Tarrings and featherings, beatings, homes burned."

Esther's intake of air signaled her commiseration.

"Thankfully, his fate was not that severe, but his shop and all his tools were confiscated. Turned over to a Whig."

"Did he get them back?"

Jared shook his head. "No, but he was able to acquire much of what you saw in that chest after the war. And pass on his knowledge to me when I was a young lad—at least, as much as he could with that odd assortment."

"Your father did not follow in the trade, then?"

Jared's chest tightened, and he paused to blow shavings from the top of a carved ivy leaf. "He owned a farm outside town. The grandfather I speak of was my mother's father."

"Oh, yes."

He frowned. Why did she sound as if she connected that confirmation to some former knowledge? What all had Tabitha prattled about?

"So the war did not harm him, then."

The bitter laugh—if one could call it that—coughed out of him before he could stop it. "I would not say that."

She blinked at him. "Was he much troubled for being married to the daughter of a Loyalist?"

"If one could call suspicion and harassment trouble, most certainly. He felt compelled to fight, despite his peace-loving nature. He..." Jared clamped his jaw over his admission, but it forced its way out. "He was not prepared for what he had to see and do. He did not come back the same." *Please, God, she would not ask about that.*

But Esther folded her hands in her lap. Perhaps her own familiarity with pain made her more sensitive to its evidence in others. She spoke almost to herself. "That does explain it.

Would that I could have kept spirits away from Liam the way you keep away from them."

Liam. Her deceased husband? And how quickly she had made the jump from his father not being the same after the war to her own spouse's apparent addiction—with the memory of Jared's opposition to alcohol the comma in between. He gazed at her a long moment. "You are remarkably perceptive."

"Oh." She gave a soft snort. "Some things are so common, they need no explanation."

Jared brushed his hand over his design and matched her tone. "Like drinking...and wife-beating?"

She nodded, and her gaze sought some dark corner of the barn.

"Perhaps what is common to you makes you think it is common to most. Or even...acceptable to God."

She shrugged. "I only know what I have observed. And that is that cruelty comes more often than kindness. Although I did think for a moment tonight, during the reading..." Esther closed her lips over the rest of her sentence and sat up straighter. "But you did not always live in a cocoon, either, then. I am sorry for that."

He scoffed, although his mind chased after that incomplete admission of hers. "Live in a cocoon? What do you mean? And why are you apologizing?"

"I might have misjudged you." She stared at the toes of her moccasins, tucking them under her hem.

"How?"

"As someone who has always received blessings."

"Always? No." Jared laid his chisel in the tool chest, but rather than reach for another size, he stared into the past. Scenes flashed before him. His father's slap, hard enough to make him stumble and shatter the decanter Jared was trying to hide from him. Hooves galloping away from home as he huddled under the covers, his mother's sobs clamping him in a vise of helplessness. A movement from Esther brought him back to the present. This wasn't the time to mire in his old hurts. This woman needed a model of redemption, not a man yet haunted by childhood pain. "God allows people to make choices, Esther. And sometimes they make bad ones. But we can decide not to be like those people and not to let them break us."

She stared at him a long moment, cheeks flushing, then she raised shaking hands to cover her face. "But sometimes, they do." The quavering admission escaped through her slender fingers.

Jared went over and knelt beside her. He dared the lightest possible touch to her arm. Even still, she jerked away. Words, then. "God can heal you."

She kept her face hidden. "How?"

Jared prayed for the Spirit of God to interweave his own logic. "Well, He often begins by putting you in a safe place. I believe He brought you here on purpose. Then He uses His children to show how good and kind He really is."

Esther lowered two fingers, peeking at him. Her tears negated any misperception of levity in the gesture. Jared fished in his pocket and came out with a clean square of fabric, offering it to her. She blotted her eyes.

"It's true," she said. "You are kinder than you should be. I don't know why you'd take in someone like me."

That made his heart wrench. "Because you are a child of God, deserving of respect and every good thing He has for you. You've been beaten down, Esther. Told lies."

"Only told what has always been true. I am lame, clumsy, worth—"

Jared shushed her, his finger snapping to her lips before he could consider.

Her eyes rounded, but she did not pull away. He did.

He resumed in a sterner tone than he'd ever used with her. "I'm sorry, but we won't tolerate such talk here."

Her eyelashes dropped, matted with tears, and his heart almost melted. She sucked in a tremulous breath, then let it out. "I did think earlier..."

He sat back on his heels. "What did you think?" Finally, she seemed to be circling back around to whatever she had started to say once before...and hopefully, the reason she'd fled the house to begin with.

Esther wouldn't look at him, turning the handkerchief in her hands. "The verses...they were talking about being set free, seeing the light. They made me think that maybe God sent you."

"I do believe that." Jared reiterated his opinion softly, then waited.

"Even though things have changed, they haven't changed in here." Esther tapped her temple, the agitation of the gesture and set of her mouth revealing her frustration. Tears slipped from her eyes. "I can't seem to escape my past, the voices in my head. I...have not been free in so long. Do you think it is possible?"

"I know it is." Conviction firmed his tone. "Although it may take some time."

"You don't know what my life has been like. How low..." Her throat worked, and she stared at the handkerchief again. "How low I have fallen."

Jared laid his hand on her arm once more, and this time, she did not shrink away. "Regardless of how low man may have brought us, God would lift us up—to be His children and heirs."

She wet her lips as she studied the wood shavings on the ground. "I would like to learn more, if you and your family would teach me."

A sense of purpose swelled Jared's chest. "Nothing would bring us more joy."

It all made sense now—even the draw to Esther he couldn't explain. He'd thought he'd enlisted to serve his country, to right the wrongs of his fathers, but God always had a higher purpose. Suddenly, the winter stretched before him, long and cold, yes—but bright and full of promise. And maybe even the sweetness of surprise, just like Christmas morning.

CHAPTER 9

The familiar smells of Maltbie and Moore's—tobacco, whiskey, gunpowder, fur, leather, and unwashed bodies—took Esther back in time as she stepped through the door. This store, however, carried a wider variety of goods than her father's, which had focused on beads, blankets, metal trinkets and tools, and firewater—items most often bartered with the Indians. As Tabitha led Noble to examine a feather mattress, Esther froze just inside the threshold, her mouth dropping open at the confusing assortment of cooking and dining implements, saddlery, and tin trunks.

Jared struggled to close the door behind her. "You can go all the way in, you know."

She breathed out her trepidation in a low-spoken sentence. "Father always forbade it." The words came out on a puff, for mid-December's chill had settled over the piedmont, and the warmth of the fire crackling in the hearth did not reach past old Mr. Moore's counter.

A chuckle rumbled from Jared's chest. "Freedom, remember? Your father is not here. And I want to show you my furniture."

Esther turned to him. "Your furniture is in here?"

"Right behind you." Jared swept his hand toward a walnut sideboard and corded bedstead in the corner. "I made those back in the summer. I'm hoping someone will purchase them as a Christmas gift."

She moved that direction. "Oh, they surely will, but it seems a shame to sell them." She ran her fingers over the smooth wood, glossed with a protective walnut-dye stain. "They are amazing."

"I can make more. I *will* make more once this trouble with the Creeks subsides."

Of course. For his new cabin, the one Tabitha had told her would be located on the nearby rise. The one he would share with Keturah. Esther turned away.

The readings from the Bible this past week had spoken of her worth in God's eyes. If that was true—she lay awake into the night, struggling to believe—she needed no man to affirm her. A respectable widow could make her own way in the world. With Aunt Temperance's help, she should be able to gain that respect in Savannah. So why did the thought of a girl she didn't even know living with Jared make her chest as hollow as a dried gourd?

He hovered near her elbow. "What do you wish to look at?"

She wished him gone so that she might right her thoughts. "I will only pass through and admire everything." She did not need to remind him that she had no coin. But the whispers and chuckles of the others had carried on the frosty air this morn as they traveled to the settlement. She had to find a way to thank them for their kindness this Christmas. She twisted the silver ring on her finger. She hadn't worn it since the visit to her old cabin, but she had a plan. One that needed Jared elsewhere. "Perhaps I might look at the ladies' items and consider necessities come spring."

He ducked his head, the picture of an English gentleman in

his gray wool greatcoat and vest, linen shirt with neatly tied stock, trousers, and Hessian boots, his hat clasped against his chest. She'd never seen him dressed so fine. When she'd descended the ladder this morning, he'd fair stole her breath away. "I'll leave you to it, then."

Esther pretended to linger at the fabric table while he went to inspect a nice-looking flintlock rifle. Was that what he wanted? It would certainly make his scouting easier. She fingered a thin twill-woven bombazet, peeking over her shoulder at Mr. Moore tending his fire.

Tabitha slipped up behind her. "That would make a lovely spring dress."

"Oh no. 'Tis far too fine." Esther thrust it away as though her touch might sully the worsted cloth.

"You'll need something fine for Savannah. And that olive-green would look lovely with your coloring." Tabitha cocked her head and narrowed her eyes, studying her.

"I have plenty of clothing. Two short gowns—linen and wool—to go with my other petticoat, besides this dress." Esther rubbed her hand down the front of her rust-colored bodice. "Father said it was a great extravagance, but he wanted me outfitted before my wedding."

"That was thoughtful of him." Even though she did not say it, Tabitha's gentle examination made Esther aware the garments had been well worn since then.

She left her hostess to discuss the merits of a durable osnaburg for a rocking chair cushion with her husband and snuck over to the counter.

"Can I help you, ma'am?" Mr. Moore gave no indication he recognized her as the daughter of his previous competitor. Just as well. She'd rather him assume she was a guest of the Lockridges, perhaps a relative.

"Have you white sugar and wheat flour?" She whispered the question. Tabitha's dried apples would make a wonderful cake, and Esther hadn't forgotten Jared's reference to syllabub. The Lockridges took their corn to the grist mill on the Apalachee—a luxury compared to the hand mill Liam had expected Esther to use to grind their dried corn, and blanched acorns when that meager supply dwindled. But even well-off settlers seldom acquired wheat flour on the frontier.

Mr. Moore caught onto her secrecy, his bushy brows shooting up, then nesting above his shining eyes as he whispered back. "I do, but it comes very dear." He named the price, and Esther swallowed hard.

She twisted the ring off her finger. She'd gained enough weight that it no longer threatened to fall off. "Would this be enough for a pound of each...and one of those?" She nodded toward several nutmegs displayed in a nearby wooden bowl.

"Why, I'd say so. I don't get much jewelry here, and rings that can be used for weddings are even rarer, but ma'am..." He took the circlet to examine it. "Are you sure?"

Esther nodded. "I am sure." She picked up the top nutmeg and shook it, satisfied by the rattle of kernels in the shells covered by their streaked reddish coat of mace. The seeds had sufficiently dried to make their highly prized powder.

"Have you something we can hide your purchases in?"

She held out a cloth satchel looped over her shoulder, strung under her cloak.

"Very good. One moment while I fill your order."

As Mr. Moore turned to some barrels behind him, the door swung open with a gust of cold air. Two Cherokee young men entered bearing bundles of rolled furs on their backs. Esther slid to the end of the counter as they approached. They wore buckskin tunics, leggings, and winter trade blankets. Their long, dark hair shone with bear grease under floppy felt hats rather than the turbans favored by their wealthy brothers. The memory triggered by the smell—along with the way the handsome one's dark eyes swung to her—made Esther stiffen. He reacted to her as well, stopping momentarily and staring as though he'd seen a ghost. Did she know him? Had he indeed traded in her father's store?

The men unrolled luxurious beaver, deer, and rabbit pelts on the counter and waited for Mr. Moore to acknowledge them. He turned and welcomed them in Cherokee. "*Tsi-lu-gi.*"

"*Si-yu.*" The brave who appeared slightly older than his comrade said hello, but the younger one's gaze remained on Esther, only flickering to her right when she felt rather than saw Jared step up behind her.

Mr. Moore slipped Esther brown-paper-wrapped packets of her baking goods secured with twine, thanking her and wishing her a joyous Christmas. She slid the purchases into her satchel.

Jared touched her arm. "Are you ready? We can wait for the others on the porch."

The young brave's eyes narrowed at him, and his back stiffened, but Jared ignored him.

Esther nodded as she took the arm he offered. At the door, she glanced back, and just as she had known he would be, the native was watching them. Outside, she put her hand to her fast-beating heart. "I got the strange sense that Cherokee didn't like you."

"I didn't like him much either. I was afraid he was about to speak to you before I came over."

She took a deep breath. "I can't imagine what he would say."

Jared frowned and led her to sit on a bench. "He didn't seem familiar? He looked at you as though he knew you."

"Somewhat."

"Could he be the man who has been watching you? The one who killed Liam?"

She forced a response past the sudden dryness in her throat. "It's possible, but I couldn't say for certain. I've never seen the man's face. Even the night he tried to abduct me, he grabbed me from behind."

"Right." Jared patted her hand. "Put it from your mind. You're safe now."

With a nod, Esther focused on the rough settlement in its gray cloak of early winter. Yes, not only was Jared at her side, but children and housewives bundled in woolens darted between the stores and a sprinkling of log homes. A pair of riders dismounted and tethered their horses in front of the Hog Mountain House, the smoke from its brick chimney promising welcome warmth. Militiamen with rifles much like the one Jared had admired in the store marched up the dirt lane to the fort on the rise. As the trees had been cleared in all directions surrounding the structure, Esther glimpsed pickets on the walls.

The trading post door opened again, and relief settled over Esther as Tabitha and Noble emerged, bearing a number of wrapped packages and between them, the feather tick. Esther and Jared rose and smiled.

"Behold, my Christmas present," Tabitha declared proudly. "Although one of us will have to walk home, Esther, as Noble must fix it to a horse."

"I don't mind walking." In fact, the exercise sounded good.

Jared smiled at her. "Neither do I."

"Then I will take the opportunity to forage along the path."

Tabitha glanced up the road. "First, Noble says I should introduce myself to the woman who serves as the local midwife, Mrs. White. Her husband is the cooper."

"I know where they live." Jared stepped off the porch and offered his hand to Tabitha. "Allow me to escort you ladies while Noble secures your goods."

Ladies? Esther ducked her head as she handed her host her pouch of secret purchases. He took it with a little bow and raised his brow as its unexpected weight yanked his hand toward the ground. But he made no comment. Did he think she had stolen something? Her face flamed. Then he winked and turned toward the horses, and she released her breath. She couldn't get used to the way the Lockridge men treated her as though she were of the same quality as Tabitha.

Jared accompanied them down the street to a single-pen log house with a fenced herb garden, and beyond it, a coopering shed. She would have been drawn straight to the enclosed plot had the door not opened and a gray-haired housewife stepped out. And behind her, a Cherokee woman with dark braids, clad in an English-made ensemble over buckskin leggings and moccasins.

"Ahyoka!" The name burst from Esther's lips with a surge of joy.

Her old friend turned, and her dark eyes rounded. She held out her hands as Esther rushed and stumbled to the foot of the porch. "Esther. *No-tlv-si.*"

Why Ahyoka had always insisted on calling her *Star* mystified her. For despite it being the meaning of her name, there had never been anything bright about her. But none of her protests had ever discouraged the moniker, so they probably wouldn't now.

Instead, she squeezed the healer's hands. "It has been so long."

"Yes. Ten summers?" Ahyoka spoke very simple English sprinkled with Cherokee.

Esther's attention fixed on a pewter button on a rawhide string around Ahyoka's neck—the only sentimental object she'd had to give when last they'd met. "You still wear that silly button?" She reached up and touched it.

Ahyoka nodded vigorously. "A gift. Special." Her gaze swept Esther, taking in every aspect of her appearance and then moving to those behind her. "*Tso-ga-li-i?*"

98

"Yes, these are my friends." She drew Tabitha forward and introduced her, then Jared.

"*U-ye-hi?*"

Esther's face heated. "No, he is not my husband. Or hers. He is her brother, *di-na-da-nv-tli*." She chose the simplest way she could think to communicate about a brother-in-law.

"Ah." Ahyoka nodded, her braids sliding up and down over her chest.

Jared dipped his head and smiled. "Pleased to meet you." His questioning gaze fell on Esther.

She responded to the unspoken prompt. "Ahyoka is the healer I told you about."

Tabitha frowned and looked between them.

Before they could explain, Ahyoka gestured to the woman behind her. "Mag-gie White." She chattered something else Esther did not understand, but Tabitha took over, coming up the steps and offering her hand.

"You must be the midwife."

"Yes, my dear. That would be me, merely by merit of how many births I've attended."

"I am Mrs. Noble Lockridge. Tabitha."

The older woman pressed Tabitha's hand between her own. "Honored."

"I have some questions for you and am hoping you might attend me as well when my time comes."

Mrs. White assessed Tabitha's ever-rounding belly. "From the way you're carrying, I'd guess you will have a son in a couple of months."

A brilliant smile broke across Tabitha's rosy face. "That is what I am hoping."

The midwife nodded. "I will do all in my power to help you, of course, but I must warn you, I'm no expert. Not like Ahyoka here. I have learned much from her about herbs."

Ahyoka smiled at Tabitha. "Mag-gie do good. I also teach

No-tlv-si, many summers ago." Her Cherokee friend ran her hand down Esther's arm, and Esther warmed at the gentle touch she'd missed so much.

Mrs. White folded her hands at her ample waist. "That does not surprise me. Ahyoka has been so good as to bring me roots needful for feminine complaints and childbirth."

Jared cleared his throat behind them. "At that, I will leave you women to visit, if you will be a few minutes." Their giggles at his sheepish manner gave way to agreement. "Good, then. I will return shortly. I have some unfinished business at the store."

Mrs. White extended her palm toward her door. "Do come in out of the cold. We'll have a pot of tea."

Tabitha followed her in, and Esther nodded at Jared, who raised his hat, turned, and strode down the street. Ahyoka looked after him with her lips pressed tight.

"He is good to you?"

The familiar heat flooded Esther. "He is not mine." Had Ahyoka not understood Jared's role earlier?

Ahyoka faced her, seemingly undiverted. "Better than *u-ye-hi*?" Her brows drew together. "I still mad at your father. He pick *u-yo-i a-s-ga-ya. Ni-da-tse-lv-na yv-wi.*"

Bad man. Ugly person. Indeed. A band tightened around Esther's chest, and she reached again for Ahyoka's hands. "Yes, but how did you know that?"

"I see." She pointed to her eyes. "I look. Right there, in front of nose."

"I missed you, missed talking to you." Esther dropped her head. Why hadn't Ahyoka warned her? But would it have mattered? "I had no choice."

"I know." Ahyoka patted her hands. "I could no longer come to trading post."

But why not? The question stuck in Esther's throat. She had assumed Ahyoka no longer cared about her when she had disappeared—just another confirmation of how little she mattered to anyone. When she asked her father about her, he'd explained that she lived quite a distance away, near Suwanee Old Town, and only came to Hog Mountain occasionally to trade. But why did she no longer come even for that? And now, here she was. Esther's mind spun with the conflicting evidence.

Ahyoka put a finger under Esther's chin and tipped it up. "I must go now."

"Already?" The loss surged afresh in Esther's chest. "I have so much to talk to you about."

"Hold thoughts here." Ahyoka tapped Esther's breastbone. "We talk again. But promise...these people, they are good?" Her gaze went to the door Tabitha had gone through.

Esther nodded firmly. "They are good. Kind to me. They are letting me stay the winter with them to help Tabitha, then I will go east in the spring."

Sadness pooled in Ahyoka's eyes, and she squeezed Esther's hands. "We talk again," she repeated. Then she hurried down the steps and toward the settlement.

Rapid blinking allowed Esther to clear the tears from her eyes as her old friend joined two men who had been waiting under a tree—the two Cherokees from the trading post.

CHAPTER 10

The thumping and cracking sounds made by Noble as he chopped firewood provided the rhythm for the final swipes of Jared's polish rag over the completed headboard. By peeking out the window ever so often, he was able to ascertain the moment his brother went down to the spring. He grabbed the unwieldy piece of furniture and, after securing the entrance, hurried away from the barn with an awkward sidestep. Then he cracked open the cabin door and peered inside.

Thankfully, both women focused on whatever they were doing at the hearth, Esther standing and Tabitha seated. Their recent trip to Hog Mountain had provoked a return of difficulties for Tabitha, who had until then sworn that Esther's help had been enough to normalize her pregnancy. But Tabitha's laughter assured him all was well today, and the savory smell of the roasted turkey—shot by Jared two evenings prior and hung until dressed this Christmas morning—promised that the women had succeeded in producing a mouth-watering dinner. Before they could spot him, he whisked into the bedroom. There, he moved the bed away from the wall and slid the headboard behind it. He would attach it later. He was out the door with a gust of cold air before Esther could finish whirling around.

Back in the barn, he gave the animals extra feed. Then he wrapped a length of linen around Esther's gift before setting it inside the finished crib. Several evenings, she'd sat with him while he'd worked on his gift for Tabitha and Jared. She'd asked questions about his tools, his process, and his background. What little he'd managed to get her to share about herself painted a picture of neglect and hardship that had further softened his heart toward her. And made him certain the arrangement he'd made with Mr. Moore—after the merchant verified what Jared suspected about the packets he'd glimpsed Esther slipping into her satchel—had been the right one. But would she be touched by the sentimental nature of his gift, or would it remind her of the painful part of her past?

Jared waited until Duchess's bark alerted him that his brother had returned to the house before carrying the heavy cradle to the front porch. Singing wafted from inside—Tabitha's bright soprano and his brother's reluctant tenor. "'The second day of Christmas, my true love sent to me two turtle doves and a partridge in a pear tree.'" Jared lowered the crib down next to the door before entering on the third verse.

Tabitha stood behind the bayberry tapers glowing bright and steady in their pewter holders in the center of the table. An embroidered cloth from her hope chest spread the length of the board, embellished with holly and magnolia leaves. She laid pearlware plates between Old English flatware at each setting.

"Oh, good, Jared, you must join us. We need your deeper voice. Singing 'The Twelve Days of Christmas' is a tradition in my family, and I must feel at home." She glanced to Esther, who was ladling something into a tureen at the sideboard. "And maybe you can convince Esther to chime in before the twelfth round."

Esther's face pinked as Tabitha continued on about "colly birds." Did she even know the rhyme? Sight of Esther made Jared almost forget that he did, for she wore a dark-green dress —Tabitha's?—with a square neck and fitted quarter-length sleeves and bodice that confirmed that her childlike figure had filled out with decent rest and nutrition. Her hair shone in the firelight, tied back with a white ribbon but swirling down her back in freshly washed waves.

When she lifted the tureen and sagged under its weight, Jared hastened to relieve her, whispering, "Let us sing if it makes her happy." He winked as he placed the container on the table. Then he joined in with "five gold rings."

On the next verse, a surprisingly rich alto at his elbow described "six geese a-laying," prompting him to offer Esther a smile of approval. Averting her eyes, she pointed to the turkey on a large platter, and he moved it to the place of honor between the bayberry candles. Esther followed with a plate of golden Johnny cakes. They all took their seats as they concluded the song, Duchess at the end, still tall enough while seated to watch every transfer of food with drooling jowl and hopeful eyes.

Jared likewise offered admiration to the victuals before him. "I see that you have done justice to the turkey."

"To be fair, Esther did it. She hardly let me lift a finger." Tabitha smiled at their guest. "And wait until you see what she has prepared for dessert."

Esther drew her shoulders forward. "Which I couldn't have done without your receipts and your advice."

Tabitha glowed. "Regardless, I have never felt so rested and happy."

"Recipes?" The plural hadn't escaped Jared. "There is more than one dessert?"

"It is a surprise. My gift to you all."

"On that note, let us pray." Noble extended his hands on both sides.

Esther took Tabitha's but stared at Jared a moment before finally lowering hers onto his palm. He closed his fingers over hers, so delicate, yet roughened by hard work. His heart lurched, and he tightened his hand, trying to convey his appreciation with a gentle smile. Her calluses endeared her more to this family than the soft hands of a pampered lady ever could.

After the *amen*, Noble carved the turkey while Jared served up stewed root vegetables—parsnips, turnips, and sweet potatoes. Esther passed the cornbread.

"I was taking the pigeons I shot to our neighbors, the Howells, yesterday when you got home from Hog Mountain." Noble handed Jared back his plate. Before he could get around to his point or question, his wife chimed in.

"How is Catherine Howell? And her new baby?"

"Both are well." Noble smiled at her. "And the eldest daughter was pleased with the pigeons to make a Christmas pie."

"I am glad you could offer them, since Mr. Howell is needed close at home right now and Jared had such luck with the turkey."

"Wasn't luck." Jared mumbled the words before stuffing in a tender bite of the bird.

Tabitha pressed her lips together and leaned forward. "Of course. I meant your *excellent skill*. What blessed women we are, Esther, to have two such mighty hunters to fill our table."

Esther blushed and glanced his direction. Did she feel as he did? As though this scene was all too comfortable...like two couples, a real family, joining together at the holiday? Already, it was growing hard to picture not only her absence, but the presence of another. A face he'd begun to forget. He frowned and studied his meal.

105

"As I was saying," Noble resumed with a throat clearing, "was there any news from the settlement?"

Jared glanced at his brother. "While my delivery was readied in Hog Mountain, I visited the fort. I found everyone in good spirits. The structure has been completed at last. They had been supplied brandy rations and corn meal from James Clements and beef from Isham Williams. Major Key will relinquish command to Captain Joseph Whorton, the commander of a detachment from Colonel Jones's regiment of the second brigade of militia. His men will serve through the rest of winter."

Noble lowered his fork, his eyes lighting. "So we won't be needed, then?"

Jared flattened his mouth. "I wish that were so." His gaze swung to Esther, then to Tabitha, shifting uncomfortably on the bench with her hand on her rounded belly.

"Did you not say a full detachment will man the fort?"

"Of infantry, yes, and supposedly nine horsemen. But there is a problem." Jared cut into a turnip.

His brother frowned. "What's that?"

"There are only two horses among them."

"How can that be the case?"

Jared spread his hands. "Not enough men with their own mounts, I suppose. You know most settlers are lucky to have a mule. But it will be hard to deploy the needed scouts without them. Benjamin Reynolds and Isham Williams, who took the last stint, will be seeking a reprieve. In fact, I heard that Isham is hiring on to help grade the road to Standing Peachtree after an initial crew lays it out—he, William Nesbit, and Bob Young. As stock raisers, they have sufficient horses, knowledge of the area, and extra hands to help with building the road to the new fort that will be constructed on the Chattahoochee."

"So you feel we ought to volunteer our services come January." Noble's tone bottomed out.

When Tabitha covered one side of her face, Esther reached over to rub her shoulder.

"What I feel doesn't matter," Jared said. "I know where my responsibility lies."

"Of course you do. Upstanding and loyal Jared, who always does his sacred duty."

The tang of bitterness in his brother's voice made Jared's eyes flash up. "I didn't mean to imply anything about you. I speak only for myself. I don't have a wife to consider." Awareness prickled through Jared even as he spoke the words, and he returned his focus to his plate. He did, however, have someone else to consider. Someone relying on him for protection. How must Noble feel?

"Only two from the fort have horses." Noble's mouth tightened. "That would leave you to scout alone, a dangerous undertaking should bands of Creeks sweep up the line again."

"Must we talk about it now?" The soft inquiry made them all stare at Esther. Her lashes fluttered, and her cheeks reddened, but she didn't lower her eyes. "Forgive me. I am sorry. But your conversation is stealing our dear Tabitha's Christmas cheer. Perhaps you can save it for another time."

Bravo for her. Leave it to Esther to find her backbone in defense of another. Amazement and admiration rushed over Jared, and he said quickly, "Of course. My apologies."

Noble sighed and sat back from the table. "No, it is I who must apologize, as I first brought it up and then pressed for information."

Tabitha folded her hands in front of her, her lips puckering. "Seeing as it is Christmas, it might take a bit of bribery to solicit my forgiveness."

"I think I know just the thing." Jared folded his napkin and stood. "May I?"

Tabitha blinked at him. "May you what?"

"Fetch your present from the porch, if Esther will hold the door for me."

"Of course I will." Esther got to her feet, and Tabitha clapped her hands while Esther and Jared crossed the room. She gave him a conspiratorial smile.

He brought in the crib to the hoped-for cries of delight. Tabitha clamored up and waddled over to inspect it, bending to feel the wood and test the smoothness of the rockers. "Oh, Jared, it's beautiful. I thought our gift was a headboard."

"It is. That is in your room already, if you wish to go see."

She squealed and clasped her hands under her chin. Then she raised herself on her tiptoes while he braced her arm, and she planted a kiss on his cheek. "You are forgiven. More than forgiven. But what is this?" She pointed to the wrapped parcel inside the crib.

Jared lifted it out. "I'm afraid this third gift is not for you. It's for Esther."

Esther froze as he turned to her, her eyebrows winging high on her delicately creased forehead. "But I don't have anything like that for you. For anyone." She looked around at them.

"We know." Tabitha hugged her. "Your gift went into our dessert, and I can't imagine a finer treat than what you have made. The smell alone made me feel I was back home in Augusta. I have something for you, too, but first, open Jared's present. I have a good guess what it is."

"You may, but there is a reason I rode into Hog Mountain yesterday." Jared led them back to the table and placed the bundle next to Esther's plate. "I had something of value and sentiment added to the practical item I made."

With her lips parted, Esther sat and gently unwrapped the linen. She gasped at the sight of the mahogany box with its vine pattern carved on top, and her finger flew out to rest on the clasp in front. "Is that..."

"Silver, yes. Your silver. You can put a lock on it now, if you wish."

Esther's eyes filled with tears. She stared at him in wordless wonder. "My silver?"

"From your mother's ring." Jared nodded toward his brother. "When Noble told me what he suspected you'd done outside the trading post, I went back in and bought the ring back from Mr. Moore. Then I had the blacksmith melt it down and make this clasp. I couldn't let you part with it."

A sob broke from Esther's lips. "It's perfect...better like that than as a ring."

Emotion swelled in Jared's throat. Her reaction was more than he'd hoped for. "Open it."

With trembling hands, she pushed the lid up and drew in a quick breath. She inspected the double trays carved with multiple slots. "For my herbs." Voice breathless, she passed her finger gently over the indentations. "This is perfect. Twice the size of my old chest." She turned to him with her eyes shining. "Thank you."

"You're most welcome."

Rising, Esther flung her arms around his neck. She pressed the side of her head to his, and the lavender scent of her hair filled his senses. He couldn't speak, so great was his astonishment. Warmth flooded him, and his eyes slid closed for a brief moment—basking in the softness of her nearness and her gratitude.

When he opened them, Tabitha was frowning.

Her expression cleared the moment Jared noticed her and pulled back. She tossed her hands up. "Well, as wonderful as that is, I still haven't seen my headboard. Let's all go look!"

"These presents have overtaken the end of our meal." Noble plucked a strand of dark meat and stuffed it in his mouth, then tossed the bone to Duchess. Chomping and slobbering sounds competed with the snapping of the fire.

Noble's wife pulled him up by the hand. "Your meal will wait."

Esther brightened. "And when we return, I will serve my gifts to you all. It will be but small thanks for all you have done for me, but I do hope you will enjoy."

"I have no doubt we will." Jared lowered his head closer to hers and murmured as his brother and Tabitha hurried into the next room. "Might I know what it is?"

She bit her pink bottom lip, then the admission spilled out. "Apple cake and syllabub."

He'd known it was something sweet, something special, but this, he hadn't expected. Just like he hadn't expected her. "You remembered." He curled his hand around hers, nestled in the fold of her skirt.

Shock that she didn't pull away coupled with amazement at the smile that spread over her features. It turned her beautiful, stealing the breath from his chest.

~

The mixture of the syllabub's sweet cider, grated nutmeg, milk, and brandy had already gone to his head, for he couldn't keep his eyes from Esther as she cleaned up their supper. Her manner delighted him more than the 1803 Harper's Ferry flintlock that could strike a deer at a hundred and fifty yards his brother had so generously gifted him with. Probably more than Tabitha's gift of olive-colored bombazet fabric had delighted Esther herself. The selfless way she waited on them all when Tabitha was indisposed spoke volumes about her character. Jared promised to take the dishes to the spring later if Esther would join them by the fire for the reading about the birth of Jesus.

Noble settled his wife on the new osnaburg cushion on the rocking chair while he fetched the family Bible from the shelf.

He lowered himself into the ladder-back chair with a creak and offered Esther an explanation. "We pass the Bible around, taking turns reading aloud from Luke, chapter two, on this final night of Advent. I will begin. 'And it came to pass in those days, that there went out a decree from Caesar Augustus that all the world should be taxed.'"

As he read about Mary and Joseph going to Bethlehem, Esther's bodice rose and fell, her eyes fixed on the fire. Was she remembering hearing the story as a child? When she finally shifted, Jared gave her a reassuring smile.

Tabitha shared the verses about the birth of Jesus. "'And, lo, the angel of the Lord came upon them, and the glory of the Lord shone round about them: and they were sore afraid.'" With a questioning glance, she slid the book onto Esther's lap.

Sore afraid was what she looked. Esther's hand trembled as she smoothed the page and bent toward the tiny print. Could she not see in the firelight? Jared moved the bayberry candle closer. He helped her find her place on the page. But still, her mouth only opened, then closed.

Tabitha made a tentative declaration. "I don't think...that is, I don't think Esther is up to this."

Jared looked between them. "What is wrong?" Esther's statement in the barn that night that she wanted to learn more about God had served as a springboard. Since then, her childhood faith had slowly grown. Was something triggering her old fears?

"Tabitha is right. I...I can't." Esther met his eyes, her brows knit. "These words are too hard for me."

"Hard? But these are words of the greatest good news."

"I know." Her shoulders sagged. "I mean they're...too hard for me to read. My father only taught me enough to get by."

"Oh." Relief surged through him. "Well, that is something easily remedied." He reached for the Bible, sliding it onto his leg. "To start, why don't you sit next to me as I read? I'll go slowly and trace along under each word."

Esther nodded and sighed, her curled fingers relaxing. "Thank you."

He extended his hand, wrapping it briefly around her far shoulder as she scooted closer. Then he used it to indicate his place, the warmth of her arm pressed close on his. "'And the angel said unto them, Fear not: for behold, I bring you good tidings of great joy...which shall be to all people.'"

Her head bent near his, nodding as he enunciated longer words, her lips moving along with his. The comprehension and delight that crossed her features brought the burn of deepest joy. This was the meaning of Christmas, this very moment. What could get sweeter?

When Noble went to put away the Bible, Jared and Esther stood to clear the platters from the table. He leaned close to murmur, "If you like, we can read together again soon. Other passages that you might find helpful." He already had several in mind.

Her gaze met his, still full of light. "I would like that very much." She turned in a swirl of lavender to gather and carefully stack their dishes on a tray on the hutch.

Stepping over to the peg near the door, Jared shrugged into his overcoat.

Tabitha drew up beside him, her tone laced with a warning that brought an interior frost. "Jared, *this* is an appropriate moment to speak of loyalty. Pray, don't make me regret my kindness to our guest."

CHAPTER 11

Confusion tangled Esther's emotions when Jared entered the cabin as the light of the sunny, early-January afternoon filtering through the windows began to fade. The men had been gone all day—hunting, she supposed, since no one had said otherwise in her hearing—and she had been too busy with wash day to take notice. But her whole being leapt to a painful attention now. An awareness no longer born of fear prickled her skin as she peeked through the damp garments she'd strung from the rafters to dry. Uncomfortable, unfamiliar, the unbidden sensation made her want to hide behind a woolen petticoat.

"Ah, Esther, I see you've been busy, as always." Jared laid aside his new rifle, shrugged out of his coat, and ran a hand through his wind-tousled blond hair. It fell in casual waves over his strong neck.

"Indeed. I apologize for cramping our living quarters with laundry, but it would freeze stiff as a salty mast outdoors."

"Of course. I appreciate your hard work on our behalf." His glance swung to the closed bedroom door as he rightly implied that Tabitha had been of little help. She'd started off the morning feeling poorly and gone downhill from there.

Esther spoke in a low voice. "She tried to at least transfer the garments between the wash and rinse tubs, but even that was too much for her." She went back to preparing Tabitha's tea, adding some mint in an attempt to disguise the flavor of the sneezewood root, black haw shrub bark, and partridge berry leaves she'd procured from Mrs. White and made into a tonic. Hopefully, Ahyoka's herbs would help stop the expectant mother's spotting. She froze when, with a flutter of laundry, Jared appeared beside her, reaching for her hand.

He inspected her nails and palm with a sober expression. "I see you did all the scrubbing and wringing by yourself." Despite the roughness of her skin, it tingled at his touch. Liam's grasp had only ever been rough, impatient, or demanding. Jared's was gentle, evoking a strange response ... pleasure mixed with wariness.

"It couldn't be helped." She curled her fingers to hide the chipped nails and chapped flesh, still raw after applying salve. "After all, it is what I am here for. It is Tabitha who deserves concern." He frowned at her assertion, but she continued before he could make a protest. "Is Noble not with you?"

"No. He must still be hunting." His brow lowered yet further. "Does Tabitha need him? Do I need to go back out and find him?"

Esther pressed her lips together. "It should be all right if she drinks this tea and rests." As she moved toward the bedroom door, she nodded to the hearth. "There is chicory coffee in the pot."

She found Tabitha drowsing, but the young woman sat up long enough to drink her tea. Reassuring her that she had supper well in hand, Esther waited until she'd lain back down and tucked the quilt around her chin. Returning to the hearth, she moved the crane holding the pot closer to the fire. The men had not eaten any stew for the midday meal, so they would find no fault with having it for dinner.

Jared sat at the table with the Bible open beside his earthenware mug. He patted the bench next to him. "While she sleeps, come. Join me a minute."

Esther straightened and clasped her hands before her as a rush of nervous anticipation made her weak—hunger to be fed by the words of the Good Book, anxiety at being near Jared, and guilt. This wasn't the first time they had snuck reading time while Noble's wife was otherwise occupied. Tabitha had never confronted Esther directly but made her disapproval felt at any sign of closeness between Esther and Jared. Tabitha couldn't possibly be concerned that Esther posed any threat to her friend, perfect lady that Keturah was. So it must mean she found Esther unworthy of the Lockridge men's attention—or worse, unworthy of efforts to better herself.

The possibility made Esther scramble onto the bench beside Jared to seize the opportunity while it presented itself. She would need this knowledge for her future if she was to hope for any future worth speaking of.

Jared's blue eyes glowed with the approval she craved. "I chose a short passage. Psalm 139, verses 13 and 14." He placed his finger on the spot on the page. "See what you make of it."

Esther bent closer and drew a breath, then slowly began reading aloud. "'For thou hast pos-pos...'"

"Possessed."

"'Possessed my r-r-eee...'" Already stuck again. The order of the *e* and *i* always confused her.

"Reins."

"Reins. 'Possessed my reins.' What does that mean? God has control of us?" She looked up at him.

"He has ultimate control of our lives. Direction, as in the way we lead a horse."

Esther nodded. She did not blame God for the bad things

that had happened to her. She'd always thought she deserved them. "'Thou hast cov-covered me in my mother's womb.'" She pronounced the last word wrong, and he corrected her, but so gently as to not offend. "'I will praise thee; for I am...'" The next bit took multiple starts and stops, but finally, she got it out. "'Fearfully and wonderfully made: marvelous are thy works; and that my soul knoweth right well.'" Could this actually apply to her? If so, she was far from knowing it *right well*. She stared straight ahead, into the fire.

Finally, Jared said in a low voice, "God doesn't make mistakes, Esther."

"I am not a mistake."

"No."

"My foot is not a mistake?"

He took a sip of coffee and sighed. "In a perfect world, God would not have you struggle with a lame foot. Sin and disease entered for all of us way back in the Garden of Eden. But the trickle down of that does not mean any of us are less worthy or less loved than another. Do you understand?"

"God does not see me as flawed." Or dirty, though she couldn't bring herself to say that in front of Jared.

"No. No more than the rest of us, as we all fall short of His glory."

She tried to read the long, momentous words again, *fearfully and wonderfully*, but they blurred before her. When a tear dripped onto the page, she jerked upright, wiping it away with her finger and an ever-ready apology. "I am so sorry."

Jared's finger on her chin turned her face to his. "Stop apologizing, Esther. Do you see, if God thinks you have value, no man has the right to look down on you?"

She tried to fit that new puzzle piece into her brain, but his tender touch, his eyes earnestly boring into hers, unhinged both thoughts and tongue. "I-I—"

The door to the bedroom opened, and Tabitha spoke. "I thought I heard voices. How did the rock hunting go?"

*J*ared dropped his hand to the table and glared at his sister-in-law while Esther swiped at her eyes. Just when they'd been on the verge of a breakthrough. If Tabitha had but taken a moment to listen, she'd have waited to barge in. And her introductory topic was no accident.

"Rock hunting?" Esther looked between them with furrowed brow. "I thought you were game-hunting."

"Noble is. I was." Nothing for it but to tell her, though doing so might diminish the hope the Bible reading had ignited in her eyes. "We spent the early part of the day finding and moving stones from the creek bed to the far ridge. Large, flat stones, fit for a foundation—or a chimney."

"Oh." She drew a quick breath and folded her hands in her lap. "I see."

With her silent acceptance of this inevitable future, the curtain that had drawn open between them fell back into place. There was no way to sugarcoat it. She would leave, and Keturah would come.

Jared tried to picture Keturah, her strawberry-blond hair, her big blue eyes, her perfect form. The ringing of her teasing laughter. Spirited, that was what people called her. They also said Jared and she looked as though they belonged together, remarking on what beautiful children they would have.

When he was near Keturah, she boggled his brain and fired his senses. No matter that his memory of the girl had faded. It would all come back when she arrived. Wouldn't it?

It didn't matter. He had made a promise. He had asked a hard thing of Keturah, waiting so long, accepting so many changes to her life to come to this rough place. He had to keep his end of the bargain, even if the only woman he could now envision at the fireside next to him was this one.

None of that mattered. What mattered was that Esther grasp the fruits of the Good Book in front of them. His job was to show her the truth and protect her until spring. And on that note...

"You women should not go near the creek now."

Tabitha, who lingered in the doorway with her arms crossed, awaiting his penitence, straightened. "Why is that?"

"We saw panther tracks leading to and from the canebrake." Jared glanced back at Esther as he explained. "They hole up there in the cane and fallen logs, but the bitter cold of deep winter drives them out. Hunger makes them a great danger. We'll need to start lighting the pine knots around the house at night."

Esther nodded. "We did the same last winter."

He met her gaze briefly. "You know where I keep the kindling." The uneasy task would fall to her.

With an expressive shudder, Tabitha relaxed her arms. "I thought I heard a tyger scream far-off last night. Chilling, like a woman." Distracted from her disapproval, she drew near and scooted onto the bench across from them.

Jared sought to lighten the mood. "At least it's not the legendary Wog."

"The Wog?" Tabitha's eyes widened.

He peeked at Esther again, judging her reaction. He'd forgotten his sister-in-law hadn't been in these parts long enough to hear all the local legends, but Esther's attempt to suppress a smile confirmed her familiarity with stories of the creature. "A jet-black animal the size of a small horse with a long tail, tipped with fluffy white hair. They say you know it's near by the whizzing sound the tail makes as it swings down. That and the way the other animals go crazy. The Wog is said to have red eyes and a long forked tongue which can fit in the openings between logs." His description petered out at Tabitha's horrified expression.

"But it's ridiculous," Esther hastened to add. "I've heard its front legs are shorter than the back ones. Seems more a laughable sight than a fearsome one. How does it walk?"

"On its back legs?" Tabitha squeaked.

Esther made a face. "I'm sure it's just a tall tale, something made up by the local settlers to frighten their children into good behavior."

"Local?" Tabitha batted her lashes. "It's been seen around here?"

"In this county, yes." Esther waved a dismissive hand. "But closer to Jug Tavern, not here."

Jared's appreciation for Esther's sensitivity rose again as Tabitha let out a whooshing breath and leaned closer.

"I'm sure Esther's right," Tabatha said. "It's just a fable. What are you studying?"

He hastened to embrace the change of subject. "A passage in Psalms. One that tells of the way God views us."

"Oh. One-thirty-nine. Yes, that's a good one." Tabitha shot a smile at Esther. "You and I can keep up your reading when Jared is gone scouting." Her gaze swung to him, pointed despite the corners of her mouth lifting. Taken together with that look, her smirk seemed a pretension to generosity. No doubt of it, Noble's bride possessed an edge that her friend Keturah lacked.

Esther's eyes widened a moment. With surprise? Had she not recognized Tabitha's true fear until now? Under his perusal, Esther's lashes swept down, and she curled one of her hands over the other. "I'd very much appreciate that."

Did they have any choice but to agree? He should be delighted Tabitha would continue the instruction he had begun. It was appropriate. Wise. Yet half the remaining light seemed to have drained from the room.

"Good." Bracing on the table, Tabitha hoisted her unsteady weight onto her feet. "After all, Jared will be leaving soon. Very soon."

She had turned to check a pot on the fire and Jared had closed the Bible when horse hooves sounded in the yard. Duchess, who would have alerted them moments earlier, was out with Noble. On the frontier, the arrival of unexpected visitors called for caution over delight. Jared sprang for his rifle and a peek out the window.

At the sight of the figure dismounting in the swept-dirt yard, he relaxed. "It's young Benjamin Reynolds."

Tabitha lowered the lid to the stew pot. "One of the scouts from the fort?"

Jared flung the door open and called a greeting. The women followed him onto the porch. Now that he'd confirmed there was no danger, the sight of a fresh face and whatever news might be forthcoming was not to be missed.

Benjamin doffed his hat, his hair sticking up helter-skelter. "Afternoon, Jared." He clasped the floppy brim against the dirt-smeared front of his hunting frock. He looked sore in need of a bath. "Ma'ams."

"What brings you hereabouts?" Jared stepped down from the porch.

"I'm on my way home from reporting with Isham to the fort. I heard you might be volunteering in my stead, so I wanted to tell you some things direct-like."

"I appreciate that. You saw some action on your stint, then?"

He gave a nod and a wary look at the women. "Ever heard of Keziah Willis?"

Jared cocked his head and scratched his chin, searching his memory. "The mean old coot who lives near the Snow brothers across the line into Clark—father to the Brushy Creek miller?" He'd learned the hard way that despite his son Hampton's congenial personality, the elder Willis's cabin was not one to approach, even neighborly-like.

"That's him. He's dead—shot, and his place put to the torch much like Mrs. Andrews's. But he was also scalped." Benjamin's eyes darted to Esther, then back. "Not that anyone's much aggrieved. He was respected for his service in the Revolution, and for that reason, folks listened to him—even when he said we shouldn't send out a search party for those women from the Snow settlement."

Jared grunted. "I'd imagine that didn't set well with their men. Could it be the same two warriors that fell upon Bledsoe? Same general area."

"Same area, but there were three sets of tracks this time, not just two. And the third was shod."

Jared tipped his head to avoid the white-gold splinters of sun setting through the bare branches. "The raiders I followed were undoubtedly Indian. Could be the new horse was stolen from a white man."

"Could be." Benjamin went on to describe the route he'd used to track the intruders and a rocky glen about two miles west of the river where he suspected they often made camp. Jared was familiar with the area. A small creek—the banks of which were overhung by a number of boulders—and an abundance of evergreens made it a perfect winter hideout. Finally, the young scout planted his hat back on his head. "Captain Whorton wants these troublesome Injuns rounded up posthaste before they attack again or burrow deeper in their territory. He requests that you ride direct from here."

Jared nodded. Much as he might wish to pass on this duty to another, there was no one else available and equipped to fill this particular need. "I understand, Private. When should I report back?"

"The other volunteers are serving January fifth through March fifth."

Jared ran his hand over his face. Early March? Much longer than the ten-day rotations of the past fall, and in the harsh grip of winter, but nothing could be done about it. "I will ride out at first light." Perhaps if he brought the troublemakers in...

"One more thing. The commander asks that your brother go with you."

Asked? Or ordered?

Tabitha stifled a gasp behind him, but Jared didn't bother to point out that Noble's child was due two months hence. Noble would barely make it back in time for the birth...if he was lucky. Benjamin had no say over the matter. With a regretful nod, the young man mounted and rode out of the clearing.

Jared's chest squeezed as he turned to the women, who stood silent and grim. Their manner confirmed they understood the dangers of facing the winter alone and unprotected. Understood. Accepted. But still, wisely, feared.

CHAPTER 12

*T*iny flecks of precipitation boded the coming of a winter storm as Jared and Noble rode into the clearing surrounding Ephraim Snow's cabin. A deerskin strung in the process of being tanned near the back door and a thin trail of smoke indicated occupancy and gave rise to hope.

They'd spent the last three days in an A-frame shelter of evergreen boughs camouflaged with dried leaves, a fallen tree their ridgepole, staking out the camp Benjamin Reynolds had described. Indeed, the site had been used, but a week or more prior. The overhang of a large boulder had been insulated, pine branches laid at the back of the crevice, even a stone ledge oven constructed near the entrance. But no one had returned while Noble and Jared waited in ambush...no one even passing through. And the old tracks to and from the glen led in every direction.

One set had led here.

Perhaps the warning they brought would secure hospitality. Jared's stomach rumbled, and he was so cold he could barely move his hands inside his gloves. A troublesome fact, for he'd need them to remove his booted feet from his stirrups.

Noble unwrapped his scarf from his mouth and nose, a small cloud curling forth with his summons. "Halloo, the house."

They waited on their horses until the door opened and a young man, tall and skinny as a ridgepole, stepped out with a musket propped in one arm. He gave no greeting, not even a nod ... merely stared at them.

Jared hadn't seen this face when he'd visited in the fall. He made a guess. "Enoch Snow?"

"Who's askin'?"

"I'm Jared Lockridge, and this is my brother, Noble. We're serving as scouts from Fort Daniel."

"A little out of yer neck of the woods, ain't ya?" Enoch tilted his head of long, stringy black hair, then a frown darkened his angular face. "You ain't that scout what came by here askin' questions in November, are ya?" His fingers tightened on the stock of his weapon.

Enoch's demeanor gave fair warning of his frame of mind, but it was not in Jared's nature to lie. He'd witnessed the destruction wreaked by deception firsthand. "I am. I spoke with your brother, Ephraim. Allow me to offer my condolences on the loss of your father and the abduction of your sister-in-law and niece."

"Some good your fine words do, just as they done then. You and old man Willis told the folks hereabouts it would do no good to track Ephraim's wife and child." A break in Enoch's voice betrayed the grief behind his accusation, prompting Jared to respond with humility rather than defensiveness.

He dipped his chin. "I'm truly sorry, Enoch. I've never once heard of captives being retrieved by pursuit. You hold more hope in bartering for their exchange when General Jackson subdues the Red Sticks."

"At least you was tryin' to keep our border safe." Enoch

swiped his rough wool sleeve across his eyes. "Served myself. If more had, none of this might've happened."

"I agree."

Noble shifted on his mount, his tone betraying his growing impatience. "Is Ephraim home?"

A shutter squeaked open, and a dirty little face sighted along a musket barrel. Enoch leapt toward the window, pushing the shutter closed. "Seth, what did I tell you? You're too little to handle that weapon."

A female voice piped from inside. "Sorry, Uncle Enoch. He went and got it when I wasn't looking."

"Stay inside like I said." The portal successfully secured, Enoch shook his head. "Ephraim ain't here. I have charge of his younger kids while he and Micajah are gone west."

Jared exchanged a glance with Noble. Micajah must be the cousin's name he couldn't recall after the attack here. "Why are they riding west?"

"What do you think? Askin' everyone they can if they saw Nancy and Patience. They woulda gone earlier, but they had to wait until I got shed of my duty. Micajah's half out of his mind since his bride got killed. He ain't fit for watchin' kids."

Jared removed his hat, smoothing his hair back before replacing it. "We understand."

Enoch's eyes narrowed again. "Mighty kind of you to be so understandin', especially since you helped make sure no one would go with them in the first place."

"Not out of any lack of sympathy." Why did Jared bother to argue? When the potent cocktail of grief mingled with bitterness flowed through a man, he wasn't apt to hear reason.

Before the exchange could deteriorate further, Noble pressed on to conclude their business. "You best keep a sharp lookout in the meantime. We're tracking a trio of what we believe to be Red Sticks, and some old tracks led from a temporary camp on Brushy Creek up the gulch to this place."

"They won't catch me unawares. I done heard their fake birdcalls in the woods when I was huntin' 'bout a week ago." A grim smile tightened Enoch's thin lips. "I laid my own traps." He turned for the door. "Best stick to the main trail as you leave."

∼

*E*sther dreamed Duchess was growling. She should be afraid, but Duchess liked her now. In fact, her warm fur was pressed against Esther's back, soft and comforting.

A thump on the porch was followed by an explosion of barking and scrambling as the mastiff launched her massive body at the door, baying and scratching the wood. Esther shot to a sitting position, quilt clutched at her neck. Only embers glowed in the fireplace beside her. She'd taken to sleeping at the hearth and keeping a log burning since the men had been gone and the water had started freezing overnight in her upstairs washbasin. The faint light of dawn lit the edges of the window and the door.

Probably not a wild animal, then. Her spine sagged. Duchess whined and turned in a circle, begging to be let out, but Esther would take no chances. Cold as it had been this past last week of January, they'd heard both wolves and panthers in the distance. Another possibility made her breath lodge in her chest. What of a beast that went on two legs?

She eased off her pallet, reaching for her musket propped by the fireplace. A floorboard creaked, and Tabitha's door edged open. Her belly appeared first, then her wide eyes. Esther put her finger over her lips and pointed to Duchess. In her woolen undergarments, Tabitha came forward to restrain the dog, whispering a command as she slipped her fingers inside the mastiff's leather collar. Fully dressed and in her moccasin feet, Esther crept to the door.

She lowered her voice to what she hoped resembled a man's gruff tones. "Who's there?"

No response.

Her heart hammered as she lifted the heavy wooden bolt as quietly as she could.

In one quick motion, she cracked the door and stuck the muzzle of the musket through the opening. "Who goes there?" She made the demand as she scanned the porch. No one stood in view, but something was lying at the top of the steps. A dying animal, maybe? No. The heap of light tawny fur wasn't moving.

Esther glanced back at Tabitha and the dog, which was growling with her head lowered. "Heel, Duchess." Until she knew what they faced, she didn't want to risk the animal any more than she wanted to risk herself. Tabitha put her arms around the canine's massive neck and murmured near her ear. The mastiff could easily break from her hold, but Esther had come to know Duchess would never use force against her family. A whine signaled reluctant obedience.

Esther eased the door wider and searched the clearing. Empty. No movement in the woods beyond either. She closed the door a moment and leaned on it, squeezing her eyes shut.

"What is it?" Tabitha gasped.

She opened her eyes. "Something lying on the porch...a deer, I think."

"Where did it come from?"

"I don't see anyone. But it occurred to me that when I go out there, I'll be in shooting range of anyone watching from the woods."

Tabitha's brows shot up. "Or grabbing range of anyone under the porch."

She hadn't thought of that. Her knees nearly knocked together. Blast this war, leaving womenfolk such as themselves —one pregnant and one lame—to fend for themselves. She slid the bolt. "I can't do it."

"Maybe Mr. John Howell left it."

"Then why didn't he call out when he came up to the house? We'd have thanked him with coffee and porridge, as well he knows."

They stared at each other for a good minute, listening, thinking. Not for the first time, Esther wished the men would stop by and check on them, as they'd promised to do when they'd ridden off several weeks before. Jared had taken Esther aside and told her that in case of emergency with the birthing, she was to take Duchess and go to the Howells. John or his boys could fetch help from the settlement if necessary. So far, by keeping inside the house as much as possible—not even venturing to the spring—they'd managed. But winter's relentless siege drained their resources with surprising efficiency.

"The men left us a goodly store of food and firewood, but our meat is running low. What if Jared and Noble sent someone by with a deer?" Or what if someone had been watching them and guessed their need? That would mean someone knew she and Tabitha were alone. She kept that possibility to herself. Esther drew a deep breath and palmed the musket again. "I'm going out to investigate, but keep Duchess in here with you. We don't want her running off or attacking a neighbor. And if something happens to me, you will need her."

A small moan broke from Tabitha's lips, and she hid her face on the mastiff's back. "Oh, for one day, just one day, to feel safe again."

Esther couldn't concur more. But of the two of them, she was now the stronger—an unfamiliar but oddly empowering position. So she opened the door and, bold as brass, stomped onto the porch with her gun leveled. She swiveled, surveying the whole yard.

No shots erupted. Nothing moved except a red cardinal flitted onto the branch of the oak tree, watching her. At her feet lay a neatly gutted deer carcass.

A COUNTERFEIT BETROTHAL

~

*E*sther and Tabitha enjoyed a delicious noonday meal of tenderloin seared in the iron spider, but on the frontier, even a gift brought a cost. Esther worked all day, separating out the cuts of meat. She was a bloody mess when she was done. They let the fire die down to string jerky on two iron racks Noble had fitted into the chimney for smoking, although Esther added a layer of soot to her skin, clothes, and hair in the process. Then she fetched kindling while Tabitha diced meat and vegetables for a stew. As she passed by the carcass remains on the front porch, she cringed. Liam had brain-tanned his hides. She'd watched him do it once or twice but loathed the idea of taking on the task herself. And she lacked the time and efficiency to scrape the fat and flesh from the skin.

"I don't know what to do with the carcass," she told Tabitha as she added knotty wood to the fire. "I'm afraid to leave it there any longer. Maybe I should just drag it into the woods, away from the house."

Tabitha shuddered. "It may still draw predators."

Duchess dashed past Esther on the way out the door, barking. Esther grabbed her gun and followed to the porch.

A middle-aged man dressed as though he belonged to the militia drew up his horse in the yard, eyes wide as he stared at the mastiff.

Esther called her, and the dog trotted back to her side. "Can I help you, sir?"

"I am Sergeant James Montgomery." He dismounted and approached with slow steps and a rueful chuckle. "You have a fierce hunter there, ma'am." His gaze flicked to the carcass on the porch as Duchess emitted a low growl. "That's a nice-sized deer."

Let him assume Duchess had taken it down. "It has

provided much meat, but I'm a bit overwhelmed at tanning it." Esther blew a strand of ashy hair from her eye.

"That is indeed quite a task." Montgomery glanced at the fleshing beam and rack near the outbuildings and then back at her, fixating on her right cheekbone. She must have soot smeared there. At least she had removed her blood-stained apron earlier. "I understand the Lockridge men are away scouting."

Esther stiffened, her knuckles tightening over the stock of her musket. "How do you know that?"

"I come from Fort Daniel. We rely heavily on the intelligence of our scouts. And as the former tax collector for Jackson County, I'm acquainted with Noble Lockridge."

Tabitha had come out of the house, wiping her fingers on a cloth. She nodded at the visitor. "I am Mrs. Noble Lockridge."

"Pleased to make your acquaintance, ma'am. As I was telling Mrs. ..."

"Miss." Esther rested the muzzle of the musket on the ground. With a flash of certainty about her changing identity, she gave her maiden name. "Miss Esther Venable." Thankfully, Tabitha didn't react as their guest continued.

"I was telling Miss Venable that I'm now a U.S. Army wagon-master tasked with the building of Fort Peachtree, some thirty miles west of here on the south bank of the Chattahoochee."

"We've heard about the road that was built." Tabitha stepped down from the porch. The glare of the winter afternoon turned her face an ashen color to match.

Esther frowned. This sergeant needed to conclude his business so that Tabitha could rest while Esther tended the stew.

"Yes, ma'am, and I have already sent a corps of artificers, a boatwright who will oversee the building of several flatboats we'll use to ship supplies to General Jackson's men, and a strong contingent of workers to the site with Lieutenant Gilmer.

But this past Sunday, I discovered none of the tools we ordered had arrived at Fort Daniel." Removing his hat, Montgomery extended both hands. "I am having to range far and wide to procure what we need. I did hear that the younger Lockridge was a woodworker, so I thought I might try my luck here."

"I'm afraid your luck's run out." Esther drew herself up. "Jared Lockridge's fine woodworking tools are not meant for constructing forts and boats." She almost gasped at herself. Where did such boldness come from?

Sobering, Montgomery returned his hat to his head. "Pardon me, miss, but I believe a tool is a tool. I would not ask were the construction of this fort not only for the good of our state, but our new nation."

"And I'll not let you cart away his livelihood, especially while he's off fighting for his country!"

Tabitha gawked at her, but Esther stood firm. Such a thing would be worse than what had happened to his grandfather.

Montgomery pursed his lips, doubtless preparing to inquire who Miss Venable might be to rally to the defense of Mr. Lockridge. But he thought twice and relaxed his posture. "I ask only for the basics." He waited a moment while Esther glared at him. "Has either Mr. Lockridge a saw? An ax?"

Tabitha came to stand beside Esther. "Would this saw or ax be returned?"

The sergeant gave a brief bow. "I will personally see that the tools of any settlers from Jackson County are returned to Fort Daniel as soon as the Peachtree structure is complete."

Tabitha's expression softened. "I believe we can help you, Sergeant Montgomery. Miss...Venable can stable your horse while you come in for a cup of cider." She extended her hand toward the house. "And of course, you'll stay for stew."

A light sparking in his eye at the mention of vittles, Sergeant Montgomery relinquished his reins to Esther and headed for the porch.

131

Esther caught Tabitha's elbow before she could follow and hissed a question in her ear. "What are you doing?"

Tabitha whispered back, "Giving you the chance to hide Jared's tools. Noble has an old whipsaw and a broadax in the box in the far stall. In exchange, Sergeant Montgomery will leave us with a clean hide and dispose of the unpleasant parts."

Esther's mouth fell open, then a smile bloomed forth. Why hadn't she thought of striking such a bargain? Well, feminine charms were hardly her strength. "Mrs. Lockridge, I don't believe you require any help to make you a frontierswoman."

CHAPTER 13

*J*ames Montgomery's visit had taxed Tabitha. During dinner, Esther had watched her shifting on her bench as the sergeant told them all about the flatboats that would be built for the Chattahoochee River. The enthusiastic light in his eye must have blinded him to his hostess's strained politeness, but Esther didn't miss the way she kept catching her lower lip between her teeth. Duchess only stopped rumbling at the man when Esther gave her a meaty bone. Finally, as winter's hazy twilight liquefied into flurries, the sergeant mounted and trotted his horse away bearing the promised whipsaw and broadax. And leaving behind a cleaned and salted hide.

After tending the livestock in the barn and lighting the pine knots 'round about the yard, Esther returned to the house. She bolted the door with a sigh and leaned the musket against the wall. "Finally, we can rest."

"Long-winded as he was, I do believe the sergeant was a godsend."

"An insensitive one. The man must not be married." Not that it made any difference in Esther's experience.

Tabitha braced herself with one hand on the hutch and the other under her mound of an abdomen. "Yes, I think I need..." Her voice caught on a gasp.

"What is it?" Esther hurried to her side. "Is it the baby?"

Tabitha grimaced, then waved. "A few contractions is all. Mrs. White told me I could expect this, and probably more than once in the month leading up to the birth."

"Are you sure? Should I take Duchess to the Howells' while there is still light?"

"No, no. They would laugh me off as a silly woman. I just need to lie down a bit."

"Of course. You did too much today." Esther offered her arm and escorted Tabitha to bed, helping her remove her shoes and swing her legs under the quilt. "Call me if you need anything."

Tabitha nodded, and, leaving the bedroom door ajar, Esther set about cleaning up the stew. She'd just sat down with the Bible when a stifled moan came from Tabitha. Snatching up a candleholder, Esther hastened to check on her. "Should I prepare some partridge berry tea?"

Tabitha rolled onto her side and pulled her knees up to her chest. When her contorted face relaxed, her eyes sought Esther's, wide with fear. "I think it might be too late for that."

~

*T*abitha labored all through the night and into the next day. Shortly after noonday, Esther placed a squalling male infant—tiny but pink—into his mother's arms. She sank onto the bed next to Tabitha, weak with profound relief. It had been all she could do to rush between the hearth and the bedside up until the time Tabitha refused to let go of her hand. She had managed to cut the cord and, following an infusion of blue skullcap root, help expel the afterbirth and apply a yarrow poultice. Finally, she changed the linens.

A COUNTERFEIT BETROTHAL

In the throes of bliss, clutching her baby, Tabitha declared Esther superior to any midwife. But Esther knew better. She thanked the Good Lord little Micah hadn't been born unresponsive, for she had no idea what she would have done had that been the case.

Now one set of her knuckles protested along with her left leg and foot. She had partaken of the black cohosh root infusion she'd prepared for Tabitha's childbirth since it also helped the pain in her joints at times, though to little effect. Her stomach felt shriveled to the size of a pea but had moved past hunger to hollow. And uncontrollable emotion overtook her as she looked over at Tabitha trying to get Micah to nurse. Not just relief, but gratitude, joy, and a piercing wistfulness that she wished to cull out and toss into the slop bucket. Her empty arms ached. Tears ran down her face so fast she gave up trying to chase them with her fingers. As she blinked moisture from her lashes, the sleep of the exhausted beckoned.

Sometime later, the scream of a panther popped her eyes open wide. Her heart raced. The candle had guttered and the room fallen almost completely dark. Must be the middle of the night. Cold fingers of air swept under the bed and wrapped around Esther's uncovered form. She shivered.

"Did you hear that?" Tabitha whispered.

"Yes." Esther sat up. What time was it? "It was far off. I can't believe I slept that long."

Blankets stirred. "I can. You spent all of one day butchering a deer and the whole night and most of the next day attending a birth." Tabitha shifted the baby in her arms. "He hasn't eaten except the littlest bit right after he was born."

"He is merely tired like we are. I will get a light."

Duchess lifted her head from her paws and thumped her tail as Esther stepped over the threshold. Speaking softly to her, Esther stirred up the embers, putting a wick to the small flame that listed and danced. She'd fetch more kindling when she

135

went to feed the animals. How hungry they must be! She hastened to deliver the candle to Tabitha's chamber, where the fitful baby whined and mewled.

Tabitha looked up with worry lines on her forehead. "I can't get him to latch on."

"Keep trying. I'm sure it just takes practice. I must light the pine knots in the yard." Calling Duchess, Esther swung on her cloak and exited onto the porch, where she stopped abruptly. "Oh no."

A blanket of snow covered everything—the ground, the trees, the roofs of the outbuildings. A bitter wind raked her loosened hair into her eyes.

She would have to clear a spot for each pine knot. But first, she needed to feed the animals—after she ducked back into the house to struggle into Tabitha's boots. Duchess dashed into the woods, presumably to do her business. She would undoubtedly check the perimeter before returning. Esther reminded herself that in Queen Elizabeth's day, mastiffs had been bred to fight bears. Having such a formidable guard offered comfort indeed.

She clumped to the barn, struggling against the weight on her foot. She took extra time to feed and pet Simon and Daisy, bedded down in their stalls. Then she dug Jared's toolbox out from the pile of straw where she'd hidden it from Sergeant Montgomery and lugged it back to its rightful place on the workbench. She stood for a minute caressing the smooth top. A pain she didn't understand pierced her heart. Somehow, it connected to the memory of Tabitha holding her son. It was not something to be examined.

She grabbed up the flint, steel, and box of tinder Jared always left in the barn. Then she let herself out the door and bolted it firmly.

Duchess had not returned. At a baying in the distance, Esther's breath caught. Lifting her hand against a whistling eddy, she called the dog. Only the sighing of the pines and the crackle of last year's beech leaves answered. She cleared four circles in the snow where they'd last lit their watch-fires and called again. No shaggy shape bounded from the woods. A chill went down her spine. She gathered pine knots from the woodshed and set to placing and lighting them, but the wind kept putting out her flames. At last, all but one took, and she hurried for the house with her fingers near frozen.

She called from the porch one more time. "Duchess! Duchess!" Where was the slobbering beast? Her heart squeezed, but with one last look into the night, she went inside and bolted the door.

Tabitha's voice came from the next room. "Esther? I don't think I have milk."

Esther divested of her armload of kindling and her cloak, calling back. "From what I hear, you don't for the first couple of days. But the baby should be getting a liquid he needs."

"I don't think he's getting anything." Micah's wail rose above Tabitha's, drowning out the end of her sentence.

What did Tabitha expect her to do? Esther drew a deep breath, then—*boom-ba-bloom!*—let it out on a cry at the sudden thumping on the porch. Duchess's whine sounded from near the door. She opened it with thanks to God and ushered the dog in the house, inspecting her for injury. Duchess was huffing, but only wet fur attested to her foray into the woods. She shook all over Esther.

"You naughty girl." Esther wiped the moisture from her face and pointed to the fireplace. "Go. Lie down."

After a hearty drink from her bowl, Duchess complied. But as Esther checked on the new mother, the dog kept getting back up and walking in circles.

Esther paused in her tea preparation and cocked her head. Was that a panther's cry again?

The fur on the back of the mastiff's neck rose. She faced the door and growled.

A pit opened in Esther's stomach.

"Did you hear that tyger again?" Tabitha asked when Esther brought her porridge and tea.

There was no point denying the obvious, but Esther did her best to lighten the new mother's concern. "No need to fret. I think Duchess might have chased it away earlier." She ducked her head and placed the dishes on the bedside table, chancing a glance at Micah. He fussed and wiggled in Tabitha's arms, his shrill cries piercing the night. "You should eat and then try to feed him again." His wailing made her nervous. Was the panther drawn by the crying?

"Would you hold him?" Tabitha held the baby out.

"Oh…" Esther couldn't finish her protest before Tabitha pressed the swaddled form against her chest. Her arms came around him before she could think. Staring into the wrinkled little face, she perched at the end of the mattress while Tabitha took her own nourishment. The baby's cries made her painfully aware of her inability to satisfy him. She stuck the tip of her pinky finger between his lips, but he only protested more.

Would she ever hold a child of her own? If a year and a half without conceiving offered any indication, she should surrender that dream. Her best hope might rest in marrying a widower in need of a readymade mother for his children. The notion made her more than willing to return the child to Tabitha.

Esther had just stepped back into the main room when a thud on the floorboards outside made her freeze. Duchess threw herself at the door, barking and snarling. A bone-chilling scream answered from the other side. Esther's hand flew to her throat. God help them. A panther was on the porch.

"What is happening?" Tabitha yelled the same moment Esther ran for her musket.

With a furious scratching that splintered the wood separating her from her prey, Duchess assaulted the door. But the prey could kill her.

"Heel, Duchess, heel!" Esther's command was pointless.

A *thunk* sounded at the front corner of the house. The cat had leapt to the roof! Esther swung the barrel of the musket toward the spot where she had heard the solid body land, though any footsteps were lost to the mastiff's baying.

Tabitha appeared in the doorway, her eyes wild, Micah clutched against her chest. "What do we do?"

Eyes and gun muzzle trained on the ceiling, Esther tried to trace the panther's path by faint creaking and Duchess's barking. She darted a glance to Jared's musket, which he'd left propped by the hearth. "Take the extra gun. It's loaded. Go back into the bedroom and try to nurse the baby."

"Nurse him?" The question shrieked out with disbelief and a curl of terror.

"You must try. His crying—" A new sound paralyzed her. Scratching. The beast was attempting to scratch through the wooden shingles on the roof. "Go!"

Tabitha snatched the gun and ran. Her frantic, sobbing breaths came from the bedroom.

Should she shoot? But wouldn't that weaken the roof? Should she let Duchess out, after all? But the cat would leap on her from above, and the disadvantage could mean the mastiff's life.

The scratching stopped.

Then Tabitha screamed. "Esther! It's right over me!"

Oh, God, what do I do? An image formed in Esther's mind— the sugarcane cone they used with black tea. She thumped to the hutch as fast as her weakened limb would take her and fumbled for the right box. Sugar in hand, she hurried for the bedroom.

She could hardly hear or think for the screaming and clawing of the cat, the baby's wailing, Tabitha's sobbing, and

Duchess's barking. In the spluttering light of the candle, Esther brought the pointed tip of the cone to Micah's mouth. She laid her hand on Tabitha's shoulder, an unspoken plea to settle. *Oh, God, please.*

Tabitha gulped in deep breaths, and Duchess's barks turned into low growls. An unnatural peace washed over Esther from head to toe.

Lo, I am with you always.

Tears flooded her eyes as the baby sucked and the scratching stopped.

Then came another thump and a scraping that turned her to ice. Her eyes met Tabitha's. A horrified whisper rasped out of her. "It's in the chimney."

Musket in hand, she hobble-ran to the main room. Duchess almost knocked her down as they both tried to squeeze through the threshold at the same time. In the fireplace, ashes and debris fluttered down onto the neglected embers. Esther grabbed a fistful of kindling and threw it on the fire, then stood back with her gun leveled and the dog at her side, steeling herself to meet her foe.

CHAPTER 14

Sunlight glared on fresh-fallen snow and undeniable panther tracks leading from the canebrake toward the cabin. Jared's eyes met Noble's for a fraction of a second before both men spurred their mounts up the gulch. Esther's name tore from his throat as quickly as Tabitha's did from Noble's. Visions of what horrible sight could be awaiting them flashed before his eyes. But smoke poured from the chimney, and the door flew open as they rode into the clearing.

Duchess's massive tan-and-black form almost knocked him down as he dismounted, but behind the dog, a slight figure limped and leapt across the snow. Esther, running to him with her hair streaming down her back and her arms outstretched. He caught her, and his insides sang with relief as he wrapped his arms around her. But she was sobbing so hard that she could make no reply to Noble's frightened inquiries. Jared could only brace her head against his neck while his brother took off for the house.

"What happened? Is it Tabitha?"

A head shake, then a nod. His gut tightened. She drew back to look at him but still couldn't form words.

"Is she all right? We saw the panther tracks."

Esther grasped the lapels of his coat. "Th-the baby—"

The baby? Was it born? Dead? "Breathe." He cradled her face in his hands, and she puckered her lips to do as he instructed as tears streaked down her cheeks. Whatever she had undergone had been terrible, indeed, to so unsettle her, but no benefit would come of hysteria now. "I'm here, Esther."

Her eyes closed, and he pressed a kiss to her forehead. Didn't think, just did it. It felt right, like a parent comforting a child. Only, the way his heart squeezed when she laid her face against his chest resembled something else altogether. He stroked her back and held her while Duchess sat with a whine at their feet.

Finally, Jared whispered, "Can you tell me now?"

Esther nodded. "The baby is here."

His eyebrows shot up as she looked at him. "Here? And alive?"

"Noble's son is fine."

"Did the midwife—"

She shook her head. "There was no time. He came early."

A chuckle broke loose, ripe pleasure for his brother. "He surely did. And you...you delivered..."

She bit her bottom lip. "Thank God there were no complications."

Jared cupped her chin. "That's amazing. I'm so proud of you."

Esther took a shaky breath. "The next night, the panther came. It was on the porch before we knew it. Then it jumped on the roof. I-I couldn't bring myself to let Duchess out. Although, she did almost claw down the door." She drew back enough to lay a hand on the mastiff's huge head.

When Duchess licked her, Esther knelt and wrapped her arms around the dog's thick neck. "If she hadn't been there..."

"Good girl." Jared rubbed Duchess's short coat. "Good girl."

He took Esther's hand to draw her back up. "She scared the cat away?"

Her throat worked as she swallowed. "Not exactly. It tried to scratch through the roof."

As a shudder passed through her, Jared slid his arm around her again and squeezed her hand. "Oh, Esther. I'm so sorry we weren't here. That must've been terrifying."

"Indeed. I truly thought we might die. The animal must've been half-crazed with hunger...or upset by the baby's crying. Micah wouldn't stop." She ran her hand through her hair, separating strands that floated in the air with a wintry charge. "I put the sugarcane cone in his mouth. I thought that worked, but then...then..." Her wide eyes swung to his.

He waited, breathless with anticipation. "Then what?"

"Then it climbed into the chimney."

Jared's brows shot up. "What did you do?"

"I built up the fire and waited with Duchess and my musket. But I had forgotten about the jerky."

He cocked his head. "What jerky?"

"The day prior, someone left a gutted deer on our doorstep. We thought maybe you sent it."

He shook his head, increasingly uneasy. "I didn't send it."

"Well, I had butchered it and made a stew, which Sergeant Montgomery helped us to eat in exchange for a saw and an ax, but we did make him clean the hide—"

Jared put his finger over her mouth. His breath escaped in a sound that meant to become a question but couldn't, so many puzzle pieces floated in his head. Sergeant Montgomery? "None of this makes sense. But Esther, tell me what happened with the panther."

She raised her face to his, her cheeks pink in the February cold. "I had strung jerky to smoke on Noble's racks. The cat snatched some of the meat and went away to eat it." Her eyes rounded. "We could hear it growling and chewing in the yard. Then we heard its screams as it went away into the night."

"Thank you, Lord." Overwhelmed with the incredible tale, Jared pulled her close again.

The impossible had just happened—her arms slipping around his waist—when Noble's proud voice carried from the doorway of the cabin where he'd appeared, holding a small bundle. "Brother, come see your new nephew!"

∼

The moments Jared and Esther had embraced, taking comfort in each other following the women's harrowing ordeal, an invisible wall had toppled between them. A new awareness connected them as Esther moved about, cleaning up after supper. Jared felt it keen as heat lightning. Did Noble and Tabitha notice the stolen glances, the little touches? No. They were absorbed in their new son. Noble stood behind his wife's shoulder as she rocked the babe by the fire. They exclaimed over his every expression or sound. Wouldn't they be shocked to know Jared experienced a joy almost as intense each time he looked at Esther?

Esther passed behind him as he settled back at the table with his rag, oil, and rifle. Her fingers fluttered to his shoulder, and she set a pewter mug in front of him. When he glanced up, she winked. "Real coffee."

His mouth fell open, and not because of the coffee, though that was a rare delight. He couldn't fathom the changes in her. She moved with her shoulders back and her chin up. And a wink? Had he ever seen her wink?

Tabitha caught him staring. Her brows drew down. "Are you men sure you shouldn't hunt the tyger down? As much as I fear for you to, neither do I want it to come calling again."

Esther moaned. "Now you joke about it."

"Oh, trust me, that was the worst experience of my life." She rolled her eyes.

Noble took a step back at that. "Worse than childbirth?"

"Worse than childbirth. Because I already felt like I had died, then I thought I was going to die again. And far more terrible because"—Tabitha bent closer to her wee babe and smoothed the blanket around his face—"Micah was in danger."

Esther stepped around the dog at the hearth, bending to pet the mastiff's head. "Duchess would never have let it get to you." Did only Jared notice her voice cracked at the end of her firm declaration?

"*You* would never have let it." The look of admiration his sister-in-law sent Esther ignited a glow in Jared's chest. Something passed between the women as sure as it existed between him and Esther now. Their ordeal had forged a bond.

But Esther's old ways were not so easily broken. She frowned as she set the coffeepot in the ashes. "Had I not fallen asleep and then gotten busy and let the fire die down..."

Jared wiped his ramrod, shaking his head. "We won't hear it, Esther. We all agree you should accept our gratitude with no self-depreciation." As she ducked her head, he deflected further attention from her. "To answer your question, Tabitha, I will keep the fire stirred up all night. And Noble will stay here with you for a week or so to make sure all is well."

Tabitha tipped her face up to her husband. "But will you get in trouble?"

He smiled at her, smoothing back her hair. "I will rejoin Jared before the term is out, but no, I don't think so. We are local volunteers, not part of a regular company."

Esther settled beside him with her drop spindle. Did the woman ever sit idle? Perhaps the change between them made her nervous, and she sought something to busy her hands. She glanced up at her sister-in-law. "Remember, Tabitha, Sergeant Montgomery indicated that the fort would probably be abandoned, anyway, when this last stint of service is done. He said the action has moved deeper into Creek Territory now."

Tabitha shifted in the rocker. "I seem to recall something about that, but vaguely. I was a bit distracted that night." Everyone chuckled, she having filled the men in on the whole story earlier.

"Understandably." Esther peeked at Jared and uttered a soft query. "But must you ride out again?"

He'd asked himself the same thing.

Bending to tend the fire, Noble answered for him. "While we were gone, we lodged often with Hampton Willis, the miller on Brushy Creek, to thoroughly scout the area where most of the trouble occurred. Our search came up with naught but rabbit trails and dead ends. The Jackson Line is quiet. It seems the renegades we were sent after have melted back into Indian Territory."

Esther halted the motion of the spindle and wrapped a length of yarn around the stem. She raised her brows at him. "Well, then?"

He returned the ramrod to its position under the rifle barrel. As much as he'd like to seize inaction as an excuse to resign... "It's not in my nature to fail to see something through. I will make another pass down to Clark County, then report at Fort Daniel, to whomever may remain there."

Noble chuckled. "I'll be thinking of you from my warm bed. Speaking of which, I believe my wife and son and I can all use some rest." He held out his hand to Tabitha.

She rose from the chair, sweeping them with a sober glance. "I trust you to keep vigil."

When the door closed behind them, Jared packed up his gun-cleaning kit. Putting it away, he fetched his bedroll and spread it before the hearth. Esther had taken up a candle as though to climb to the loft—although he'd seen her quilts folded next to the rocker—but she hesitated at the foot of the ladder. Was she afraid to pass by him to fetch her covers?

Jared swept a hand toward his own blanket. "Sit with me a while?" When she worried her lower lip between her teeth, he added, "There are things I did not get to say to you earlier that I would share."

Leaving the candle on the table, she approached, and he helped her to sit before lowering himself to the blanket beside her.

She studied her hands, folded in her lap. "Will you leave in the morning?"

"I will. So you can resume your place here if you prefer it." Now it was his turn to wink.

She blushed. "It seemed wise to be close to Tabitha before the birth, but I think I will return to the loft now that Noble is home. "

"And that brings me to what I didn't get to say earlier. This family owes you a huge debt of gratitude." Amazement clogged Jared's throat for a moment. "I can't say how much I admire all you did—birthing Tabitha's baby, running the household alone, fighting off a panther."

A deep shiver took her, and he reached for one of her quilts. He spread it around her but left his hand there with the other side draping his shoulders. She sat stock still, staring into the flames, but her parted lips told him to wait, that she was about to speak.

Finally, she whispered, "I've known fear. Much fear. But not like that."

"And now?" He almost held his breath.

"I'm not afraid now, for you are here." Esther turned her face toward him. "I've never been so glad to see anyone in my life as I was today to see you, Jared Lockridge."

His name coming from her rang so sweet in the charged air that he leaned forward to taste the remnants of it on her lips.

The moment his mouth touched the softness of hers, he realized what he'd done, and he froze. But she didn't pull back. She didn't move either. For a second, he pressed her closer, his tentative breaths mingling with hers. When they separated, they stared at each other. Perhaps most astonishing of all, wonder, not terror, filled her face.

"I knew fear too."

Her eyelashes fluttered up. How had he ever thought her plain?

"When I saw the tracks leading to the house, I thought my heart would beat out of my chest."

Perhaps it was his voicing intense emotion, but Esther made a move as if she would get up. He gently caught her hand. Her eyes flew open wide, and he drew his fingers back.

"I will never make you do anything you don't want to do, Esther. I hope you know that." He angled his body toward the fire.

The next moment, Jared held in a swell of joy as she resettled beside him, tucking herself into the crook of his arm. She fit like a mortise-and-tenon joint. As if she'd been designed by the Master Carpenter to go there.

Suddenly, cold realization doused him. For he'd already selected someone to go there. Someone who—in his admiration for Esther and eagerness for her to accept tenderness—he'd completely shoved to the back of his memory. And yet... how could he let Esther go?

CHAPTER 15

*E*sther blinked sleepy eyes. Where was she? Ah, on her pallet in front of the fire, but—

Alarm raced through her as awareness jangled through her body—for Jared dozed beside her. She lifted her head from his arm. She must have fallen asleep leaning on him before he drifted off himself, doubtless as exhausted as she had been after attending Micah's birth.

What if Noble or, worse, Tabitha, came out and saw them thus? Her heart lurched. She must get up. But Jared didn't stir, and Esther slowly lowered her head as something in her whispered that it wouldn't hurt to linger just a moment, to absorb the fact that a man slept beside her, yet terror did not stiffen her limbs. That the beat of his heart under ear actually calmed her, the spicy scent that clung to his clothing drew rather than repelled her, and the slight scratch of his shadowed jaw did strange but pleasing things to her middle. That hollow of his throat, where his pulse beat—she had noticed it before. What would it be like to kiss him, just there, only softly?

Her breath caught. What was happening to her? Had relief at his return overpowered her better judgment? It was as if his words of gratitude and admiring glances filled a void she hadn't even known existed. More importantly...could he really want her, with her backwoods raising, over a real lady? Or was it only the fever of a lonely man that had shone from his eyes? Could he look past her childlike frame, her twisted limb? Esther's stomach plummeted. Not when he learned that frame might never bear him a child of his own.

Something scraped in the next room, and Esther scrambled up. Wrapped in her quilt, she scampered for the ladder, and just as she had the first night she arrived, she launched herself into the darkness beyond.

~

Something had shifted between night and morning. Esther's porridge stuck to the roof of her mouth and almost refused to go down, for Jared wouldn't meet her eyes. It was all she could do to act normal in front of Tabitha and Noble while her mind spun. Did he think ill of her for falling asleep with him by the fire? Or for fleeing upstairs? Worst of all, did he now regret their whole exchange—her first hint that intimacy with a man might not bring fear and shame, the first indication that he might care for her—and the kiss that she had relived in her mind a dozen times on her cold bed? It could hardly be considered a kiss, just a touching of lips and a moment of breathing together. For her, it had been a test. She'd thought she'd passed. But had the moment's gentle innocence been naught but a deceiving bait?

This unspoken dissatisfaction from a man was nothing new. It always built to a climax of some sort. But where Liam had exploded in anger, the way Jared told his family and not her of his plan to return to Hamp Willis's place hinted that his would ebb into a proper reserve. Liam's blows might have broken her body, but distance from Jared could break her soul.

Sometimes, the dread of a thing was worse than the experiencing of it. So Esther returned Jared's flint and tinder box to the barn while he was saddling Chestnut. The soft sighing of the wind and clucking of the chickens filled the tense silence. When he didn't speak, she hesitated by his work bench, tempted to run out the door. But she found her voice at last.

"I wished to apologize before you left."

Jared stepped out of his stallion's stall, his lean form formidable in layers of buckskin and wool. "For what?"

She cast her gaze down. "For whatever I did that displeased you."

"Esther." He came forward and gently took her hands. "It is I who should apologize. I have much on my mind this morning but never meant to make you think you were at fault. If anything..." He sighed, running a thumb over her knuckles. "If anything, I took advantage of a traumatic situation."

Esther blinked at him. "Advantage?" She'd been taken advantage of many times before, but never had it felt so sweet and innocent. No. She couldn't bear to think he saw it that way.

"I care deeply for you. I feared for you. But I should not have pushed the bounds of propriety, especially considering your past...and my future." He met her eyes, and the meaning pierced her with a thousand arrows. Keturah.

Esther slid her hands from his and hid them in the folds of her skirt. Only a dignified response could offer her any protection now, but her voice rasped as she spoke. "I know you meant nothing more than kindness to me."

"Esther, what I meant—"

She extended her palm toward him and shook her head. "I should not have presumed on your friendship. Your generosity. It has been"—she choked—"a great honor to work for your family."

"Esther..."

She fled from the barn, unable to look on him a moment

151

longer. She hurried toward the woods. What feared she from panthers and wolves when that tender man's rejection ravaged her insides? Why insulate herself from the cold when already she turned to ice?

She found a place under a massive hemlock and curled at its trunk, making herself small until the sound of Jared's calling her faded. But the sentinel of the forest failed to bring her the usual sense of peace. She sobbed, but—her reaction more like unto shock—no tears came out.

Why are you surprised? Didn't I tell you no one would ever take you but me?

Esther stopped her ears against the voice that she'd thought gone for good, but it was pointless. It came from the inside.

He saw you for what you are. Trash. A trollop.

She'd thrown herself at him from the moment he got home and let him take liberties that were only appropriate between a betrothed man and woman. Even she knew no upstanding female should allow such a thing, even a widow. Worse, he already had a fiancée, and it wasn't her. She'd shown him she cared nothing for honor or loyalty. He would never want her now.

She must be gone before he returned.

~

"Tabitha, would you help me make a dress with the olive-green material you gave me for Christmas?" Esther held her place in the Lockridge family Bible with her index finger. Asking a favor, even one implied by a gift, made her uncomfortable. She had waited until today, the day after Noble departed to join his brother's final scouting mission.

Tabitha had positioned her rocker closer to the window for better light. She kept Micah's cradle at a soothing motion with an occasional push of her foot while she embroidered the baby's initials on a length of linen that would become the front panel of his christening gown. She and Noble had agreed that, when fair weather came, they would take the child to a service at the new Baptist congregation, Mt. Moriah, near Hog Mountain. An immediate smile lit her face. "Of course. I had meant for us to start it long before now. This little gentleman's early arrival took me quite by surprise." She beamed down at the sleeping infant.

It must be the most amazing thing in the world to give a son to the man you loved. Esther swallowed hard. "Thank you so much. I would have started it myself, only...I'm not sure I know how to make a dress so fine."

"Pawsh." Tabitha waved her hand. "There's nothing to it if you have a pattern. You liked my dark-green gown, did you not?" When Esther nodded, she added in a satisfied tone, "We can use it as a pattern."

Esther dipped her chin. "Such a dress would be well met in Savannah." If she wore gloves to cover her calluses, someone might even think her a lady.

"Savannah?"

Esther glanced up. "Why, yes."

Tabitha drew her threaded needle up slowly. "Of course. I had thought perhaps..."

"Thought what?"

The young mother shrugged. "Only that you might stay in these parts a while."

Esther gently smoothed the page in front of her. "There is nothing for me here." Come spring, Keturah's name would be written in the front of this precious book as Jared's bride. That she could never bear to witness.

"Nothing?" Tabitha's voice offered subtle encouragement.

"I will miss you, naturally. And I will miss reading this book." Esther flattened her palm on the text. "You and your family have restored the gift of faith to me. Nothing feeds me as

153

the words on these pages. But I feel certain my uncle has a copy. I remember Aunt Temperance reading from it."

"I'm glad of that. If you take a renewed faith away from here, Esther, it will be recompense far beyond all you have done for us. But I had wondered...that is, I had thought that perhaps you had found another kind of love as well."

Esther met Tabitha's steady stare. She tried to read something in it. She couldn't. She made a tentative offering. "The love of good friends."

"I see." Tabitha pursed her lips and applied her needle again. "Do you say that because you fear I might disapprove of more?"

"I say that because it's true."

Tabitha laid her sewing in her lap with a little huff. "Esther, I am quite certain something happened between you and Jared when last he was here."

Esther ducked her head again. "Whatever happened, he made it clear his future is already set."

"I see." A soft breath eased from Tabitha's chest. "I am sorry. Jared is nothing if not loyal. It is one of his most admirable qualities. But I want you to know..." She waited until Esther looked up. "I will be deeply sorry to see you go. No one could have been a better companion...and teacher...and even savior to me as you have."

Tears filled Esther's eyes as the balm of friendship offered a temporary salve to the sting of rejection. She sought words, but they jumbled and piled in a lump in her throat.

"I mean that." Tabitha frowned. "*No one*. I also dare say that, despite his determination to honor his promise, Jared feels the same."

"Thank you." Yes, he was an honorable man. Would she have fallen for any other kind? "It means more to me than I can say that you have shown me what it is to have a friend."

CHAPTER 16

"Thank you for a fine supper, Mrs. Willis." With a contented sigh, Jared settled into Hamp Willis's Windsor chair, a finely crafted piece that inspired all sorts of ideas for furnishing his new cabin. Had he been home these past months rather than scouting the Jackson Line, he'd have been hard at work with his tool chest, making the most of the shortened days before spring demanded planting and cabin-raising. He'd a great deal of catching up to do.

"You're most welcome." The heavily pregnant miller's wife managed a smile as she refilled his cup of cider, but her slumped shoulders and shuffling steps revealed her weariness.

Hampton looked up at her from kneeling before the hearth, where he was lighting a pine knot from the single, flickering flame that remained after dinner. "Effie, you're plumb tuckered out. Why don't you go on to bed? I'll see to our guests."

She replaced the pitcher on the sideboard and gave a sigh. "Suppose'n I might. Goodnight, all."

They echoed her goodnight, and she let herself out the door of the dogtrot cabin. For a moment, the chorus of early peep frogs could be heard from the mill pond. Then she headed across the breezeway to join her seven-year-old daughter and ten-year-old son in the newer portion of the home Hampton had added under the same roof of this original cabin when his mill business became brisk.

"I'm sorry for the extra work we've required of your wife." Noble tamped some tobacco into his pipe. "However, your location on the border between our counties provides an ideal place to watch the renegades' camp."

"And keeps us from freezing," Jared added with a rueful chuckle. These first couple days of March had brought a hint of a thaw from the cruel winter—just in time for their ride back to Fort Daniel on the morrow.

The flare of the fatty wood Hampton placed in the corner of the hearth brought out the auburn hues in his shoulder-length hair. "We're both pleased to be of service. Naturally, we want nothing more than to see the men who murdered my father brought to justice."

"We are only sorry we've not had more to report." Jared tightened his fingers around his tankard. The uneventful weeks away from home felt wasted, especially leaving as he had, at odds with Esther. But no one could predict when the same or another war party might lay siege to the frontier. The only sign of movement near the renegades' camp had been that of solitary hunters passing through—following their four-legged prey. "Perhaps the enemy is merely waiting for spring when they can burn crops and easily thieve foraging livestock."

Hampton stood and brushed off his trousers. "That would be my guess, but perhaps the war to the west in Creek Territory will soon end. Everyone expects decisive action from Jackson and his army in the next month or two. He's only been waiting for fair weather to finish what he started in the fall."

"Indeed, that is the hope." Noble nursed his pipe a moment, then puffed out a breath.

"Then we can all move on with life." And now, Jared finally

knew which way to move. Doubtless, he wouldn't sleep much tonight for anticipating the journey home.

"If Jackson subdues the Red Sticks," Hampton said, "we'll see an influx of new settlers. With the Cherokees our allies, they'll be naught to fear from the natives. That will be good for business."

Jared nodded. "And likely, new homesteads will open up across the river."

Noble made a scoffing sound. "White men haven't respected the Indian boundary since the Revolution. I couldn't guess how many times the governor has imposed fines and chased settlers back across the line."

As keen as Jared was to serve his country with honor, the greed of many of his comrades for land belonging to the Indian tribes soured his stomach. "It's high time law and order was established in these parts."

Hampton crossed his thick arms over his chest. "All I've ever wanted is peace and the opportunity to make a living for my family. That's what my father fought for. Neither one of us wanted this war with the Creeks, allied to the British, and for that, we've been called traitors."

Noble cocked his head, studying his host. "You weren't tempted to enlist after what the Red Sticks did to your father?"

The miller shrugged, letting his arms hang. "The way I see it, I'm doing my part, helping supply meal to our local militia at Fort Smith and the settlers lawfully abiding in Clark County. You can't put an army in the field if you can't feed it. As for the Red Sticks, can we really blame them for fighting to keep *their* lawful land? If there's folks here who take exception to that and think me less than a patriot, then so be it."

Jared straightened. "None among present company."

Hamp grinned. "That I know well. If we weren't of the same mind regarding the Creeks, I wouldn't have opened my home to you. And on that note, I'll bid you gentlemen a good night."

"Good night." Jared stood and shook his host's hand. "Thank you for offering us lodging." The shed room behind the kitchen with its two twin cots had been much more accommodating than pine boughs and a bedroll on the hard ground.

After the man left, Jared sank back down in his chair, not quite willing yet to leave the warmth of the fire.

Noble puffed his pipe. "Are you certain of your course about your betrothal now? When I first rejoined you here, you were not in a good frame of mind."

Inhaling, Jared sucked in his lips for a moment. Then he let out a gusty sigh. "I hated to leave after dealing Esther such a blow. Guilt was eating me up. I led her on and dishonored my commitment. But I didn't stop to think about how telling her that would reinforce every lie she's ever believed about herself."

Noble crossed an ankle over his other knee and rested his forearm there, pipe glowing. "Esther is sturdier than you think. And Tabitha will help her. Those women know how to draw strength from each other. However this ends, much good has come of you bringing the widow into our home."

Jared inclined his head. "Much good." His heart, on an invisible string, strained toward the northeast.

"You didn't answer my question. Are you certain of your decision?"

"Yes." Sitting forward, he smacked his palms on his thighs and then let them rest there. "Ever since Mrs. Willis allowed me to write to Keturah and posted my letter, I've had peace. I'm only impatient to finalize things with Esther." His future course would doubtless injure one of the women in his life, but hopefully, it would do the least damage while remaining true to his conscience.

Noble nodded. "Perhaps a letter will be waiting upon your return."

Jared sighed. "One I'm none too anxious to read."

He'd just risen when shouts, thumps, and running footsteps

came from the attached cabin. He turned toward the breezeway and snatched his rifle from near the door, which he flung open.

Hamp's son, Mark, skidded to a stop in front of him.

"Fire!" the boy exclaimed in his tinny voice. "The mill's on fire!"

Across the clearing, flames licked from under the looming mortise-and-tenon structure.

"We've got to put it out." Mark pivoted toward the front porch just as a dark figure darted in front of the giant water wheel.

Jared grabbed the boy by his collar the same moment Hampton appeared in the doorway opposite and aimed his musket toward the mill.

"Get back, son," Hampton hissed.

Jared shoved the child to Noble, now crouching behind him.

Hamp's musket flashed and boomed, but the intruder had already disappeared into a copse of trees. A horse and rider emerged, headed for the main trail. Jared scampered to the edge of the porch, knelt, and took aim. Flint struck frizzen, sending a shower of sparks into the pan. His shot dropped the fleeing miscreant just as two more riders broke out of the trees. The wounded man's hat fell off, and his horse cantered away. Clutching his chest, he struggled to rise on all fours. Eyes wide in the firelight, he glanced Jared's direction. But Jared's powder horn was inside the cabin.

Hamp grunted and struggled to reload behind him.

"Down, Jared," Noble growled as the other two renegades fired back from their mounts. Jared flattened himself on the floor, and Noble got off a shot.

One of the Indians—his dark hair loose, his face painted red—hooked his arm through his fallen comrade's, dragging him up behind him. Their mounts' hooves thudded away into the darkness.

"Now, son, get the sand buckets," Hamp yelled to Mark, who cowered in the kitchen doorway.

Regardless of the danger to the mill, Jared wouldn't be caught unaware again. He grabbed his powder horn and reloaded before following the others to the burning structure. With sand buckets from both the house and the mill, followed by pails of water, they got the flames extinguished before significant damage was done.

When it was out, they stood panting and disheveled in the yard.

Effie Willis burst into tears, her daughter clinging to her skirt. "Them blasted Injuns! We leave them alone. Why don't they leave us alone? Why us? We don't do them no harm."

Jared took a step forward. "Unfortunately, that's not quite true."

"What do you mean?" Glowering, Hamp encircled his wife's waist with his arm.

"I mean, you did do your attackers harm." Jared met his host's eyes. "You and your father refused to join the search for the Snow women and discouraged others from doing so." At Hamp's blank, intense stare, he further clarified. "I got a glimpse of the man I shot tonight, and it wasn't a Red Stick. I'd recognize that long, lean face anywhere. It was Enoch Snow."

CHAPTER 17

*J*ared intercepted Noble's sideways glance as they took the trail home from Hog Mountain.

"What are you going to do with those boots?" His brother asked.

Jared trained his gaze straight ahead. "What boots?"

"The ones you bought off Mr. Moore when I was loading my supplies. The ones you've now got stashed in your saddlebag."

"Redbuds are blooming." Jared shifted on Chestnut, surveying the damp forest around them that stirred with the earthiness and sweet birdsong of coming spring. "We'll have to set to turning the garden spot and the cornfield as soon as we get home."

"You'll need more than boots if you want the widow to forgive you." Noble gave a grim chuckle. "You'd best be thinking of some pretty fine words."

It had been a disappointment that no letter from Keturah waited at the trading post. But there remained a good likelihood one had already been delivered to the cabin in their absence. He was almost free.

It had been strange to see the fort nearly abandoned. The sergeant he'd reported to had seemed more interested in making his way to Creek Territory before the decisive battle than recording the Lockridge scouts' tale of white men pretending to be Indians to stir war and exact revenge along the frontier. He'd assured them the authorities Hamp Willis rode to see at Fort Smith would be responsible for rounding up the Snow men.

Jared had fulfilled his responsibility to the militia. He'd identified—if not captured—the troublemakers on Jackson County's southern border. All that remained in the way of his future happiness was release from one woman, if she was willing...and forgiveness from another.

"I've got special plans for those boots," he muttered. Chestnut almost ran into the back of his brother's mount when Noble drew up suddenly. "What're you doing?"

"Hope you got your speech ready." Noble nudged his stallion off the path, allowing Jared the view ahead.

Clad in her rust-colored dress with a satchel in her hand and her eyes wide as Tabitha's pearlware saucers, Esther stared at him from the middle of the trail. Leaving. She was leaving. She wasn't even going to wait to tell him goodbye.

Jared swung down from his saddle and led Chestnut forward by the reins, never breaking eye contact with Esther. Rising panic made his voice come out sharper than he'd intended. "Do you want to tell me what you're doing?"

"Y-you're a day early."

He focused a pointed glance on her bag. "I can see that I'm not."

Noble cleared his throat. "If you'll pardon me, I'll head on home and leave you two to settle this." He tipped his hat, and when they did not respond, he urged his horse back onto the trail behind Esther.

Jared questioned Esther again. "Where do you think you're going?"

Esther's delicate throat worked, and she took a step back. "Into the settlement, to arrange a ride east."

He slowed his breathing, forcing his shoulders to relax. "And you couldn't wait for Noble to escort you, to procure and pay for that transportation with someone reliable?"

"Tabitha gave me the money." As his eyes widened, she looked to the side. "She didn't want to, but she understood."

"Understood what?"

After a beat of silence, Esther's reply whispered out so softly he had to bend closer to hear. "That I couldn't bear to see you again."

Almost all the air left Jared's chest in a single rush. "Oh, Esther." So her feelings hadn't hardened to the point that he couldn't bend them—even if she still held anger against him. He forced himself to speak slowly, not to frighten her or deluge her with the emotions he'd held so tightly in check. "This is my fault. When I woke the morning after...after I held you by the fire, all I could hear in my head was the hammer of my own guilt. I've always been so...*proud*...that I was a dependable man."

She blinked at him. "To be a dependable man is a good thing."

"But pride is not. You see, it wasn't as much about being loyal, noble, and dependable—all good things—as it was about not being like my father."

"I don't understand."

He glanced around, and spotting an overturned tree, gestured to it. "Will you sit with me? Just hear me out for a minute?"

Esther remained planted on the path, her expression pinched. She shifted her weight off her lame foot as her fingers tightened on the handle of her bag. Finally, she nodded and followed him through the crunching leaves of last autumn. Jared tied Chestnut to a purpling Eastern redbud and sat beside Esther as she settled her bag at her hem. She wouldn't look at him.

"I told you my father came back from the war much altered." He waited for a nod. "Now I must explain what I meant. He had nightmares and...day-mares. Loud noises, stressful situations, would make him flash back to moments in the war."

Her brow creasing, she looked at him now.

He'd rather she didn't for this part. He plucked up a stick and started snapping off little pieces. "He drank to deal with the memories. He drank a lot. And he was different when he was drunk, like we talked about. He turned his anger on us boys and on our mother."

Esther's fingers fluttered almost to his sleeve, then away. "I'm so sorry."

"But what was worse were his absences, because I knew that when he was gone, he was not only drinking, but gambling away any money he had left and taking up with other women. My mother thought he blamed her for having to go to war. For everything."

"Because her father was a Loyalist?"

"Yes. I...hated him for what he did to her." Jared dropped what was left of the stick. Hands on his knees, he hung his head. "I couldn't do anything to help her." Admitting the darkness of those days took him right back to that feeling of helplessness he'd despised. This time, he could've sworn Esther touched the back of his neck, but he couldn't raise his head. "I vowed I would always do what was right and never betray anyone I loved."

She sat back quietly. "I see. A big vow for a little boy."

He dragged in a deep breath and looked sideways at her. "But he returned."

Her eyebrows rose. "He did?"

Jared nodded again. "Days before my mother was due to take us and sail back to her extended family in England. Sober and resolute. He'd found God at a Methodist camp meeting."

"Did your mother take him back?"

"The condition of his return was that he would come here, to work this bounty land for a year as part of the requirements to file a claim to it. He fulfilled his end of the agreement, so my mother fulfilled hers. They had more children and gave this frontier parcel to Noble and me when we came of age."

Esther laid her hand over her heart and shifted on the log. "I'm so glad their love was restored."

Jared flattened his mouth. "Perhaps their love was, but I'm not so sure about my mother's trust. To this day, I believe she fears the return of the nightmares, the drinking, the gambling, the wenching. And she passed that same mistrust on to me. Not so much that I watch for it in others, but that I hold myself to a standard of perfection."

"I'm still not sure why that is bad."

He clasped his hands together to keep from taking hers. "To strive for perfection through Christ is godly. To strive for it in one's own strength is folly. And sometimes, the heart does not obey."

As she watched him, the color slowly drained from her face. She managed a breathless question. "Have you fallen into your father's sins?"

A chuckle escaped, and Jared allowed his hand to stray over to nab hers. "No, but I did fall in love with you when I was engaged to another."

The quick intake of breath was the only thing that betrayed her emotion. She stared at him as still and unmoving as a deer hiding in the brush.

Since she seemed to have lost powers of speech, he might as well plow on. "I didn't realize it until Noble joined me on the boundary line. He made me see that the reason I was so miserable wasn't just guilt. That I hadn't trifled with your affections in a moment of weakness. My actions were born out of love. He also showed me that loving you wasn't a sin. It was an indication that maybe you'd make a better match for me than Keturah."

The last thing he expected was for Esther to spring to her feet. But she did, and he scrambled up after her. She paced several feet away and covered her ears. He came up behind her and sought unsuccessfully to pull her arms down.

"No." Her breath whistled in and out, fast and shallow. "I cannot listen to this. You are already promised to her. I can't think it."

"Esther. Esther!" Circling to face her, he finally got both of her hands lowered to her sides and laced his fingers through hers. Leaning forward, Jared met her moisture-filled eyes with his and whispered. "I've already written to Keturah asking to be released from our betrothal."

"Wh-what?" A tear dripped from Esther's lashes and raced down her face. "Why would you do that?"

"Without making sure you would have me first?" One corner of his mouth lifted in a lopsided grin. "Because not only is Keturah not suited to the frontier, but it would be the utmost cruelty to marry her when she has no idea my heart belongs to you. That doesn't excuse my behavior, but it finally came clear what a disservice I would be doing not only to myself but to my fiancée if I brought her here and let you go."

"But why? Why would you want me?" The words seemed to tear from a raw place deep inside. "Look at me!" It wasn't a demand. It was self-recrimination.

His heart squeezing, Jared thumbed away another of her tears. They still had a lot of work to do. "I *am* looking at you. I've been looking at you for months—as often as I could, by the way. And I see a lovely, compassionate, capable woman."

Esther covered her face as he kept speaking.

"A hard-working woman who takes care of everyone else ahead of herself. A courageous woman who stands up to Indians and wild animals and hunger and whatever nature throws at her. A woman who wants to better herself, one who is just beginning to accept who God says she is. And God willing, if you are willing, I want to see who you become. I want to be a part of that."

She flung her hands down again. "You speak so beautifully, but for the life of me, Jared Lockridge, I don't understand what you are saying half the time."

Laughter momentarily eased the stranglehold of suspense. "Then let me come to the point. I want you to come back home with me. We'll build a cabin and furniture for it. We'll put in a big vegetable garden we can share with Tabitha and Noble, and we'll plant you an herb garden. We'll wait until we get the letter from Keturah releasing me from our betrothal, and then we'll go up to the county seat at Jeffersonton and get married."

Her mouth fell open. "But—"

He held up a finger. "Don't worry. I promise to ask you proper-like when that time comes."

"But what if Keturah refuses to release you?"

Jared shook his head, squeezing Esther's hands. "That won't happen. Keturah is too proud to marry a man who prefers another." She drew a breath, and he narrowed his eyes, hurrying on. "Before you pity her, you should know that she's also too selfish. She isn't happy unless all the attention is focused on her. Tabitha told me a young lawyer—Shaw or somebody—had been paying suit to Keturah. She will quickly find another—if not this lawyer, someone else."

Esther dropped her head. She seemed to struggle, starting to speak and then falling silent twice. Finally, she raised her chin. "Be that as it may, how could you want me instead of her, flawed as I am?" She gave a nod toward her feet. "You may find it worse than you imagine."

It was all he could do not to take her in his arms, but her manner held too much reserve. "No doubt, you will find flaws in me as well. But if you give me the chance, Esther, I will cherish all of you. You don't see yourself rightly yet. I hope that with time, with love, you may come to see yourself through my eyes."

"But I am not a maiden." Another tear coursed down her cheek. "And you deserve a maiden."

He squeezed her hand. "There is no shame in widowhood."

She covered her face again. "But there is shame in mine."

"Not anymore." Finally sensing his opening, Jared drew Esther to his chest. "With God, you're a new creation. Let me show you how a man is supposed to love a woman." A sob bubbled out of her, and a new fear stabbed his breastbone. "That is, if you think you can love me."

What an idiot he had been. He'd thought he'd seen the signs, but what if her reactions to him had merely portrayed a grateful admiration for his kindness? What if she had decided that their brush of a kiss was the extent of her desire? That she truly only wished to be his friend? And now, what if she decided to leave him?

Esther raised her tear-streaked face and shook her head.

His heart almost stopped. "No? You don't think, perhaps in time..."

Then that beauteous smile transformed her countenance. "No, I don't *think*, silly man. I already do."

"You do? You love me?" Blood raced in hot relief through his veins.

She squeezed her eyes closed and murmured, "I love you," as though the admission exacted a deep toll from her. And she trembled in his arms. When he cupped her chin, her lashes flew open. "Pray, do not kiss me again."

"Why not?" Jared touched his thumb to her full lower lip, his breath catching.

"Because, right now, I think it would be more than I could bear."

She sounded so serious, he took that to heart. He stepped back and instead pressed a light kiss to her forehead. "Very well. I won't kiss you again until we are well and truly betrothed, just as long as you will let me take you home now."

With a faltering smile that begged he live up to his words, Esther gave him her hand.

CHAPTER 18

The chirp of a wood-cock high above in an alder tree filtered down with pale sunshine on Esther and Tabitha as they mounded little hillocks in their new garden spot. Catherine Howell had sent clippings and plants over with her husband this morning. They laid out the edibles and the medicinals as the ring of axes carried from the far rise—the ridge Jared was clearing for his cabin. Just the house site, for Tabitha said many more men would come soon to clear additional acreage for planting.

"We'll have a regular log rolling when that happens." Baby Micah in a sling on her chest, Tabitha looked up from brushing dirt around a clump of lavender. She paused to give her hands an appreciative whiff. "Mm."

Duchess, lying just outside the open gate of the sturdy fence Jared had built, lifted her head and sniffed the air. Then, apparently finding nothing of interest, she lowered her muzzle to her paws again.

Esther inspected a strange plant with a reddish, fleshy stem and succulent leaves. How puzzling that she'd never seen the species before. "A log rolling?"

Tabitha's mouth dropped open. "You've never attended a log rolling?" When Esther shook her head, she hurried on. "It's when the girdled trees are cut into lengths and piled to be burned. Word will go out to neighbors for miles around, and while the men roll the logs down into the field, the women quilt in the house. At night, we feast on a roast hog, and there's a dance. A real dance." Her eyes sparkled. "It will be a perfect time to wear your new dress."

Dismay filled her. Had Tabitha forgotten about Esther's lame foot? "I don't think so."

Tabitha's tone turned teasing. "Perhaps you want to save it for your wedding."

Heat flushed Esther's face. She had yet to work up the courage to speak to Jared of her barrenness. She was a coward. A needy parasite who would suck up the love and affirmation of this fine family for as long as she could. "What is this plant? I've never seen it growing in the wild."

Tabitha's hand flew to her waist. "Esther Venable, don't you change the subject on me."

"I need to know where to put it."

Tabitha pointed to the far corner. "By the lamb's quarters. Settler women grow it and the purslane to eat raw or cooked. Both are full of healthful benefits."

"Very good." Having such plants mere steps outside the door would certainly be easier than foraging through the forest. With a smile, Esther turned to her task.

A warning cry was followed by a loud *swoosh* and a tremendous *crack*.

Esther froze and held her breath, only relaxing when hoots of triumph filled the silence.

"Makes you just as nervous as it does me, doesn't it?" Tabitha shook her head. "Those trees are so big."

Esther swallowed and applied the hand hoe Jared had fashioned for close-up garden work to the manure-enriched soil. "I have no right to be as nervous as you."

"You will soon enough, after your wedding."

"There may yet be no wedding, as there has been no letter from your friend."

"You are my friend."

Pausing in her digging, Esther glanced over her shoulder. "Your other friend."

Tabitha sighed and adjusted the sling that held her sleeping babe. "I must admit, I'm puzzled, and a bit concerned, as to why there has been nothing from Keturah."

"What will Jared do if no letter ever comes?" She'd been too afraid to ask him for a timeline.

"If none ever comes, I daresay, from the way he looks at you, he hasn't the patience to wait long."

Duchess leapt up and ran into the woods, barking, and Tabitha's chuckle died on her lips.

Esther struggled to her feet and grabbed the musket she'd left propped against the fence. "Perhaps it's Jimmy Howell." Mr. Howell's twelve-year-old son had taken the morning to hunt in hopes of bringing them a hare to roast for dinner. "Stay here until I see what it is."

Tabitha nodded, cradling Micah's head.

Past the massive hemlock where Esther had once hidden from Jared, Duchess had cornered something in the spreading branches of a red oak. Esther gasped. A man! Not just a man, an Indian. She swung the muzzle of the weapon up and sighted on his chest.

His hands flew up, and he crouched on the branch using the moccasined arches of his feet alone. "*A-le-wi-s-do-di!*" *Stop.* Then, in halting English, he added, "I come in peace."

"*You.*" The breath rushed out of her chest with the word. "I saw you at the trading post."

The young brave gave an eager nod and placed a hand on

his buckskin-clad chest. "Friend. Brother. I warn." He motioned toward the snarling dog, and Esther bid her come to her side. Duchess obeyed but remained tense, ready to spring, her own warning rumbling from her massive chest.

Given that Esther had seen this man with Ahyoka, she lowered her weapon a mite. "Warn? Of what?"

The Cherokee deftly dropped to the ground. He switched to his native language but kept it simple enough that Esther could grasp his meaning. "We must hurry. Leave this place. Bad white men come, men who pretend to be Indian."

Esther felt the blood leave her face. "How do you know about that?" The man shook his head in response, his expression frustrated, anxious, but uncomprehending. Raising the musket again, she demanded, "Who are you?"

His eyes narrowed on her, and he spoke in emphatic English. "I am Oukonunaka. White Owl. Ahyoka's son."

~

The moment Duchess's strident barking carried from Noble's cabin, Jared and his brother mounted their horses and tore down the ridge. They found Tabitha in the garden, clutching Micah close. Unblinking, she pointed around the house and spoke in a raspy voice just over a whisper.

"I think Duchess treed something—or someone."

Heart thudding in his ears, Jared plunged into the woods with his rifle stock on his shoulder. The sight that met his eyes stopped his feet.

Esther stood with her back to him, the mastiff at her side, both but inches from an Indian. The brave's head was bent to Esther's, and she fingered something at his neck.

Jared barked out an order. "Stand back!" Esther blocked a clean shot, and he wanted nothing more than to get her as far from that Indian as possible, as quickly as possible.

The man's hands flew up. He retreated a pace as Esther whirled.

"Jared! Don't shoot. Oukonunaka came to help us."

Jared cocked his head. She knew the Indian?

"He is Ahyoka's son. Look." Esther lifted something on a string around the brave's neck. "The button I gave her as a child."

Noble held his musket at the ready beside Jared. "Why does he wear it?"

"Please. No time." Oukonunaka waved his hands, palms down. "Bad men come. Women leave!" He gestured toward the river, almost-black eyes above high cheekbones intense.

"Esther, come here." Jared nodded to the ground beside him.

After hesitating a moment, she complied. "Don't you remember, we saw him at the trading post?"

He did. He also remembered the man's stare had disconcerted Esther so much that he'd taken her outside. "Are you the one who's been watching Esther?"

He received only a frown and a confused head shake in response.

Esther answered instead. "White Owl speaks little English. But he told me the men who pretended to be Indians are coming."

Noble lowered his weapon and edged forward. "Coming here?"

The Indian gave a sharp nod. "Yes. Women go." He faced Esther and spoke in Cherokee. Jared had picked up enough of the language at the fort to understand that the young brave wanted to take Esther and Tabitha to the settlement.

"Whoa, whoa, whoa." Jared tucked the rifle under his arm and waved to halt the flow of conversation. "Why should we trust you? Why would we let you take our women anywhere?"

The baby's whimpering revealed that Tabitha had come as close as the hemlock, waiting in hearing range.

White Owl fell back into his native tongue, speaking quickly and with harsh hand gestures.

Esther's brows tucked down as she listened, then she translated. "I think he's saying the men are angry at you. One of his people was hunting and learned this." Her eyes entreated him. "I believe him, Jared. Before you came, he said Ahyoka asked him to watch over me. I think he made me so uneasy in the post because I had encountered him before...when he tried to take me away from Liam."

Silence fell in a frozen moment. Confusion swirled in Jared's head, and he turned to White Owl with a challenging glare. "Is that true? You killed Esther's husband?"

The brave gave a slow dip of his head. "Bad man." But it was the way he looked at Esther, hooded eyes glowing with a gentle light, his molded lips softening, that made up Jared's mind.

"You're not going anywhere with him."

The beating of hooves broke the quiet of morning. They all stilled, casting glances at one another.

Jimmy Howell's youthful voice called out, "Mrs. Lockridge! Mrs. Lockridge?"

Tabitha hurried for the yard, and they all followed her. "I am here, Jimmy."

The young redhead—hatless and windblown—reined in his pony as soon as he spied them. "Thank God! I had just bagged this hare"—he indicated a small, furry carcass dangling from his saddle—"when I heard voices on the path. Got a glimpse of them and thought they was Injuns, but they was speakin' English. And they was talkin' about you, Jared. Named you by name."

He stiffened and shot a glance at White Owl. "Saying what?"

"That it was a good day for the man who killed his brother to die."

Killed? Jimmy went on explaining how he'd taken a shortcut to the Lockridge land, but Jared flashed back to the memory of Enoch Snow sprawled on the ground, a bloodstain on his chest. He must not have survived that shot. Jared met White Owl's eyes. "You spoke the truth."

Noble gathered his wife and child under his arm, his expression fierce as he addressed the Cherokee. "You will take the women to the Howells' cabin. Duchess will go with you. And Jimmy will fetch his father back here, then hasten home to help defend the place." The boy had already curled the reins between his fingers to turn his horse. Noble's gaze sought Jared's, unwavering in his commitment. "We will be waiting for the Snows."

The words had no sooner left his mouth than the crack of a rifle reverberated through the trees.

CHAPTER 19

With Jimmy's high-pitched scream ringing in his ears, Jared jumped forward to catch the boy as he slid off his rearing pony. Blood stained his thigh. The shot had come from the woods near the trail. Had the boy not moved his horse, Jared might be dead.

Everyone bolted for the cabin, but White Owl grabbed Esther's arm. "Come!" He nodded to the forest on the other side of the house. "Horses."

Esther's wild gaze swung to Jared's. The intense need to protect her would have wrenched him to her side, but he held the unconscious Howell boy. They must take cover—instantly. If White Owl could keep her safe...

He nodded. "To the Howells'."

All in a split second, Jared transferred the boy to White Owl as Tabitha and Esther ran in the direction the Cherokee had indicated. Jared grabbed his gun from where it had fallen. He caught one last glimpse of the swirling skirts of the fleeing women as he slid behind the rain barrel at the corner of the porch—the nearest obstruction. Noble had taken cover behind the wide trunk of a lone pine tree halfway to the woods. Like

Jared, he searched the forest near the trail. Where had the shot come from?

A hint of movement from a juniper drew Jared's first bullet.

An answering crack came from the other side of Noble. Noble flattened himself, eyes going wide. His brother was caught between the two attackers! One of them had circled around through the woods.

"Blast!" Jared struggled to pour the powder down the muzzle while keeping his extremities behind the barrel.

Noble fired back toward the assailant behind him. Nothing indicated he'd hit his target. He crawled on his elbows toward a clump of rhododendron, dragging his legs behind him. Another gunshot.

Had his brother made it?

Jared had just tamped down his patch with his ramrod when something swooshed overhead, followed by a small thud. Then another. A flicker just above the nearby stone piling caught his eye. Burning arrows!

A voice carried from near the mouth of the trail. "Your death will be worse than my brother's, Jared Lockridge!"

Jared sucked in a dusty breath. "You're a wanted man, Ephraim! Turn yourself in, and maybe they'll go easier on you."

A wicked laugh sashayed across the clearing. "I got nothin' to lose. You, however..."

Cover me, Noble. Jared struggled out of his hunting frock, then straightened and flapped the garment at the small orange tongues of fire. Muskets boomed twice. A lead ball contacted wood with a *thud* as he used the tunic to beat out the flames.

Ephraim called out again. "When we finish here, we're goin' to find your womenfolk. Ain't that nice of us? Even after no one wanted to find ours." Another *swoosh* followed his taunting.

Jared's fingers tightened on the butt of his rifle. "Come out and face me like a man!"

"Now why would I do that when I got you trapped with the porch burnin' down around you?"

Sure enough, a dreaded popping and crackling came from near the front steps.

A sense of movement behind him had him whipping his rifle toward the back of the house—just as a thick figure in buckskin whisked around the corner, musket pointed in Jared's direction.

~

"Will he lose his leg?" Catherine Howell wailed as White Owl eased her son's limp body onto the table. As Tabitha and Esther had shared a second pony he'd picketed in the woods, the Cherokee had cradled Jimmy in his arms during their dash up the trail. But the boy's entire trouser leg was soaked with his blood, and his skin was white as a heavy frost.

When he roused and moaned, Esther laid a hand on the heavyset woman's shoulder. "Shh, you must not speak like that."

"Mama?" Jimmy raised a trembling hand, and Catherine grabbed ahold of it.

"I'm here, son."

While White Owl cut away the trouser fabric, Tabitha went to comfort two girls, the older one hugging the younger on a low rope bed in the corner.

Esther surveyed the nearby shelves. "Have you any spirits you can give him?" But when she glanced back, Jimmy's head again lolled to one side, his pupils disappearing under the top fringe of his ginger lashes.

Her heart pounded. This was much more serious than Jared's grazed arm. Most gunshots to the leg did indeed result in amputation. Whatever would she do if such a thing became necessary?

Across from her, White Owl caught her eye. "You help, *No-tlv-si.*" *Star.*

Ahyoka had told him the meaning of Esther's name. And apparently, he believed it.

~

Jared pulled his rifle's trigger, and Ephraim Snow—for the man who'd taunted him must not be—fell backward, a hole through his chest. His hands trembled as he lowered the smoking weapon. He'd aimed for Snow's arm, but the man's movement had taken him straight into the path of death. His first kill. It felt awful.

John Howell's ruddy face peered around the edge of the house. "I was coming to help, but I guess you took care of that."

"Get back!" Jared made a shooing gesture. "There's another one. He has Noble pinned down."

Rather than take cover, John sauntered toward him. "No, he doesn't. Your brother's comin' into the yard with his gun trained on 'im." He nodded toward the woods.

Jared peeked past the rain barrel. His jaw dropped at the sight of Noble with his musket to the back of Micajah Snow's greasy head. *Now* he remembered the name?

~

Between her blood-soaked fingers, Esther held up the bullet that had lodged deep in Jimmy Howell's thigh. "It did not shatter the bone."

"Oh, thank God." Catherine dissolved into sobs.

Esther plunked the projectile onto a rag on the table. "We can be thankful it was a rifle rather than a musket."

As Esther finished stitching up the wound, Tabitha hurried onto the porch, a girl at each side and a basket on her arm. White Owl, who guarded the clearing from the open doorway with his musket over his arm, moved aside to let her pass. She laid Micah in the cradle with Catherine's infant son. "I have the herbs you asked for."

"Good." Having tied off the stitches, Esther set aside her needle and turned to wash her hands. "With proper care..." Catherine's continued weeping would make it impossible for her to hear Esther's instructions. She wiped her hands on a rag, then took the young mother by the elbows. "Catherine. I'm going to show you how to tend his wound, but you must listen. And do exactly as I say."

Where did such confidence come from? Ahyoka. The teaching she had given Esther, a tiny seed of strength when she was weakest, still under Liam's control. But her spirit had been open, and that seed had fallen into fertile ground.

She had just finished explaining to Catherine how to care for Jimmy's wound and what warning signs to watch for when White Owl stiffened, aiming his musket at the clearing.

Catherine gasped.

"Don't shoot!" Mr. Howell shouted. "It's us."

While the other women ran out onto the porch, Esther remained at Jimmy's side should he rouse and, becoming startled, roll off the table. As much as her eyes longed to gaze on Jared's beloved face and her feet longed to hasten to his side, she should refrain from such displays. Their pledge to one another couldn't be termed a promise, much less a betrothal. When she had returned to Jared's home, Esther had determined to do nothing that would bring him guilt while he waited to hear from his fiancée. And if she threw her arms around him this moment, she would also kiss him.

But when John Howell and Noble filed into the cabin with

the womenfolk and White Owl closed the door, her pulse raced. Where was Jared?

Mr. Howell rushed to his son, reaching for his hand. "Jimmy?" His eyes sought Esther's as Jimmy's lashes fluttered. "Is he all right?"

"He should be if your wife cares for him as I told her to. I removed the bullet, sutured the wound, and applied a healing poultice." Esther stepped around John's formidable form, seeking Noble's face. She swallowed to clear the thickness from her throat. "Your brother? Why is he not with you?"

He uncurled his arm from Tabitha's shoulder and laid his hand on Esther's back. "Never fear. Jared is delivering Micajah Snow to the authorities in Jeffersonton. From there, the miscreant can be taken back to Clark County to stand trial."

Briefly, she closed her eyes, breathing a prayer of thanks, and the band around her chest loosened. She raised her head. "And Ephraim Snow?"

"Jared killed him. He was trying to stop the man, but Ephriam ran head-on into the bullet."

"Oh no." Esther covered her mouth. Surely, such an act would take a toll on one of Jared's gentle nature.

John glanced up from smoothing Jimmy's hair. "I had him in my sights if Jared had failed."

"I'm just sorry you had to be involved," Noble told him. "And at great cost, I might add."

"Cost?" Mr. Howell spluttered. "Soon enough this one here will be limpin' about, fillin' the ears of any who will hear with his adventure of helpin' capture an outlaw." The bravado in his tone made Esther's heart squeeze again.

Please, God, let the boy heal. This talking to the Almighty like a friend was new to her but gave her a sense of comfort. She especially liked the way the Bible described God as the Great Physician. Picturing Him as such came easier than relating to Him as her Heavenly Father. That might take some time,

Tabitha said. She pointed to Noble's gentleness with their son. And there was another example before her just now.

"Pa?" Jimmy's frail voice drew Mr. Howell's attention back to the table. "Did we get 'em?"

Relieved laughter rippled through the room. As the others gathered around Jimmy, lauding him and preparing him to be moved onto his bed, Esther gravitated toward the tall, silent man in buckskin, standing near the door, watching her. As if awaiting her leave to go. He'd brought them here and guarded them with such grave respect that any fears about him harming them had melted away. Now, the lines around his eyes and mouth curved into an approval that both alarmed and reassured. It was like unto the way Jared looked at her, yet different. She couldn't quite fathom it. Protective, without being passionate. Almost proud.

She stood before him and tipped up her head to meet his gaze. "That we are all here is probably thanks to you. Had you not warned us—"

"I watch." White Owl tapped two fingers below his eyes. "I see."

Hadn't Ahyoka said something similar? She cocked her head. "Why do you watch me?"

He studied her for a moment, his granite brow smooth. But in his eyes, some deep emotion she couldn't read flickered.

"Did you bring the deer? *A-wi*?"

As Esther touched her chest to indicate herself, White Owl offered a single nod.

"You did? Why?"

The firelight caught in the centers of his dark pupils, but there was no malice there, only gentle regard. Nevertheless, she jumped when his fingers closed around her forearm. "*I-gi-do.* Sister?

He released her and turned for the door.

"No!" She followed him onto the porch. For some reason,

her heart burned at the thought of him leaving. "I don't understand. I have so many questions. Won't you stay and talk to me?"

"*Nu-li-s-dv.*" *Soon.* He brought his fist to his chest in a gesture of farewell, but he added in Cherokee, "Wait. I will come with my mother."

CHAPTER 20

*L*ess than a week after the attack, Esther finished sprinkling ashes from the fireplace on the turnips, radishes, and spring onions in the vegetable garden and raised her face to the far ridge. She drank in the fresh coolness of the March evening and the loamy scent of early spring. On this side of the creek, Noble's freshly planted furrows glowed red in the twilight. On the other, girdled trees awaited removal from what would be Jared's fields, the underbrush already cleared away. She could just spy the plot of earth where his cabin would soon be raised. Between the land of the two brothers, a greening thicket surrounded the creek, studded with the spidery white flowers of the serviceberry.

She swallowed, and a chill overtook her. As much as her spirit strained toward the day she might live on that far ridge, thought of it left her numb with an anxious uncertainty. Could she truly allow a man to get that close again? Would Jared even be given the chance? As yet, no letter had arrived. If he was wrong and Keturah demanded he honor his commitment, Jared was the sort of man who would.

Her mouth went dry. The longer she lingered here in what might prove to be vain hope, the harder it would become to go to Savannah. And even if Keturah released him...

Micah's cry, lusty now, warbled from the cabin. Could Esther ever give Jared a child of his own? Would he come to resent her if she couldn't? She couldn't marry him without at least discussing her fear of barrenness.

She turned toward the barn, where the light of the lamp on his workbench chiseled light around the window and door. Jared had only been home from Jeffersonton for two days, and they'd scarcely been alone since. She longed for those intimate moments but feared them too.

Tabitha would be sitting in the rocker to feed Micah, Noble casting adoring glances their way from his chair. She should not intrude on their solitude. They had precious little of it. The couple was patient with Esther and Jared's continued presence, but doubtless, they looked forward to their departure. Tabitha was forever bringing up *when this* and *when that* moments they would share after Esther's wedding, and she pressed Esther to add goods to her hope chest with such fervor one would think she prepared for her own nuptials.

Yesterday, Esther had found the courage to ask Tabitha if the probability that Keturah was no longer coming saddened her. Tabitha had admitted the prospect had given her cause for melancholy at first, but now she had Esther and Mrs. Holloway, and wouldn't she make more friends at the log rolling? And if they could start attending the new Baptist church? All these were friendships that could be deepened through the coming year. Her connection to Keturah had been forged in girlhood, a tie that would probably linger sweeter in memory than if they attempted to take it up again now.

Perhaps Jared was working on something that she could help him with. Esther moved the bucket to the edge of the porch and made her way to the barn. She knocked before pushing the door open.

Across his workspace that was scattered with furniture projects in various stages of completion, Jared dropped something into his tool chest and slammed the lid shut.

Esther cocked her head as she entered, closing the door behind her. "Did you just hide something from me?"

He propped a foot on top of the wooden box and offered his lopsided grin. "What would make you think so?"

She stifled a smile. "Besides your haste to stow it away? The fact that you never put your feet—or anything else—atop your grandfather's chest."

"Oh." He lowered his moccasin to the floor. He preferred the native style of footwear to boots when he was around the house or workshop. He cracked the chest's lid and nonchalantly searched until he came up with a small bit. "I suppose I am delaying the start of this chair."

"Understandable, when you put in a full day planting corn already."

"We finished Noble's acreage. After the log rolling, we start on mine...ours." Jared rose, watching her with a restlessness that made her second guess her decision to visit him here alone.

She approached the bench, where a thick square of wood had been clamped onto one corner with wooden braces. The faint indention of a seat had been etched on top. She gasped. "The Windsor? You are attempting it?"

"Pray, don't sound so confident." With a wry chuckle, he came up behind her, laying a square, a compass, and the bit he'd selected on the table.

"Oh, I have every confidence in you." She ran her finger along the curves of the seat outline.

"It is only the continuous arm design. Even so, the Windsor

is the bane of every woodworker. Especially in these primitive conditions."

Esther shook her head. "I marvel at the lines, angles, and measurements. I don't know how such math and vision can come from one person's head." She turned to offer an admiring smile, but he stood closer than she'd anticipated. The corners of his mouth lifted, and his gaze swept over her face. "All that you do amazes me. You're a scout, a tracker, a farmer, a woodworker. Is there anything you aren't?"

Jared's fingers cupped her jaw. "A husband." The breath of his soft admission stirred her hair...and her heart. "All this preparation for the future, and yet the future is not settled."

Which was why they should not stand thus. Esther drew back, but the bench only gave her a few inches. "Truly, any woman would be pleased enough with a ladder-back chair." Or had he realized Keturah would not be?

He grunted. "How long at a time have you sat in Noble's?"

Moving away, Esther gave a light laugh. "Then we'd best beware, or Tabitha will snag your new chair before you have a chance to carry it to your cabin."

Duchess's bark from inside the cabin drew them both to the door of the barn. Two figures approached from the main trail, one tall and broad-shouldered, the other petite. Esther's breath hitched. "Can it be?"

"White Owl returns?"

"With Ahyoka." She took a step, her feet light, but Jared drew her back.

She turned back to find a frown on his face. "Wait. We will go together."

"But it is Ahyoka! It is perfectly safe."

"Is it?" Jared's eyes sparked. "I will be eager to hear a good reason why White Owl tried to take you from your husband. Does he also seek to take you from me?"

"What?" Esther breathed out the incredulous word. "You

can't still think so. He called me *sister*, as I told you." The word he'd spoken before leaving the Howells' cabin, *I-gi-do,* had settled her own uncertainties on that score. "Ahyoka asked him to watch out for me."

"But why was he so willing?" Jared ducked back inside the barn for the lamp before stepping out and securing the door. He offered her his free arm, but Esther frowned.

"And you say I should believe a man would want me."

"Well, yes, but not *him*. The distance he traveled, the lurking in the woods—"

Esther didn't wait to hear more. White Owl's promise to visit had intrigued her and remained forefront in her mind, but she'd feared that if circumstances allowed him to return at all, it might be many weeks. She hurried ahead as the door of the cabin opened. When Duchess witnessed Esther calling a joyful welcome to the two guests, her barks faded to friendly yelps, and Noble and Tabitha joined them with cries of greeting.

Esther embraced Ahyoka around the blanket that circled her shoulders, then smiled up at White Owl. "You came. Thank you for bringing her."

He nodded, his stoic bearing forbidding any display of affection. But as always, his eyes glowed like coals when he looked at her. What a mystery that the brave's silent affinity for her made Jared more uncomfortable than it did her.

Once the guests were invited into the cabin, Tabitha insisted on serving them while Esther sat beside Ahyoka. As their hostess brought leftover stew to the Cherokees and tea to Esther and Jared, White Owl ignored Jared's frowning stare. The two looked as though they balanced a child's seesaw, so far apart did they sit on their bench. Esther might have found it amusing had she not been so eager to learn why this brave had taken up his mother's concern for her.

While Tabitha and Jared settled before the fire, Ahyoka related in her broken English that White Owl had fetched her from the village and taken her by the post to trade. She reached for Esther's hand. "Then Oukonunaka say, time come for *du-yu-go-dv*."

"For truth. Yes." Esther squeezed the healer's fingers. "When I last saw you, you said you would explain why you stopped coming to Father's trading post. Why you had to stay away."

Ahyoka nodded, one braid settling in front of her shoulder. "I know your father before you are born. His wife die...very sad." She traced the track of an imaginary tear down her own cheek.

"Yes, he was too sad to care for me. He sent me away for a time."

"Still sad." Ahyoka shook her head emphatically. "I tell him, bring you back."

"You did?" Esther's lips remained parted. "And he listened to you. Why?" Her gaze strayed to Jared. Until Liam, her father had been the most stubborn man she knew, unlikely to take any council, certainly that of a woman...and a Cherokee woman, at that.

Ahyoka sighed, her lashes creating dark crescents against her high cheekbones. So lovely. Looking at her, Esther's heart clenched, and she sat up straight. She guessed what Ahyoka was going to say before she spoke. "Long ago, I think he marry me."

Tabitha's rocker stopped rocking. Noble's pipe stopped puffing. And Esther could only sit in frozen silence.

Ahyoka spread her hands. "But he no want Cherokee wife. I return to village. Not tell him he has a son."

Esther twisted the folds of her skirt between her fingers. The room narrowed down to Ahyoka's face, her honest brown eyes. Her lips speaking long-held secrets. "A son?"

"Raised Cherokee, to be my son. Not his." Ahyoka's mouth

firmed, and her eyes fired with conviction. Her gaze shifted to White Owl. "Oukonunaka. Your brother."

The truth of it shone from White Owl's eyes.

Esther buried her face in her shaking hands. "All this time, I thought I was alone. I had no one."

Jared's forearm thumped on the table, and Esther sensed him shifting to reevaluate the man next to him.

Ahyoka ignored him, stroking Esther's back and hastening to finish her explanation. "Oukonunaka did not know. I only tell him when you marry bad man. He vow to watch, to take you away." When Esther raised her face, she traced a semicircle between her own collarbones. "I give him..."

Esther blinked back tears. "Necklace?"

"*V-v*, neck-lace. To show you he good."

"The necklace was the reason I trusted you when you warned us of danger, although I always felt you were good." Well, almost always. Despite her words, Esther could hardly bear to look at White Owl, to imagine the sacrifice and thankless protection he'd offered when she'd been completely unaware—had even feared him at first. She searched his face for signs of their father. Thankfully, except for skin that was slightly lighter than his mother's, none could be found.

She turned to Ahyoka, reaching for her hand again. She craved the consolation of a reassuring touch. "I don't blame you for keeping him from Father. He would have ruined him. Instead, look at what a fine man you raised. A man as fine as..." Her eyes strayed to Jared, watching her with tenderness and joy. "As fine as the other man who has taken care of me."

Ahyoka nodded, opening her hand to include all the Lockridges in a slowly sweeping gesture. "We see...you good people."

Esther looked at White Owl. "That was why you let me stay?"

"Yes." If possible, her half brother drew himself up even more. "You will stay now?"

Jared laid his hand on the table, angling toward White Owl as he answered for her. "You should know that I love Esther. I plan to make her my wife. And I will take good care of her."

White Owl's straight dark brows made his young face fierce when they drew downward. She did some rapid figuring. He must be two or three years younger than she was—yet his stern manner made him seem older. He focused on her rather than Jared. "You agree?"

She swiped a tear from the corner of her eye. This would be the first time in her memory not one man, but two, had wanted her. Her heart felt nigh unto exploding. "I agree." And now she must pray to high heaven that Keturah would release Jared, for Esther could never leave this area. How could she? If she went to Savannah, she would never again see the half brother she'd only just met.

"It is good, then." Holding his beaded bandolier bag against his wide chest, White Owl stood abruptly.

"But you are not leaving?" Esther leapt up as well, seeking reassurance from Ahyoka. "I have many questions, and it is dark now." Clutching the edge of the table, she turned a pleading expression on White Owl. "Your mother must not travel at night."

His lips twitched, and that light flared in his eyes.

Esther flushed. Of course, Cherokee women were well-accustomed to traveling at night, and in any type of weather.

Tabitha sat forward. "Indeed, you should stay. You would be most welcome." She rose from the rocker. "I am so happy for Esther to learn she has a near relation. You must take some time to get to know each other."

White Owl hesitated. Finally, he nodded.

Ahyoka tipped her head toward the door. "We stay with animals."

"No." Jared rose, extending his hand to White Owl. "I will. You will take my place by the hearth." His firm handshake, followed by a warm glance Esther's way, illustrated his immediate acceptance of her half-Cherokee brother as a new member of the family.

Her heart swelled. How was it possible to love him even more?

CHAPTER 21

※

*E*sther couldn't sleep. She had a brother! And his deep, even breathing confirmed he dozed just below her loft. Joy sang through her, tinged with a thread of regret. How different her life might have been if her father had not been too proud, too selfish, or too grieved to marry a Cherokee woman. Esther would have grown up with not only a stepmother, but a brother as well. No doubt, Ahyoka would have softened Thomas Venable. The four of them—and maybe other siblings—would have shared a home near Hog Mountain, and her father's death would not have forced her to marry Liam. She might have met Jared when she was yet an innocent maiden. He might have courted her properly...before he promised himself to Keturah.

And that brought her to the fear lingering in the back of her mind as she tossed on her cot.

In their murmured conversation by the fire after the others had gone to bed—filled with animated gestures and details that had been withheld in front of the Lockridges—Ahyoka and White Owl had told her she always had a place with them if need be. Such generosity stunned her. She could meet Ahyoka's other children, White Owl's brothers and sisters, born to her through her Cherokee husband. Even though White Owl would doubtless take a bride soon, Ahyoka enjoyed a respected position as a medicine woman in her clan. Esther could live with her as a daughter, continuing to learn from her, and take up her mantle when she was old.

The village they described was not unlike white settlements, complete with a square, a council house, and log cabins with garden plots. While the notion of abiding among Cherokee warriors made her blood chill, the fact that she would not be expected to choose one as a husband left open the door of possibility. And of course, White Owl would be there to see that everyone treated her well. Her brother would continue to protect and provide for his sister and mother even after he married.

In the morning, Ahyoka and White Owl would leave, and she wouldn't see them again until well after her future with Jared was decided. If she was to go with them, now was the time. But how could she make such a decision? She couldn't predict how Keturah would respond to Jared's offer to annul their betrothal, but another potential obstacle to Esther's union with Jared existed. A very personal fear she must discuss with him with no further delay.

She dressed and braided her hair and shimmied down the ladder when dawn's golden fingers touched the clearing. If White Owl or Ahyoka heard her, they gave no indication. She slipped past their blanket-wrapped backs and let herself quietly out the door.

The rooster crowed as Esther entered the barn. Duchess gave a low woof from somewhere near the back. "It's me," she called softly, lest Jared greet her with his rifle.

She found him sitting up on a pile of straw, wrapped in a thick woolen blanket, blinking sleepily. Duchess wagged beside him.

"What are you doing here?" Amazement gave his words a lilt. As she approached, he opened his blanket to her. "Come. Sit. You look as if you didn't sleep a wink."

"I don't suppose I did." She lowered herself beside him, and the warmth of the thick material closed around her, capturing her body heat with his. Despite that, awareness caused a shiver to course through her. "I had so much to think about. You, however..." She plucked a bit of straw from his golden locks. "You appear not to have been put off your slumber at all by a night in the barn."

His mouth curved up in a rueful grin. "Duchess is a good source of warmth, but I can't say I'm disappointed to have a more appealing one." He ducked his head against hers in a teasing gesture, eliciting a whine from Duchess but not the smile he'd likely hoped to gain from Esther. He tipped her chin toward him. "What troubles you? For I daresay you'd not tempt propriety unless there was something serious on your mind."

She licked her lips and averted her eyes. "Last night, I stayed up talking with Ahyoka and White Owl."

"I figured you might." A shadow of unease colored his tone, though he attempted to sound hearty.

"I learned much about their family and village. They say there is a place for me there." She didn't dare to look at him.

He stiffened. "You jest."

"I could serve as Ahyoka's assistant."

"Esther, I'm delighted you have a half brother, and more delighted that his close relation explains his interest in you, but surely, you don't wish to live in a Cherokee village?"

"It is near Suwanee Old Town. There are many white people there too."

He drew back to search her face. "You wouldn't consider such a thing, would you? Not after..."

She reached for his hand and held it between her own. "If you would have me, no."

"I have said I will have you." Exasperation laced his voice. "How many times must I repeat it before you believe me?"

"Even if I can't give you a son?" There. She'd said it. It had just popped out like a log from a logjam. Heat washed over her face.

He made a soft scoffing sound and tilted his head, rubbing her knuckles with his thumb. He lowered his voice. "I would be equally pleased with a lovely daughter."

"But what if she's not lovely?" Esther jerked her chin up, defiant in her self-loathing. "What if she, or he, is born with a malady like mine?"

"Is that what you are worried about?" He stroked the side of her face. "Then we will seek treatment from the best doctors in Washington or Augusta, or even Savannah if we must, and whatever the result, I will love the child as I love you. Esther, please stop this. You pain my heart."

She scooted away, tears of shame rising. "We must speak of this, Jared. Now, before it is too late."

"Too late for you to leave me?"

"Too late for you to leave *me*. And yes, for me to go with my brother, where my appearance and my barrenness will be of no consequence." Esther blinked rapidly.

"Barrenness?"

There it was, the confusion, the hollow despair in his voice. Her middle ached, and she wrapped her arms about herself.

Jared frowned. "What do you mean?"

"Did you never wonder why I had no child, Jared, though I had been married well over a year?"

"I..." He spluttered, searching the ground for an answer, shaking his head. "I suppose I never thought about it."

"Well, I did. Many times. And as little as Liam deserved a child, you do."

A quick, indrawn breath, and then Jared reached for her hand again. She tried to pull away, but he held it fast. "Did you ever think there was no child because of God's mercy to you, not God's judgment on you?"

She bit her lip, her vision blurry.

Duchess whined and rested her muzzle on Jared's knee.

He went on. "Or because where there was such enmity between you that a seed meant to be sewn in love could never grow?"

The promise of that love in his voice made her go weak from head to toe. Made flames of uncomfortable self-awareness lick her. She slumped against him, and he wrapped his arm around her. Hiding her face in her hands, she leaned against his chest. "But what if that isn't the case? What if a child never comes? I couldn't bear to have you despise me. And I couldn't bear to disappoint you so deeply. I think that would be worst of all."

A chuckle rumbled from his chest.

Her eyes flew open. "Why are you laughing?"

"Because you do love me. This is proof of it." He smoothed her hair away from her forehead. "You know what my fear was?"

"What?"

"That the wretch had damaged your heart so much that it would take too long to heal. That your shame and fear would hold you too far away for any good thing to grow between us. Oh yes. I see the way you look at me, the little sideways glances when you're uncertain of my intentions. The way you still sometimes shrink from me." He ran his hands down her temples and kissed her forehead. It was true, he continued to take great pains to make his every gesture gentle rather than demanding. "But you would rather me despise you than feel disappointed in you. That's love, Esther."

He had doubted her feelings? As difficult as she found that to believe, he must listen to her now. She shook her head. "Because of that love, I would rather you have ten children with

Keturah than none with me." Though even the mere speaking of it nearly choked her.

A groaning laugh seeped from deep within him, and he pulled her back with him to recline on the straw. "Oh, do not wish that upon me, pray."

She laid against him, stiff, blinking, uncertain of what to make of his mood. "I don't understand."

"Oh, my sweet Esther." He trailed a loose strand of her hair through his fingers. "In order for you to grasp how deeply and tenderly I care for you, what will it finally take?" Another chuckle vibrated his side. "Never mind, I know what it's going to take."

As his implied meaning sank in, hot horror washed over her, and she struggled to get up, but he pulled her back down.

"Be still. Stop fighting." His tone was teasing as he settled her against his chest. "For such a wee thing, you have so much fight in you. I daresay that explains how you've survived. But I won't hurt you, sweetheart."

She knew that. She did. She just had to convince her racing mind and clamoring body.

"Let me hold you in my arms just a minute. Please. And you listen when I tell you, once and for all, that I'd rather it be just me and you forever than a woman I don't love and a passel of hearty sons."

The way his arms locked around her would once have frightened her. But she knew he would let her break free if she wanted. Just as he would let her follow White Owl to Suwanee if she wanted. He'd said *please*. Even when frustration colored his teasing, even when he grew exasperated with her fears and questions, Jared asked, he didn't demand. She could relax in that. And relax she did.

Her body softened against his. Her breathing slowed. His heart beat steady in her ear as his hand made soothing circles between her shoulder blades. Yes. This was what she wanted.

Eventually, he might make her believe it was what she deserved.

An hour later, when Esther stepped back from her first hug from her brother—an embrace that filled her with peace and belonging that complemented rather than competed with that which she received from Jared—Jared drew her into the crook of his arm. She stood there, waving as White Owl and Ahyoka headed for the trail, calling out promises about their next meeting.

She would choose to believe Jared meant what he said—and that it would hold fast.

CHAPTER 22

The morning of the late-March log-rolling, the first family arrived just after dawn, bringing a pig to barbeque in a pit Noble had prepared in the yard. They'd kept coming after that until Esther wondered where they would park their wagons and stable their horses. The men and older boys with their tools joined Noble and Jared across the creek. Their shouts and the barking of dogs and the crash of falling trees soon filled the fresh morning air. Women lined the plank tables Jared had constructed with all types of delectable food—meat pies, fruit pies, wild game, cornbread, vegetables, and pound cake—then packed themselves into every conceivable spot in the cabin. While their children played outside, they pulled scraps of fabric out of bags they'd brought and set to work on a center-pieced quilt with an industry that amazed Esther.

She planned to keep the pitchers and cups of coffee, tea, and cider full, but Catherine Howell insisted Esther sit beside her at the quilt frame.

"Esther saved my Jimmy's leg," she told the women with a

proud glow. "I'd rely on her knowledge of herbs over a doctor's remedies any day. We're lucky to have her as a neighbor."

The oldest of the three unmarried Brandon girls—Marian?—turned to assess Esther as she hovered behind them in a state of uncertainty. "So you are staying hereabouts?" She blinked her long blond lashes over her hazel eyes. What a beauty. They all were. Her sisters sat beside her—fair-haired, unspoiled, full of enthusiasm for life, even a hard life. Being between sixteen and twenty, they were all of an age to leave maidenhood behind.

Esther smoothed the full skirt of her new olive-green gown and sought a safe answer. "That is my hope."

"Catherine is right, Esther. You must join us and not run yourself ragged. Bring the bits we saved from your dress. Those will go right in the middle." Tabitha offered Esther a wink that caused her cheeks to flame. This wasn't just any quilt. This was the quilt for Jared's bed in his new cabin.

"Why will they go in the middle?" Maddie Brandon asked as Esther went to fetch the material from her trunk in the loft. She felt curious gazes following her up the ladder.

Tabitha's answer followed too. "Esther and my brother-in-law have an understanding."

At the explosion of questions and cries and the answering whispers and murmured explanations, Esther sat on her bed and buried her face in her hands. If only she could stay here the rest of the day and not have to countenance the curious and speculative glances, the comments hidden behind hands. She'd already witnessed them. Now there would certainly be many more.

Tabitha thrived on the company of the other women, but Esther had been dreading this event ever since she first learned of it. It would have been hard enough to attend as Jared's betrothed. Naturally, people would wonder why a man like Jared would choose a penniless and uncomely widow such as herself. But an "understanding"? Those were broken all the time. It gave her no clout, no position. More counterfeit than commitment, an understanding could dissipate like the pretend play of a child.

She lifted her chin and stared at the herbs she'd strung from the rafters. *God, my position is in You. Help me to remember that. Your word says You will be my husband when I have none.*

She gathered her fabric and descended to the room below. She managed to join in stitching—seven per inch—and even the chitchat until she could excuse herself to package food and drink for the men in the field. The younger boys were eager to take a break from the thankless tasks of turning the hog on the spit and keeping the dogs from the food tables to make her delivery.

A brisk debate over whose initials to sew into the corner of the quilt met Esther as she returned inside.

"Seems to me, they should be hers." Catherine's gaze cut to where Esther stood at the door.

She lifted her hands. "Oh no. I hardly worked on the quilt compared to all of you."

Catherine joggled her fussing, teething baby on her knee. "Well, that's not the point in question, now, is it?"

The ample-chested Mrs. Brandon leaned forward and hissed out her opinion. "They're not married yet."

Cheeks hot, Esther folded her hands in front of her. "Tabitha is our hostess. She should sew her own initials."

Tabitha considered her with her lips pressed tight, then rendered her verdict. "I will merely stitch our last name, *Lockridge.*"

After nods of agreement, she set to work while the others cleaned up scraps and stray threads, then stirred stews and puddings.

Tabitha had just finished when deep voices and laughter carried up the hill.

Relief spiraled through Esther. "The men are coming! We must prepare to serve the food."

Cries of, "Hurry, hurry!" filled the cabin. The quilt was removed and the quilting square raised to be stored against the ceiling. Chairs and tables scraped the floor as they were slid back into place. Bags were stashed in Tabitha's bedroom. Women bustled to the hearth and out the door. And, with a wicked glow in her eye, Tabitha shoved the beautiful new quilt into Esther's arms.

"What do I do with this?" She made inquiry over the scratch of a fiddle from the yard. To her growing confusion, the unseen musician broke into "Granny, Does Your Dog Bite."

"It's the custom around here to wrap the man of the house in the new quilt, seat him at the head of the table, and serenade him while serving him the meal."

Esther stared at her. "Noble?"

"No, silly. Jared."

"But Noble is the head of this house." She glanced out the door. The group of men were coming closer, the fiddler dancing at the head as he drew his bow over the strings.

Tabitha rolled her eyes. "This house, yes, but this log-rolling and the cabin-raising tomorrow are for Jared. That makes you the best woman for this task."

Esther couldn't bear to be the focus of so much attention. "No!" She tried to shove the quilt back at Tabitha, but her friend raised her hands and shrugged away.

The knot of men broke up, and Jared was funneled to the front with cheers and thumps on his back. His blond locks blew loose around his face, highlighted by the sun, and his thin white linen shirt accented his muscular chest. His eyes—so blue in a face tanned by hours spent working outdoors—locked on her as she stood there, frozen. His gaze swept her head to toe. He hadn't seen her in the new dress, as she'd still been getting ready when he'd gone out to assist with the barbeque.

She'd even tied her hair in rags the night before to produce a cluster of curls down her back. A slow smile spread over his face, and whoops and hollers rose from the neighbors. Butterflies tumbled in Esther's middle. When he walked forward, there was naught to do but meet him at the steps and hold the quilt out.

He turned around for her to drape it over his shoulders. Securing the edges with his fingers, he faced her. "It's beautiful." He reached for her hand. "And so are you." Bending, he planted a light kiss on her knuckles.

Tabitha initiated a wave of clapping and cheering that did not spread to the Brandon women, who stood at the edge of the porch in their rainbow of fine cotton dresses.

Esther ducked her head. "Please come inside, and I will fetch you a plate."

He came, but not before draping the quilt around her as well, making her already warm face burn. She should be delighted. Affirmed. He was making a statement to all present that he chose her, but Esther wasn't blind to the sideways glances and raised eyebrows. If she truly loved him, should she selfishly wed a man she'd only bring down in the world? A man as talented and respected as Jared Lockridge?

~

The busyness of the dinner hour did little to relieve Esther's discomfort. The Lockridges made excellent hosts, humble and focused on others despite the advantages that came with being well-born. Everyone jockeyed for a place at the table near them or a moment aside for a personal chat. Esther, by contrast, felt like a servant. Few spoke to her as she hurried between the tables. Some outright ignored her. Worse, she stumbled right upon a little boy imitating her awkward gait, to the great amusement of his friends.

It was all she could do not to retreat to her loft when the fiddle again sang out after dinner. But the laughter of young girls preparing for the dance by weaving flowers in their hair and adding lace and ribbon to their collars filtered down from her once-semi-private retreat. With a sigh of resignation, she joined Tabitha on the porch. Perhaps once the dancing and drinking distracted everyone, she could slip away.

Momentarily freed from her maternal duties by a pack of doting grandmas, Tabitha wove her arm through Esther's. Her face glowed in the light of many torches and the bonfire now sizzling and popping in the barbeque pit.

Esther looked around. "Where is Noble?" *And Jared?* She might have asked had her tongue not tied at the notion of inquiring after him.

"Just there." Tabitha nodded to a group of men.

With an excess of laughter and back-thumping, eight of them got into a formation, the Lockridge brothers at the head.

"What are they doing?"

"Dancing."

Esther's mouth fell open. "With each other?" How little she knew of the workings of even this rustic society.

Tabitha chuckled. "The men always start the dancing with a rigadoon. Then one of them will perform all the steps that will be used this evening in the *Laedan*, or Leader. After that, the women join in."

Would Jared dance with as much skill as he did everything else? Now clad in a silk waistcoat and clean linen stock along with his shirt, trousers, and boots, he laughed and joked with those around him, posture erect but relaxed, laugh lines quick to appear. The fiddler broke into "Billy in the Low Ground," and the men called and performed exaggerated moves including the Double Shuffle, Jump Jim Crow, Cut the Pigeon Wing, and Hop Over the Moon. Sure enough, Jared moved fast, light on his feet, clapping and harassing the other men with pokes and slaps during the round and round, adding to the general spirit of hilarity.

A deep ache flowered in her chest—to be like the Brandon girls, pretty, lithe, and graceful. A likely match for such a man. And wasn't Keturah a blonde? Doubtless, Jared preferred fair young girls. She sighed. "He's quite good."

She hadn't realized she'd spoken aloud until Tabitha answered, following her gaze. "Yes, he is." She looked back at Esther, then ran a gentle hand down her back. "But dances only happen once or twice a year. Real life happens every day. And for that, I can think of no one better suited to partner him."

Esther managed a return smile. What a treasure to find a friend who so gently tended her feelings even when she would prefer to bury them.

Someone called Tabitha off the porch, and Esther stowed away a sense of loss. Jared's name from the shadows at the corner of the house alerted her that she was not the only one watching the second Lockridge brother.

"I heard he is still betrothed to Mrs. Lockridge's best friend from Augusta." The nasal voice belonged to the youngest Brandon girl. "If you ask me, it's a scandal, him carrying on the way he is with the Andrews widow."

Marian tossed her head as she faced the clearing. "I'm glad you feel that way."

"Why?"

"Because you won't interfere if I seek him out. The fiancée isn't here. And if I can't steal his notice from a crippled older woman, I'll hang up my cap this very night."

CHAPTER 23

An arrow of unworthiness pierced Esther's breast. Her breath coming short, she hurried down the steps. She grabbed two brass pitchers from the table designated for water rather than the refreshing mix of water, honey, and spice known as metheglin and headed for the spring where she had the best chance of being alone. The shadows closed their merciful cloak around her even though the music and laughter followed, unwelcome stalkers, taunting her.

Esther sat on a boulder near the springhouse. The starry white flowers of dogwoods studded the dusk of the forest, and she could barely make out the trickle of water in the moonlight. She would not cry. She would not. But neither would she remain at an event where she clearly did not belong—nor could she compete. To do so would only invite humiliation. At least she knew enough now to recognize that she did not deserve that. She raised her chin.

A stick cracked and her heart raced. She rose as a figure approached.

"Something told me I might find you here." Jared's voice allowed her to release her breath and relax her shoulders.

"There are people everywhere else." She sat back down.

"You don't like people?" His gentle teasing allowed her to be honest.

"Certain people. Others I can do without."

He gave a wry chuckle and settled beside her, lowering a canvas bag to his feet. Her curiosity stirred.

"There are some rough folks on the frontier, I grant you that, but most would give you the shirt off their back. Give them time, Esther."

Had he forgotten her raising? "It was not the rough sort that made me uncomfortable." She tucked her feet under the overhang of the rock.

"Ah. I see." He leaned over and chucked her chin. "They just don't know you yet."

She pursed her lips, then gave her petulance voice despite her resolution to remain detached. "Some would rather have me out of the way."

He reached for her hand. "Then come dance with me, and we will show them you shan't go anywhere."

"Dance?" Esther snatched her hand back, stiffening. "Why would you taunt me so? You should know such a matter is not one I would jest about when I want more than anything..." She swallowed, halting her unbidden flow of words.

He waited a minute in the silence that lay above the noise of the frolic. "What is it you wish, Esther?"

She wrapped her arms around herself. "You know what I wish. To be by your side. But that isn't realistic tonight."

"I'm not so sure about that." Jared bent and tugged at the opening of the small sack at his feet. A hopeful lilt to his voice conveyed a certain nervous enthusiasm as he continued. "I'm not sure if this will help much, mind you, but it's worth a try if you're willing. I wanted to give these to you earlier today but didn't get the chance. I just finished them last night."

"Finished what?" She attempted to make out the blurry

shape he held up on his palm. A soft gasp left her lips. "A shoe?"

"A leather boot. I picked the pair up for you at Moore's post. He knew your size from when you'd purchased moccasins."

"But Jared, boots are harder for me to get in and out of, heavier, and more tiring to my leg. And their poor fit creates blisters. That's why I always wear moccasins." Hadn't she explained that to him before?

He began loosening the laces. "But moccasins don't give you the height you need on your shorter leg. I've been altering this boot for your left foot. I removed the sole and added one of cedar, the lightest wood I could procure. I carved it so that the arch will better support your foot. Feel." Reaching for her hand, he guided her fingers inside the leather.

Sure enough, the raised platform curved up in just the place her foot would—but with the addition of some sort of cushion. "It's soft inside!"

"I added a woolen pad. It's all glued and fastened so it will stay in place. And feel it." He passed the shoe to her, and she weighed it in her hand. "It's light, isn't it?"

"Much lighter than I would expect any boot to be." She stared at him with her lips parted. "I can't believe you did all this for me."

"I can't believe no one has done so before."

It took everything in her not to kiss him.

"Will you try it on?"

Esther nodded, reaching down to slip off her moccasin beneath her skirt. "But please don't be disappointed if it doesn't work. My foot will still turn inward, and it is swollen from being on it so much today. I'm not sure I can get it into the boot. It may do better tomorrow."

"But tonight is when I want to dance with you." Jared eyed her as she struggled to position the boot and hold open the top. "Will you allow me to assist you?"

She froze. He would touch her twisted foot, her shriveled leg? "Why would you wish to do that?" The question stumbled over her thickened tongue.

Rather than answering, he rose and gestured to a rock closer to the spring. "You said your foot was swollen. Come, bathe it a moment in the cool water."

While his back was turned, Esther removed her other moccasin and her cotton stockings. Balling them in her grip, she took the hand Jared extended to her. Carrying the new boots, he helped her across the rocks to the spot he indicated. Slowly, she lowered herself. Drawing her skirt aside, she edged her toes toward the silver trickle. Very well she knew a lady did not raise her skirt before a gentleman. She could ask him to turn away, but she didn't, even though the darkness would not hide all she might wish for it to. Maybe some perverse part of her thought this could serve as a test.

Maybe she just wanted to trust him.

He knelt beside her, tucking her dress under her knee—and reached for her left foot. Before touching it, he glanced up. "May I?"

Fingers twisting in her skirt, stomach twisting in a knot, Esther nodded.

He ran his fingers ever so gently over toes, arch, and heel. Her roughened skin tingled at his touch. Her breath caught in her throat.

At least he gave her the consideration of not looking up at her. Or perhaps he couldn't bear to. But the tender way he lowered her foot into the water and softly splashed it up to her ankle spoke of protection, not rejection. He cupped water in his hand and allowed it to run down her thin calf and shin. She couldn't stifle a low gasp and a shiver. Tears sprang to her eyes as Jared lowered his head and massaged her foot.

Finally, angling her body to face him, he sat below her and rested her heel on his knee. "There now, that was not so bad, was it?" He reached for the boot while Esther slid her stocking back on. As if knowing she couldn't speak, he held the shoe open and helped angle her toes into the bottom. Once he had it secure, he pressed on the end of the shoe. The leather gave, indicating the location of her toes. "Seems to fit. Let's get the other one on, then I'll lace them."

As he did, Esther wiped tears from her face while he pretended not to notice. He'd glimpsed and even caressed her withered foot, and he was still here! Her heart rose into her throat, and she bent forward and tangled her fingers in his hair, breathing in the scent of him as she kissed his crown.

She whispered the front edge of a confession. "If I could only say what I feel right now..."

Jared looked up and cupped her chin. "You don't have to."

If he had tried to kiss her, she would have let him, despite her resolution to reserve any such future favors for betrothal. But the awareness that hovered between them warned the time was not right, for Esther's walls had crumbled. Her fear had vanished. Everything in her yearned to belong to this man.

He tied off her right boot, rose, and held both of her hands. Gingerly, Esther stood. For the first time, she did so without leaning to one side. A small cry escaped her lips.

"You are even, yes?" Jared dropped her hand. "Take a few steps."

She walked—not limped—toward the woods. The boots were light, like an extension of her own feet...feet that matched properly. As she had said it would, her left foot still turned to the inside, but with careful movement, she could almost conceal any unsteadiness in her gait. She turned around, hurried back to him, and threw her arms around his neck. "Thank you. I don't know how you did this, but thank you. Didn't I say you could do anything?" Pulling back, Esther pressed a kiss to his cheek.

A grin spread over his face. "I'm sure they'll take some

getting used to, and you probably ought not to wear them very long at first."

"I'm not sure I can dance in them." Esther made her tone as placating as possible, trying to alleviate any disappointment he might feel. "Most of the dances require so much hopping and leaping and passing to other partners, and I can barely comprehend that I don't have to move in the ways I always did just to walk."

He straightened and squeezed her hand. "Then I would be happy if you would simply walk with me back to the party and stand at my side."

His gracious acquiescence made Esther long to rise to the occasion. Would such an attempt end in disaster—and ruin the evening he'd just rescued? On the other hand, wouldn't her willingness demonstrate a commitment equal to Jared's gift of the shoes?

"Perhaps...perhaps I could try." Her offer, spoken just above a whisper, teased the smile back to his face.

"Only if you feel comfortable."

Jared placed her moccasins into the canvas bag and offered his arm to escort her through the darkened woods. Esther found the feel of the boot strange, the lack of need to limp far stranger, the change making itself known all the way up into her hip. But to be able to walk without the rolling dip in her stride! She only had to lift and place her inverted foot with care, but Jared had thought of even that, having created small ridges on the bottom of the shoes for solid purchase.

The tang of barbeque and wood smoke hung heavy on the air as they returned to the lighted clearing. And there, Esther's hope evaporated.

The fiddle squeaked and twanged, the dancers leapt and sashayed, and the crowd clapped and sang out the words to "Hop High, Ladies." Several people nearby heartily chanted different lyrics on top of each other. "Did you ever go to meetin', Uncle Joe, Uncle Joe?" and "Did you ever see the devil, Uncle Joe, Uncle Joe?" And then the chorus, "Hop high, my ladies, three in a row. Hop high, my ladies, the cake's all dough...don't mind the weather so the wind don't blow."

Esther started to shake her head. There was no way she could keep up such a pace.

Jared handed her the canvas bag, patted her arm, and leaned closer. "Wait here a moment. I'll see what I can do before they're all gone on the Georgia Gallop."

Even Esther had heard of the dance that continued until the strongest present collapsed in exhaustion. She stashed her moccasins under the porch and leaned against the edge, moving her feet inside her new boots—not confident enough yet to keep a rhythm, merely trying to accustom herself to them. She watched Jared weave through the crowd, approaching the fiddler's brother before she lost sight of him.

A few moments later, he returned with Noble and Tabitha, John and Catherine Howell, and an older couple Esther had met briefly earlier. Tabitha and Catherine grabbed her hands and pulled her out into the clearing as the rousing tune ended.

"Oh, Esther, look at you! So much less of a limp." Tabitha hugged her to her side and gave a little squeal. "I can't tell you how hard it's been keeping those shoes a secret."

"Thank you, but I don't know if I can do this." Esther sent the others an apologetic grimace as they formed a square, ladies on the gents' arms.

The fiddler lowered his instrument and called out with a country twang that belied his dignified enunciation, "The Spinning Wheel Cotillion."

"Jared picked a perfect dance." Tabitha clapped her hands. "Much more dignified. We'll all talk you through it." The smiles on the other ladies' faces communicated support. "We start with a walk step with just a little dip in it. You can forgo that if you wish," Tabitha added as all the groups of eight that had formed joined hands in circles and rotated clockwise.

Although her heart rested in her throat, Esther made a little joke. "That should be the easy part for me." Then she concentrated on weaving her way around the circle in various styles of promenade. By the time she returned to Jared, she was giddy that she'd remained upright.

As they promenaded again, he kept his arms firm, crossed over hers, giving her confidence. "You are doing amazingly, my love."

My love. Esther raised her chin. The faces of those they glided past looked on, not with the thinly veiled contempt she was so accustomed to but with approval. For the first time, she didn't stand out. The realization filled her with delight. But not as much delight as every touch of Jared's hand, every sparkle of his eye. He looked at her as though she belonged next to him.

"Now a series of turns." Holding her hand, he extended his arm for her to step out. "And balancé." Esther took a tiny, quick step to one side and back. "Good, now under." He twirled her beneath his arm, taking his time, bracing her waist with his other hand with a touch so brief others might not see. After another balancé, he drew her so close for the next turn that she breathed in the crisp scent of his soap. Bliss-struck, she closed her eyes just a moment—and stumbled right into a firm chest.

Not Jared's.

Her mouth rounding, Esther looked up at a glaring, ruddy-faced gentleman in a top hat. She wobbled, and he caught her —only to cast her away so roughly Jared had to steady her from behind.

In a booming voice loud enough for everyone present to hear, he demanded, "So this is the clumsy hussy for whom you jilted my niece!"

CHAPTER 24

Jared's shock left him momentarily speechless. Eli Thompson faced him with the stature of an enraged bull. Motion in their set wound to a halt as attention turned their way.

"Mr. Thompson." Coming to his senses, Jared drew Esther to his side. "I'd thank you not to insult this lady." He couldn't rightly say *my intended*, now, could he?

Esther stared up at him with questions in her eyes.

"Lady?" Keturah's uncle inflated his chest. "I don't know what type of lady would insert herself between a gentleman and his betrothed. And yet, there she stands at your side, bold as brass. I can see what manner of bewitchment caused my niece to flee."

"Flee?" Jared's brows drew down.

"She came here to see you, and no wonder she was undone by what she discovered. Did you not have the integrity to tell her to her face that you'd thrown her over?" The buttons on Thompson's waistcoat strained, and spittle flew through the air. "You had to write her a letter?" He withdrew a smudged and dog-eared envelope from his pocket, shaking it at them.

Esther clutched his sleeve and whispered, "What is he talking about, Jared?"

"I don't know." His mind spun. "Sir, Keturah was never here. The long silence from her was what caused me to write. From what I learned from others, I believed her heart had already turned elsewhere—as mine had."

Thompson took a step closer, his voice a growl. "She came here. She and her whole family. The innkeeper told me they stayed a night last fall."

Jared released a hard breath and shook his head. "I never saw her."

As Thompson's brows shot up, the fiddler concluded the final refrain. Guests milled about in the clearing, murmuring, watching the scene.

Noble put a hand on his arm. "Take your conversation somewhere private. We'll clear the barn of human ears."

Thompson gave a grim nod. But he eyed Esther and said with sour distaste, "Including hers."

She shrank back, her cheeks red.

Jared took her hand and leaned close to her. "Pray, give me a few minutes to come to the bottom of this. I will be with you shortly."

She faded into the shadows as Tabitha's arms came about her, guiding her toward the house. His heart seared with pain for her. She had been through so much. Now this? For though he knew not what he faced, Keturah's uncle had revealed enough to show it would not be good. He followed Noble and Thompson to the barn, where Noble cleared out a knot of adolescent boys smoking a pipe in the goats' stall. Once he'd declared the building clear, he stood just outside with a promise to turn away any who might attempt to enter.

Jared took a seat and gestured to a rush-bottom chair he'd just completed for his new cabin. The one he was supposed to start constructing tomorrow. The seat creaked as Thompson lowered his substantial frame onto it, then leaned forward with his hands on his knees and expectation in his eyes.

"Do you mean to tell me you never saw Keturah nor any member of her family last fall?"

"On my honor..." Perhaps not the best choice of words. At Thompson's incredulous gape, Jared finished simply with, "I did not."

"You received no notice that she planned to come?"

"No sir. What does this mean? Why was she coming? Where is she?"

"That last is the question which has rendered me sleepless ever since I came into possession of the letter from you, addressed to Keturah, asking release from your engagement. I embraced my sister in farewell along with her husband and two daughters in early November. It would seem that Keturah couldn't rest until she saw the place where she would live as your bride. Frank thought bringing her here would settle her mind. When they did not return, I figured they had decided to remain until the wedding and perhaps a missive telling me so had gotten lost, as happens often enough."

What was Frank saying? That they'd come and never returned? Had something tragic occurred?

"Frank always had a mind for business," Thompson said. "He had spoken of several potential endeavors that might prove lucrative in a growing frontier settlement, including your cabinetry shop."

Jared raised his eyebrows. "He thought of investing in my shop before the wedding?"

Thompson shifted. "He would do anything to see his daughter well met."

"So you were expecting a letter, one inviting you to the wedding, not the one I sent." Jared rubbed his chin, struggling to fit the puzzle pieces together. His ire at Thompson's boorish manner evaporated as the reasons behind the man's desperation clarified. He was terrified for his family, his most beloved niece. Having no children of his own, he had treated her like a daughter.

"Just so."

"You said the innkeeper told you they arrived in Hog Mountain, though they stayed—"

"Only one night."

"Where else would they have gone?"

Thompson rose and paced, removing his top hat and twirling it in his hands. "I have no idea. If they were not with you, they should have returned straight home. After learning what I did at the inn, I came here straightaway, believing you could shed light on their disappearance. To make matters worse..."

"Yes?" Jared rose, a lump in his throat. Clearly, what Keturah's uncle would reveal next would be the sort of thing best met standing up. Outside, the fiddler sawed out a hot tune. They'd gone into the Georgia Gallop.

So had his heart.

"An old-timer came in for his whiskey whilst I was talking with Mr. Foote. He overheard my inquiry and volunteered information he thought could be pertinent." Thompson sighed and ran his hand over his bewhiskered chin.

"What was it?"

"He said that during the winter, before the trees could obscure the view, he'd come upon a carriage abandoned on a high hill a few miles below the settlement."

Jared's chin snapped up, horror at this implication bottling into a question he couldn't voice.

Thompson held out his hand. "He said he saw no bodies. Nothing to indicate a struggle."

"Did he say anything else about where this was?"

"Overlooking a meadow owned by a man named Williams. I was hoping you'd know where that is."

"I do." Jared walked a few steps toward the animal stalls. Chickens fluttered overhead, probably more upset by the rumpus outside than his pacing. "It's not far from here, just a little southwest."

Thompson's brows tucked together. "Which implies, they must have been headed this way when they met with some disaster."

How close he must have come to reuniting with Keturah—right about the same time, possibly even before—he'd met Esther. How differently things might stand now.

His stomach clenched as another idea hit him. Keturah had never gotten his letter. Long before he sent it, she had come seeking him. He turned back to her uncle. "You said she had doubts?"

Thompson drew himself up. "I did not say she had doubts. I said she couldn't rest."

"Then you said—"

"My niece is an honorable woman, the woman to whom you are engaged. Now, are you going to be an honorable man and help me find her, or not?"

Thompson's glare speared him to a target of accountability. If the man knew the full reason behind Keturah's trip here, he would not divulge it. To press him further would only anger him, and his desperation made him volatile. "I will do all I can to help you investigate the disappearance of Keturah and her family. We will locate this abandoned carriage—if it exists—at first light." He refrained from pointing out that a bumpkin in his cups might not prove the best source of reliable information. "But if it is as the man indicated, it makes no sense. That's not close to the river, the boundary between us and Indian Territory."

"Meaning?"

"Not a likely place for an abduction."

A COUNTERFEIT BETROTHAL

Thompson's shoulders sagged, and he released a gusty breath. "I admit, that has been my first fear."

As well it should be. A shiver passed through Jared, picturing painted braves wrapping the wrists of Keturah, her fourteen-year-old sister, and their delicate and proper mother with ropes. How terrified they would have been. Their blond beauty was just the sort to capture the notice of disgruntled Creeks looking to replace wives, daughters, and sisters. But sheltered females like the Caldwell women were not the sort to survive captivity.

Jared drew a shaky breath. Best to keep these thoughts to himself until they were proved true—or at least likely.

"Let us hope there will be no carriage, or it will be the wrong carriage. You can stay here tonight." Though Jared hardly knew where. What would he do about the cabin raising? All the men camping out here tonight were sacrificing their time and offering their skill for *him*. But he owed the higher duty to this man. "You put yourself to considerable danger, making your way here from the settlement after nightfall. I'm amazed you found us, being unfamiliar with the territory."

"The innkeeper gave good directions, and you will find I'm a very determined man, Jared Lockridge." Thompson's piercing stare hinted that he possessed little tolerance for those who did not match his tenacious qualities. "Though I am not of this wilderness, neither do I fear it. I settled my own farm when it was but frontier."

There was only one thing to do. "We will find her together." He extended his arm toward the door. "Come to the house for some victuals while I apprise my brother"—and the woman he loved—"of the situation."

He was not surprised to find both waiting with Tabitha just outside. Their anxious expressions revealed that the music, clapping, and hollering had conspired to drown out any eaves-

221

dropped information they might have attempted to snatch. At his request, Tabitha took Mr. Thompson to the house while Jared drew Esther and Noble into the shadows behind the barn. There he endeavored to relate all that Keturah's uncle had shared with him as briefly as possible, along with their plans for the morrow.

"That is the proper next step." Noble braced Jared's arm with his strong hand. "We must not borrow trouble, for as the Good Book says, there is enough trouble sufficient unto today. And pray, don't worry about the cabin raising. I will oversee it in your stead."

Jared's stomach twisted, but there was no cause to point out that Jared was particular about its construction and would do things a certain way if he were on site himself. Noble would do a sufficient job. "I thank you. But what will we tell the men?" He glanced at Esther, shivering in her pretty green dress, her thin arms wrapped around herself. "The last thing we need to invite is further scrutiny."

"I will tell them you were called away by a family emergency. They will accept that."

They might not question the half truth, but there would be talk. He couldn't even spare Esther from that much. Jared rested his hand on her shoulder, his heart squeezing. "I am sorry."

She shook her head. "You have nothing to apologize for. Of course, you must go with Keturah's uncle to find this carriage." The set of her mouth said that they wouldn't speak of what might be required of him beyond that.

Concern for the Caldwells and Keturah battled with his frustration at how little control he had over his own plans. Then guilt sickened him. How could he even consider overseeing his cabin raising when the woman with whom he'd originally planned to share that cabin had disappeared—was even now perhaps suffering and in need of his help?

Once again, it seemed fate intervened to keep him and Esther apart. Or was it God?

No matter how his heart, spirit, and body strained toward the woman who stood before him, he was not yet released from his engagement. Indeed, this strange turn of events roped him even more firmly into a twisted sort of commitment.

⁓

The mist of morning had not yet cleared by the time they came upon the abandoned carriage, situated just as the old-timer had described on a hill overlooking Williams's verdant green meadow. The gentle camouflage of budding trees and a thick stand of mountain laurel made it hard to picture any violence could have occurred here. Birds tweeted overhead, and a soft breeze teased the thick carpet of last autumn's leaves—leaves that had long ago concealed any tracks.

Jared's stomach shrank at the unnatural sight. Another week, and the carriage would be well hidden from the nearest trail. Someone had indeed parked it here, one door listing slightly open, with the hope it would not be found for a long time.

Eli Thompson offered up a mournful cry. "It is their carriage! It is their carriage!" Tears flooded his eyes and streamed down his roughened cheeks.

Jared extended a hand in his direction, though he, too, felt the tug of deep emotion. "Let us be certain." Securing Chestnut to a tree, he approached with caution. Before each step, he scanned the ground ahead, making sure he did not trample any potential evidence.

Thompson displayed no reserve. Leaving his horse unattended, he stomped through the woods and bent to survey an emblem beside the door. "It is the Augusta maker's mark."

Voice laden with grief, he jerked the door open and thrust his head inside. "Nothing. There is nothing." He climbed all the way in and conducted a search of every cushion and compartment.

Jared rubbed his temple. "Indians might riffle through the baggage and steal the horses, but they would not be slowed by taking every possession. They travel light. They would not have the means handy to transport trunks."

Thompson raised a ravaged face to him. "Then what? Who?"

Jared shook his head. "Law has long been lacking in these parts. Perhaps someone took note of wealthy travelers at the inn and followed them when they left."

"Well, that would explain a robbery, but where are they?"

Heaviness crouched on Jared's chest. The old timer had seen no bodies, but how well had he looked? "You stay here. Continue to search for clues while I make a pass through the surrounding area."

Thompson took his meaning right away, judging by the renewed stream of tears from his eyes. He passed his sleeve over his face as Jared moved away.

Jared found a forked stick nearby and used it to disturb the leaves around the vehicle. The ground was rutted leading back toward the trail. He expanded his circle, poking at any depressions in the ground cover and into thickets, keeping his eye trained for mounded earth.

Search complete, he returned to Thompson, who stood outside the carriage. "Indeed, there is nothing."

Thompson's deep breath raised his ample chest. "Well, that is something. But what should we do now?"

A metallic glint just behind Thompson caught the morning sun as it peeked through the trees. "What is that?" Jared lunged for the object that lay half buried between two small rocks. Brushing off the mud, he lifted the flat disk for inspection.

Thompson's mouth rounded. "A pewter button."

"And see how it's been scraped on this side, as though against that rock?" Jared ran his finger over the roughened spot.

Thompson nodded. "Almost as if it were ground under a heel."

Jared completed his thought. "As if in a struggle, perhaps." A lot to surmise from a scraped button, to be sure. But it was their sole clue. Only with some guesswork might they bridge between ignorance and action. "Could this belong to your brother-in-law?"

"I cannot say for certain, although I do seem to recall that he favored brass over pewter. He always preferred a bit of dash."

Jared finished cleaning the button on his own waistcoat before handing it to Keturah's uncle. "If this is not his, it could suggest the involvement of white outlaws."

"How would outlaws have made an entire family of travelers vanish without a trace?" Thompson turned wide eyes on him.

Jared couldn't bring himself to voice the obvious answer, the one that led them back in a grim circle.

225

CHAPTER 25

Esther was ladling venison stew into wooden bowls when Thompson's bellow from the yard announced his return. "Why is there a cabin raising going on? My niece—your fiancée—is missing along with her entire family, and you proceed to build your home? For whom? That hussy in your brother's house?"

The ladle shook in her hand, and a potato dropped to the floor.

Tabitha swept in with a rag. "Pay him no mind. He is out of his head with fear."

"I don't blame him. I would be beside myself too." Clearly, Esther's presence served as a trigger. But she couldn't stop herself from following Tabitha to the door. Whatever the outcome or the discomfort to herself, she must learn the developments of the morning.

In the yard, Noble and Mr. Holloway had returned from the far ridge, joining Mr. Thompson and Jared. As they dismounted, Jimmy Holloway limped forward to take their mounts to the barn.

Noble laid a calming hand on Thompson's arm. "My brother must needs have his own place to live regardless of what transpires with his betrothed, Mr. Thompson. Wisdom dictated that we start the cabin while we had the help available. But we are here now to hear your report and assist you however we may."

"Assist *you*?" Thompson blustered. "I see how this goes. Already you separate yourselves from my family's misfortune. God forbid their disappearance inconvenience you."

Jared stepped forward. "That's not how my brother meant it." He turned to Noble and Mr. Holloway. "The carriage did indeed appear to belong to the Caldwells, but it was empty. The only clue we found on site was a pewter button, which could suggest the possible involvement of white men. However..." He faced Keturah's uncle again. "Should we find evidence that the family was indeed taken west, we will do whatever we can to find them."

Esther's stomach knotted at Jared's firm tone. He did not make guarantees lightly. If he spoke thus, honor still bound him to Keturah. As well it should. She swept her lashes down, but Tabitha's hand touched her back in a gesture of silent support.

"I can ride to the settlement this evening, put out word of what's happened," Mr. Holloway offered. "The business owners will help if they can. They know everyone in these parts, including Indians who frequently come to trade, drifters, and ne'er-do-wells."

Noble nodded. "That sounds good, Holloway."

Their neighbor continued, turning his hat in his hands as he addressed Thompson directly. "And if you pardon me, sir, the men who are here to help Jared today can be of service as well. We can question each one. Someone may have heard or seen something."

Thompson grunted. "Let us do so with the utmost haste, then."

Holloway gestured toward the creek. "They are coming for the noonday meal as we speak."

Tabitha squeezed Esther's arm. "Come, let us finish serving up the stew and Johnny cakes."

Esther followed her back inside, trying not to think about Jared. About the fact that he'd not even glanced her way.

The men gathered in the cabin and on the porch, eagerly accepting servings of food and cups of cider and coffee.

Esther scurried about, doing her best to remain invisible—and thankfully, her new boots helped with that—while seeing to their needs. Oh, but the one man she did not wish to be invisible to kept his head lowered, his brow knit, his attention on their latest guest. Was he merely distressed by the turn of events, or did Keturah's disappearance stir old feelings of protection, even love? Her stomach ached to think it.

Secondhand goods, the old voice whispered. *A twisted counterfeit of a real woman.*

One man who lived near Hog Mountain had heard of a gang of robbers active the year prior, but the county had been quiet since. This neighbor suspected the troublemakers had moved on. Esther's hopes that the men present might produce a solid lead withered as Thompson's frustration grew.

"We will still inquire in the settlement," Noble reminded him.

"And if that leads to naught? What then?"

Jared answered, voice resigned. "Then we will have to consider the possibility that they were taken over the border."

Anxiety twisted in Esther's chest and almost stole her voice, but she forced herself to step forward. "If I may ..." She clutched the brass pitcher in front of her like a shield, as though it might protect her from the fiery darts of Mr. Thompson's eyes.

The man scoffed. "I cannot imagine *you* would have anything helpful to add."

Esther lifted her chin. She was not secondhand goods. She was a child of the King, fearfully and wonderfully made.

Jared waved Esther to his side. "Let her speak. Esther does not waste her words." She stood near his knee, placing the pitcher on the table in front of him.

"I have a half brother who lives near Suwanee Old Town." She twisted her fingers in her skirt. "He ranges far and wide, hunting and scouting for his people. He knows many others who do so as well, not only Cherokees, but white men and friendly Creeks."

"A half-Cherokee brother. Of course!" Thompson harrumphed.

Jared's brows drew down. "Would you take help where you can find it, or not?"

Thompson surveyed her, and Esther's face heated. He waved his beefy hand her way. "Go on."

She swallowed. "White Owl might be able to obtain information. If Creek Indians were seen with three women and a man this previous fall, there is a good chance he could find it out."

Jared reached for her hand and squeezed it, his eyes communicating his gratitude. "Thank you, Esther." He spoke quietly even though Thompson made a sound of disgust and came to his feet. Jared looked back at Keturah's uncle. "That is our next step, sir. Barring information from Holloway that points elsewhere, I myself will ride to Suwanee Old Town."

~

*J*ared left the next day. And the next, while mourning doves cooed the break of day, Esther walked toward Hog Mountain.

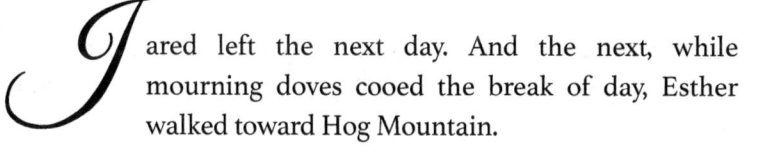

"Please stay," Tabitha had pled with her. "Stay until Jared returns and tells us what he has learned. This is something you should talk to him about first."

But she couldn't bear another day of Eli Thompson's withering glances. The man clearly felt entitled to stay with the Lockridges rather than taking a room at the inn, though he rode out daily with Noble and Mr. Howell to make inquiries about the Caldwells. And no one would dream of asking him to stay elsewhere. The enmity radiating from his presence brought back all Esther's old, queasy feelings of self-loathing. Worse were the times the man sat by the fire with his face buried in his handkerchief. His grief and anxiety were so real, so intense, that Esther could not in good conscience add to them.

Even if White Owl reported no evidence of the Caldwell party's abduction, his word was not absolute. Keturah's uncle would only be satisfied with definitive proof of what had happened to his family. How long would that take? How many miles must be ridden and people questioned and danger invited before the truth emerged? Would it ever come? Would Jared ever feel released from his obligations to his first betrothal?

Esther simply couldn't stand to remain in the middle of it. For her own health, she craved time and space to think and pray. This she explained to Tabitha with a promise to remain in the area.

Esther shifted the valise that contained her few belongings. She still had the money Noble had given her over a month ago for transportation east. She would take a room for now, and hopefully, she could find employment to sustain herself while she waited.

She entered the outskirts of the settlement with a stride made straighter by practice walking in her new boots. She drew far fewer stares than normal, a fact which gave her confidence. The most notable change in Hog Mountain was the absence of militia. Word had reached them of a great victory by General Andrew Jackson at the Battle of Horseshoe Bend in Creek Territory. All that was left was to round up the scattered foe and negotiate a peace treaty.

Scraping her boots on the cleaner at the foot of the inn steps, Esther avoided the stares of several ill-kempt men smoking on the porch. She made her way past them as unease slithered down her spine. What must they think of her, a woman arriving unescorted and on foot at a public house of lodging? Doubtless, the worst. She said a quick prayer for a position that might legitimize her presence in Hog Mountain and offer a bit of security.

Inside, she waited for two men to order their grog at the walk-up window. Then she peeked around the counter at the tall, skinny man polishing glasses. "Mr. Foote?"

"The same. Who's inquirin'?" He paused to swipe a lank strand of graying hair from his forehead.

"My name is Esther…Venable."

He pointed a skinny finger at her. "Ah, you's the widow who's been stayin' with the Lockridges. But wasn't your last name Andrews?" He speared her with a suspicious frown.

The business owners truly did know everything that went on in this part of the county. Rather than answer directly, Esther inclined her head. "I have need of a room for a while, if you have one. And I was hoping you might also have some employment."

"Talk to the wife." He hooked a thumb toward the back door. "She's in the yard doin' laundry. The inn be her business. The tavern, mine."

Despite the man's backward manner, what a forward-thinking way to approach a partnership. If only her father had been of the same mind. "Thank you." Esther hurried down the hall, her heart thumping as she passed the entrance to the noisy tavern with its malodorous smells and boisterous voices. It didn't slow down when she caught sight of the buxom woman scrubbing a pillowcase on a board, her face drawn into a pucker so fierce she looked as if she'd just sucked a persimmon. Wending her way past sheets that had been hung up to dry, Esther approached with timid steps. "Mrs. Foote?"

"What?" The woman's barked reply softened into surprise as she looked up. "Oh, I recognize you. You's the one who came around looking for work last fall."

"That was me." Esther dropped a little curtsy. "Esther Venable. I've been staying with the Lockridges but am uncertain how long I'm to remain in the area. I have coin for a room, if you can accommodate me."

She gave a curt nod. "That I can. You still willing to work?"

Esther's heart leapt. *Is this Your provision, Lord?* "I am eager to work, in fact. Do you have a position available?"

The woman lumbered to her feet. "Indeed I do. The one right here on this stool. My Sally, our older daughter, has taken to her bed with spring chills. Didn't I tell her to drink her sassafras tea so's she'd be fortified for the change of weather? But no, she can't abide the taste, she says. Now she's left me with her job and mine as well."

"I'm sorry to hear that."

"Well. Betsy's too young to have the strength in her spindly arms to scrub out the stains—tobacco and worse things we shan't speak of, as you can see." She held up the pillowcase as proof. Esther suppressed a shudder, and Mrs. Foote ran a harsh gaze over her. "Are *you* strong enough? You don't look it."

No matter how distasteful and exhausting she might find the laundry of strange men, she was hardly in a position to be particular. Esther infused confidence into her tone as she answered. "Yes, ma'am. I assure you, your linens will be white as snow."

"That's a big order to live up to." The matron quirked a brow. "We'll see how you do today. If your work is satisfactory, you may take the attic room at no charge plus a small rate of compensation to be our laundress and complete other sundry tasks." She raised her index finger. "But only until Sally regains her feet."

"That sounds quite acceptable." Esther set her bag on the ground and herself on the stool. Rolling up her sleeves and taking up a chunk of lye soap, she bent to her task.

Mrs. Foote stood over her a moment, then with a harrumph, returned indoors.

Esther let out a little sigh and surveyed the boiling wash pot, the rinse pot, the pile of fat knots, and especially, the heap of dirty linens. She would be here all day. But what had she expected? To be handed a feather duster and kindly requested to pass it over the parlor furniture?

As hard as she had worked for the Lockridges, she'd gotten soft over the winter. The men and even Tabitha after her childbed had never shirked their duties or shuffled the hardest tasks to her. There would be no such favors here. But she would take this as God's provision, her one last hope for a future with Jared. Esther scrubbed the abrasive soap over the material until suds formed and ran it over the washboard until the stain disappeared.

By the time Mrs. Foote returned to inspect her work, Esther's fingers cracked and bled, her back and gimpy leg ached, and her empty stomach growled, but all the linens were spotless and hung to dry. The matron passed around each one. Esther half expected her to whip out a magnifying glass, so intent was her examination. But finally, she said, "Very good. Follow me."

Grabbing up her bag, Esther trailed the innkeeper's wife

with a renewed limp, despite her boots. She had to use the sticky handrail winding up the narrow, creaky stairway to help support herself. At the end of the hall, Mrs. Foote showed her to a small room without a fireplace. A spindly chair and battered trunk sat beside a lumpy, narrow cot covered in a faded quilt. But the matron opened a tiny shuttered window that looked out on the main thoroughfare below and allowed in fresh air and a shaft of golden twilight.

Mrs. Foote turned back to her, wiping her hands on her apron. "Report to the kitchen at first light. I will have your supper sent up tonight."

Food. Rest. Privacy. Relief made Esther's knees weak, and she sank onto the crunchy mattress. "Thank you, ma'am."

Mrs. Foote cocked her head. "You want to tell me why you're really here?"

Esther's lips parted as the desire for a confidant warred with the need to avoid wagging tongues and judgment. Not so much on herself, but on the Lockridges. Perhaps Mrs. Foote might offer up some information that her husband hadn't. But more likely, she was just being nosy. Her brusque manner made any real compassion unlikely. "I just need some time to determine my next step in life."

"I see. Well, it's glad I am that our arrangement serves both of us. You're to let me know if you need anything, now." The glance the matron sent over her shoulder, coupled with her unexpected invitation, almost prompted Esther to call her back.

Instead, once the door closed, she fell onto the bed with a giant exhale. In a minute, she would locate the salve she used for blistered hands in her medicine box. For now, she allowed an odd contentment to sweep over her.

For the first time in her life, she was reliant on no one but herself and the Good Lord—the wisest partnership to be had. Her months with the Lockridges had prepared her well for independence. But oh, the possibility of forfeiting Jared's love raked her insides as mercilessly as she'd raked those linens over the washboard. If she didn't marry Jared, she knew one thing for sure. She never would wed again.

Please, God, if there is any way, if there is any answer to be found that will release him, will You send it?

CHAPTER 26

The heaviness that had settled on Jared ever since he'd received White Owl's news only grew as he approached home. That news would hurt Eli Thompson, and the sobering conclusion he'd drawn about his own future involvement in the search for Keturah would hurt Esther. It might even unchain the vault of lies she'd long believed about herself. But he'd wrestled these many hours and miles with duty, desire, and conscience. And he finally had reached an unhappy peace about what God expected of him.

Duchess's bark greeted him well before he rode into the clearing. The mastiff loped around Chestnut as Noble, Tabitha, and Thompson spilled out onto the porch. Where was Esther?

Thompson wasted no time on greetings. "Have you news?"

"I do." Jared dismounted and led his horse closer to the house. He waited for a slight form to appear in the doorway, but none did.

Thompson waved his hand. "Well, have out with it, man. What did you learn of my sister and her family?"

"I was able to locate White Owl and Ahyoka the day of my arrival. They allowed me to lodge with them while White Owl put out requests for information. Within a couple of days, he learned from a Cherokee who traded with the Creeks that a war party was indeed seen last November, escorting three yellow-hair captives west." Jared hung his head. His own heart wrenched at having to repeat this dire news. He couldn't bear to watch the effect it would have on Thompson.

The man made a strangled sound. "Three yellow-hairs? What of my brother-in-law?"

"No mention was made of a white man. Only two women and a young girl. I'm so sorry, Thompson."

Wheezing, Keturah's uncle wobbled on his feet. Tabitha helped him to sit on the steps. He grabbed at his cravat, loosening it, while she fetched a cup of water.

Noble met Jared's eyes, and the look shared understanding. Likely, Keturah's father had resisted or attempted escape at some point, and the braves had killed him, leaving his body along some remote path. Mr. Caldwell had always been kind to Jared, believing he was of stronger stuff than his father, entrusting him to make a good life for Keturah even on the frontier. That the man had met his end in such a way, knowing the womenfolk he loved and had vowed to protect remained in the hands of the enemy, left Jared cold with horror.

He ran his hand down Chestnut's neck as the stallion snorted and flinched. "We will provision ourselves and mount a search. I was thinking maybe we could hire on Benjamin Reynolds or the Hill brothers, expert woodsmen and marksmen. But we must move fast. I heard other important news while I was at Suwanee."

Tabitha glanced up from helping Mr. Thompson with his drink. "What was that?"

"Chief Red Eagle, the Red Stick leader who started the conflict at Fort Mims, walked into Jackson's camp and surrendered. Jackson was impressed with his bravery and let him go in the hopes that he will convince any remaining warriors to surrender. It's only a matter of time until a peace treaty is signed."

"Then the American forces will be withdrawn." Thompson appeared to collect himself. Resolution hardened his features as he struggled to rise. "Yes, we must make haste while the frontier forts are still staffed with our armies."

Noble gave him a hand up. "I can help with the provisioning and finding another man to ride with you."

"We can leave tomorrow. For now, Chestnut needs some feed and rest." Jared wound the reins around his hand.

"As I daresay you do." Tabitha's brow creased as she descended the steps and came toward him.

Finally, the question he'd been suppressing made its way out, though spoken low. "Where is Esther?"

Tabitha glanced over her shoulder at her husband and Thompson talking on the porch. Placing her hand on Jared's arm, she turned him toward the barn. "She went to the settlement."

The breath left Jared's chest, and he stopped walking. "Why?" At Tabitha's pained expression, he demanded, "Did that pompous oaf harass her?"

She pressed her lips together. "He made no secret of his distaste for her, but it was more Esther's regard for the man's feelings that prompted her to leave. She knew her presence pained him further. She promised to stay in the area until this matter is resolved, but she felt it appropriate she make her own way."

"Doing what?" Jared puffed out his frustration with the question.

Tabitha patted him. "Noble checked on her. She is working and staying at the Hog Mountain House. She is safe, Jared."

He resisted the urge to shake his sister-in-law. "And you just let her go…again?"

"I tried to dissuade her, of course, but I must admit, I

respected her reasons. No woman wants to feel like so much baggage."

"Baggage? Why would she feel that way?"

Tabitha planted her hand on her hip. "Well, who wouldn't? Sitting around a man's house while he rides off seeking another woman? And that is exactly what you are going to do, is it not?"

"It is what I have to do." He fairly growled the statement. He swiped his hat off his head and ran his fingers through his hair. "Do you think I want to be in this position, Tabitha? This is the only way I can honorably acquit myself of my promise in the Caldwells' eyes...in God's eyes."

"Oh!" Tabitha huffed a little laugh. "Did God Himself tell you so?"

"In fact, He did. I spent many hours in prayer over this. And believe me, I begged Him for another way out, not just for my own selfish desires, but so I would not have to hurt Esther. As much as I dread to tell her about my going west, I must. And she deserves to hear it from me in person." Jared drew the reins together and lifted his foot into the stirrup, but Tabitha stopped him, her hand on his back.

"Wait. First, tell me...what will you do if you find Keturah?"

He turned back to her with a pained expression. "If we find any of them, they will doubtless be in shock and will need to heal in a familiar place. They should go home with Thompson."

"And you would come back to wed Esther?"

"If she would still have me, yes."

Satisfaction relaxed Tabitha's features, and she stepped back. "Then go, but you should take Noble's mount. Perhaps you can convince Esther to return here to wait for you."

Jared led Chestnut to the barn, but the question Tabitha had not asked still chased after him. How should he respond if he found Keturah and she still wanted to marry him?

239

What was she going to do? Esther had just returned from refilling all the guests' washbasins when Mrs. Foote—taking her afternoon tea and toast in the kitchen—had told her that Sally should be sufficiently recovered to resume her duties the next day.

Esther's mind was spinning.

Jared hadn't even returned from Suwanee yet. Or if he had, he hadn't bothered to tell her. Was he angry with her for coming into the settlement? How much longer would she need to stay here? If she wasn't working, her meager savings would dwindle quickly, leaving nothing for travel. She might be forced to make her way to White Owl and Ahyoka, after all.

Mrs. Foote brushed crumbs off her bosom. "Take a tray of dumplings and coffee up to Mrs. Walton in room three as you go."

"Yes, ma'am." Esther blinked tears away as she prepared the tray. Why was she crying? She was borrowing trouble, Noble would say. *Lord, help me to trust You.* Without thinking, she fortified herself with a deep sniff and attempted to infuse some dignity into her posture.

Mrs. Foote fixed a sharp eye on her. "What's this? Are you blubbering?"

"No, ma'am. At least, I'm trying not to."

"Goodness. Does this job mean that much to you?"

"Please, don't mistake me. I'm very happy that Sally is recovered. I am just not certain of my future, but I don't know how long I can afford to stay here without working."

"Well, if it helps, you may keep the attic room at the lowest rate we offer. We don't usually let it out but use it for workers."

"Thank you. That does help." Offering her employer a grateful smile, Esther added a napkin and flatware to the tray. As her nose ran, she couldn't suppress another sniffle.

She had turned to go with her dinner service when Mrs. Foote thudded her fist on the table, making her jump. "Pray, pull yourself together before showing your face to our guests."

The tray trembled in her hands. "Yes, ma'am. I will."

Mrs. Foote huffed and rolled her eyes. "No one likes a weepy female. I once came across a pretty young miss crying her eyes out in our best room because she was pledged to a man she no longer wanted to marry."

Pledged to a man she no longer wanted to marry?

Mrs. Foote continued her rant. "I'll tell you what I told her. If you're miserable, make up your mind and take action. Do what's best for yourself, even if you displease some man in the process. Weepy females only make men believe they have power they don't deserve."

Esther set the tray back on the table. Could it be? "This young woman, can you tell me more about her? When was she here?"

~

The drum of hooves and a flash of green and brown through the trees prompted Jared to draw up on his reins. The approaching rider rounded a stand of rhododendron only to saw at his mount's bridle upon sight of Jared. Both men angled their horses off the path and eyed each other. The young dandy with his Hessian boots, silk waistcoat, and new hat was a stranger to these parts—and a foolhardy one, judging from the speed at which he was taking the narrow trail.

"Afternoon." Jared nodded. "May I ask where you are bound with such haste?"

The young man tipped his hat. "To the home of Noble and Jared Lockridge."

Jared stiffened. "What business have you with them?"

The newcomer's green eyes glinted. "What business of yours is it?"

"Seeing as I am Jared Lockridge, quite a bit." Jared laid a hand to his chest.

The other man sat back in his saddle, his eyes widening. "At last, I meet my rival."

Jared frowned, growing tired of the games. He needed time to talk to Esther before he had to return before dark fell. "Rival for what?"

"For the hand of Miss Keturah Caldwell. Shaw Ethridge, at your service." The brown-haired man bowed his head while Jared's breath froze in his chest. "Or should I say, at *her* service, for it is she I seek."

CHAPTER 27

Mrs. Foote waved her hand as she answered Esther's question. "Oh, it was last fall sometime. She came with her family to visit her intended, but she hadn't gone out to see him yet. Hoity-toity, she was. After only a glimpse of our settlement and one night here, she wanted to go home. Said she wasn't cut out for life here. Called it the end of the earth. So I told her, go home, then."

Esther sank onto an empty chair, her heartbeat surging in her ears. "Do you remember her name?"

"Something fancy. Faintly pagan-sounding." The matron quirked her mouth up on one side. "Why does it matter?"

"Because I believe you might be speaking of Jared Lockridge's intended from Augusta."

Mrs. Foote nodded, a plump finger at her lips. "Yes, from Augusta."

"A man, a woman, a young girl, and this young woman? The women all blonde?" Esther waited, holding her breath.

"All blonde, yes, and lookers they were."

"Could her name have been Keturah?"

"Could have been. Say..." Mrs. Foote's eyes rounded. "Was

they the party what went missing? I heard my William mention something about a family that stayed here a night before they disappeared. The way we learned of it was that proper old gent came through a week or two ago askin' about them. But I never put the two together."

"Yes, the Caldwells. But please, think carefully." Forgetting her place in her excitement, Esther leaned forward and seized Mrs. Foote's hands. "You are quite certain she did not want to remain here and marry her intended?"

The matron made a disgruntled blowing sound. "She spoke of a fellow back home who would make a more fitting husband for her. She didn't even have the backbone to tell her fiancé here in person. She had her papa wrapped around her pinky finger. By the time they left, she had convinced him to return straight to Augusta."

"Then they weren't coming to see Jared." Whomever had assaulted the occupants of the carriage must have diverted the vehicle to another part of the county. Esther slumped against her chair, weak with amazement.

Mrs. Foote cocked her head. "And just why are you so happy about that?"

Before she could answer, a knock came on the door, and William Foote's sparse frame loomed on the threshold. "Pardon me, my sweet, but these gentlemen be here, askin' after Miss Esther." He moved aside to reveal a well-dressed young gentleman...and Jared!

Esther sprang up and threw her arms around him, eliciting a gasp from Mrs. Foote. She muttered something under her breath that started with, "Of all the..." But Esther paid no attention, her own words tumbling out. "She didn't want you, Jared! She didn't want you."

He brushed hair back from her face with his thumbs. "What are you saying?"

"Keturah. Mrs. Foote here remembered her stay. When they left, they were not going to see you, but to return to Augusta."

"Thought this place beneath her, she did," the matron interjected with a self-righteous nod.

Almost breathless in her haste to complete her explanation, Esther added, "There was a young man in Augusta she thought could give her a better life."

Her words solicited a quick, indrawn breath from the dandy still hovering in the doorway. He swept his hat off. "I knew it. She told me she loved me before she left. It was her father who did not want her to break her engagement."

Esther frowned, looking between them. On the other side of the table, Mrs. Foote had risen, her eyes popping like a frog's.

Jared stepped back and gestured to the stranger in their midst. "Ladies, may I present Mr. Shaw Ethridge of Augusta?"

Esther gasped. "Shaw? You are the one Keturah mentioned in her letter to Tabitha."

His face colored. "Your words serve as further confirmation that I should be here."

Mrs. Foote crossed her arms over her chest. "Well, I can see now why she wanted to go back to him."

Ignoring the opinionated matron, Jared took Esther's hand. "Shaw has come to lend his aid searching for Keturah."

"Her uncle wanted me to stay home," Shaw explained. "Said I shouldn't get involved, that helping him find her was Lockridge's responsibility. But I love her." His voice tightened, almost strangling his last admission, and a sheen of tears glimmered in his jewel-like eyes. "I couldn't rest until I came. And now Jared has told me that she was taken by natives, along with her family."

"Oh." Esther deflated with this news, her gaze returning to Jared. "That is what my brother told you?"

He nodded, sorrow bracketing his mouth. "Three women were seen with a party of Creek Indians last November, although, given the evidence, I tend to believe white outlaws sold them over the border. Thompson wishes to leave in the morning for Creek Territory."

"With you?" Her voice emerged barely above a whisper.

"I had decided to go, yes." He nodded grimly. "I thought that way I could discharge my commitment to the Caldwells."

Esther's hand fluttered to her chest. But he'd said *had*. Would he still leave, knowing now that Keturah had wanted to be released from their engagement?

"I have asked Jared to allow me to go in his place, ma'am." Shaw stepped forward, addressing Esther with more respect than she would have expected from such an important-looking man. "If Keturah chose me, and Jared chose you, it is only fitting that I go instead. I won't rest until I find her and do my utmost to bring her home."

Oh, sweet mercy. Esther blinked at him. "Will her uncle allow it?"

Shaw's spine stiffened, and his voice deepened with resolve. "He must."

She raised shaking hands to her face. Jared was free, but did he know it? Would he actually choose her now? She quaked to look upon him and find out.

Gently, he drew her hands down and forced her to face him. The tenderness there almost proved her undoing. "To you, I say the same thing. I will not rest until I bring you home."

~

*H*ome lay just ahead. A soft breeze rustled April's tender green leaves, reaching into every rocky nook and damp glen. A partridge hidden in a black walnut tree called his delicate *bob-white*. And the dusky peach tint of twilight washed over the white blooms of the waxy mountain laurel tucked along the stream. No doubt, many buds and sprouts off the beaten path promised fresh edibles and medicinals, but those would wait for another day. For now, Esther had eyes only for the man cradling her in his arms atop Chestnut.

Her husband. So handsome in his finest suit.

They'd been to Jeffersonton this day, only two days since the Caldwell search party rode west, too impatient to wait for a minister to come to Hog Mountain. Noble and Tabitha had supported their decision. Setting out with the dawn, they had tracked down the justice of the peace in the county seat, and after saying their vows, partaken of a meal in a fine restaurant there.

News had just arrived that in France, Napoleon had abdicated power. The county seat buzzed with speculation that Britain's long war with France might soon conclude with a peace treaty. As good as it was to picture quiet and prosperity ahead for all, Jared and Esther were focused on more personal things. They both had preferred to spend most of the day on horseback and their first night in their own cabin rather than a loud and crowded inn.

As much as Tabitha and Noble had wanted to witness their nuptials, they had elected to stay back and prepare Jared's cabin for the newlyweds. Esther's stomach tightened with a nervous excitement as it came into view, crowning the rise with its freshly hewn timber—almost an exact twin to Noble's.

"What do you think?" Jared's arm tightened about her waist, and the breath of his question stirred her hair.

"I think it's a dream." She had seen it going up from afar, of course, but she'd tried not to linger on it, not knowing if she'd ever set foot across the threshold. And she'd yet to go inside.

"It's a dream because it's ours. I'll get to work on the outbuildings as soon as possible."

She turned to study his face. "Including a workshop for your furniture, apart from the stable, just as we agreed, right?"

He smiled. "Just as we agreed." They'd begin his business

here, continuing to consign pieces to local merchants. As word spread, and once he had the space to work, he could accept commissions. "But since we don't have a stable yet…"

She tried to keep the disappointment from her voice as she finished his sentence. "We have to ride to Noble's first to drop off Chestnut."

Jared nuzzled her ear. "Much as I dislike the delay, I'm afraid we must."

A shiver passed through her. "I can't wait to see our new home." How strange, how wonderful it would seem, living there with only Jared. With only her husband to please—who wanted to please her equally.

As they rode into the yard, Duchess barked and capered, and Noble and Tabitha, the baby on her hip, hurried out.

Jared handed Esther down to Noble, then swung off Chestnut behind her.

Tabitha swept Esther into her sweet-scented embrace. "Congratulations! Now we are both Mrs. Lockridge, and you are well and truly my sister."

Tears filled Esther's eyes. "It is good of you to say so, considering what you have also lost."

Her arm around Esther, Tabitha drew back and focused briefly on the golden-orange haze on the horizon. "My heart is sick for Keturah and her family. I pray for them almost hourly, that Thompson and Ethridge will bring them back safe. But they are in God's hands. That is another story. This is yours, and today is a day for rejoicing." She squeezed Esther again, whispering in her ear. "You will find everything you need at your new home."

"Thank you. Thank you for everything." Esther hugged her, then the man at Tabitha's side. "Thank you, too, Noble."

"You're w—" He drew back from her, his eyebrows shooting up. "Pardon me, but did you just address me by my Christian name?"

She hid a smirk behind her hand. "I believe I did."

A grin of inordinate pleasure lightened his countenance. "I suppose that means I'm no longer so fearsome, after all."

"You were never fearsome. You were always kind to me. I only wished to call you *mister* as a mark of respect. But now..."

Jared stepped up and slid his arm around her waist, finishing for her with a ring of confidence. "Now she has a new head of the house to respect." He wagged a finger at her. "But you best not start calling me *mister*."

Esther poked his side. "Only when I am angry with you."

Everyone laughed at their bantering, and Noble nodded toward the ridge with a crooked grin at his brother. "I will take care of the horse. You go."

Jared reached for Esther's hand, and together, they started toward the rise. Duchess loped behind until Noble called her back.

Jared escorted Esther up the hill with an arm about her waist. "Perhaps we can breed Dutchess this year. Would you like a pup?"

Delight flooded her, and she clasped her hands under her chin. "Oh, I most certainly would. But more than anything..." She looked away, her face flaming.

"Yes?"

"More than anything, it will be my prayer to have your child."

"That will be my prayer, too, but Esther, know this..." He paused and lifted her chin. "I'm in no hurry, and neither should you be. It is more than enough that God gave me the wife my heart desired."

"And is there any sadness in that heart?" She had to know. Did she need to prepare herself to compete with a memory? To assuage any *what if*s?

The lines by Jared's eyes crinkled. "Deep sadness for the

Caldwells, yes. But I also know this is where their lives separate from mine. I have peace about that. I do."

"No regrets, then?"

"No regrets. Well, only that it is taking us so long to get up this hill." With a teasing finger to her ribs, producing a giggle, he urged Esther along the trail.

Gentle slants of light welcomed them to their clearing. A tiny trickle of smoke from the chimney signaled that Noble had already built a fire.

On the porch, Jared put his hand on her arm. "Wait there a moment." He opened the door on the spicy smell of fresh-cut pine, hurrying inside to push out the shutters and let the light in. As he held a candle to the embers in the fireplace, Esther smoothed the folds of her olive-green gown with sweaty palms and patted her hair, upswept for today. The wife of the justice of the peace had tucked flowers from her garden into Esther's coiled braid.

"Now, then." Jared appeared before her and bent to lift her into his arms.

While she no longer feared evil spirits might follow her into her new home as the tradition implied, she did run a fairly real risk of tripping, so she made no protest to his chivalrous gesture. Instead, she linked her arms around his neck. He carried her in and set her down beside the kitchen table, where Tabitha had placed a bouquet of wildflowers, a piggin of cider, and a platter of cheese and bread.

"We will go into the settlement next week to get some supplies, but what do you think?" Hands on her shoulders, he slowly turned her in a full circle.

Though the room remained sparsely furnished, a sideboard as nice as Tabitha's stood near the table. And by the fireplace... "Oh, the Windsor!"

"Try it out. Tell me how it sits." Anticipation lacing his tone, Jared followed her to it and ran his hand along the smooth top.

Esther obliged, settling onto the curved seat with a sigh of bliss. "You may never get me up to do my work."

"Fair enough." Jared chuckled. "But can I get you up to come see the bedroom?"

Her face heated again, and she leapt up to follow him into the next room. She stopped on the threshold. "Oh, Jared, you made a beautiful headboard. And the quilt from the log-rolling..." Tears filled her eyes. "Back then, even though you told me you loved me, I did not dare to assume that I would ever sleep under it." She batted her lashes. "At your side."

"And why not?" He sat down on the bed, holding his hand out to her.

She came and stood between his legs, bowing her head. "Oft as not, I thought the understanding between us a sham."

"Clearly, it was no sham."

"I still did not believe you would really choose me."

"Esther." Jared locked his fingers around her waist. "You must know that even though I felt honor bound to help search for Keturah when she went missing, I would never have stopped fighting for you. Even if I had to go west to find her, had Shaw not shown up or Thompson not accepted him for the journey, I would have seen her returned safely with her uncle, then come back to you. You do believe that, don't you?"

Rolling her bottom lip between her teeth, Esther hesitated, then gave a slow nod.

Jared drew her onto his knee. He cupped her face in his hands. "You can trust me, Esther. Today, and every day after today, I will show you that I choose you."

He'd been true to his promise not to kiss her again until they were betrothed, and he hadn't done so until the justice had pronounced them man and wife—and then only briefly. Properly.

Now, desire flamed in his eyes, and she trembled at the thought of truly kissing him...giving herself to him.

She lowered her face to his, and the slow, gentle pressure of his lips chased away the ghosts of her fears. She parted her lips beneath his and laced her fingers behind his neck to deepen the kiss. He drew back to suck in a quick breath and stare at her with wonder.

She lifted her chin. "I choose you too." Then she laughed. For she deserved the power of choice just as much as Jared did. Jared's words, along with the way he looked at her while she let down her hair, forever erased the lie that she was secondhand goods. In his eyes and God's, she was a bride of the greatest value.

EPILOGUE

Caspius gamboled around Duchess's legs, delighted as always to see his mother. Jared shook his head at the four-month-old pup as he went inside his stable to feed their own family of goats and chickens, not to mention Chestnut and the new mare he'd gifted Esther with this past summer. Pity, she'd not gotten to ride her much. Her delicate health had required her to stick close to home this past autumn, as he had done, but their efforts showed around their homestead in more than one way.

As he came back outside, he smiled at his newly finished cabinetry shop. The increased number of Christmas orders had kept him busy since the harvest and put extra coin into his purse with which to spoil his wife with gifts. And things were only looking more and more promising for the future. The newspapers reported that their government's negotiations with Great Britain should soon result in peace, and peace in this new land of bounty meant growth and prosperity.

Jared was cradling an armload of firewood when the dogs started barking, Duchess and mini-Duchess running toward the trail.

Noble and Tabitha were already inside helping prepare the Christmas feast, so hopefully, these new arrivals were the ones who would make Esther's holiday complete. Jared broke into a grin at sight of White Owl and Ahyoka. They'd sent an invitation with a friend traveling to Suwanee for the duo to come for a visit over a week ago, but there'd been no guarantee their guests would take them up on the offer.

When he drew near, White Owl grasped Jared's free arm. "*Si-yu, di-na-da-nv-tli.*" The Cherokee word for *brother* was long...and surprising. But welcome. Perhaps Esther's half brother would stay for a while this time. There was much Jared could learn from the wise warrior.

"Welcome." Jared offered Ahyoka a half hug.

She beamed up at him. "Long walk, no snow. Come to share joy of...the baby. Holy baby?"

"Baby Jesus. Yes." He laughed. Esther had written to them about the Christ child and all the special celebrations their family observed of His birth. She'd hoped her kin would find the traditions intriguing and the feasting inviting. It was her greatest desire to share her faith with her half brother and the woman she now chose to call her stepmother. As an added bonus, they had something unexpected to share as well. "We are so happy you are here. Please. Come inside, out of the cold. We have a surprise for you."

"Surprise?" Ahyoka's dark eyes lit up like two coals.

Jared gestured them toward the house and called the dogs, who came loping onto the porch as he opened the door. The tantalizing scent of roasting meat mingled with that of bayberry candles and the exotic treat of clove-pierced oranges in a porcelain bowl. Tabitha had decorated their table and mantel with waxy magnolia, holly with red berries, and spicy-scented evergreen. The scene looked much like last year's had, only this one took place in Jared's own home, and his own wife turned from slicing bread at the sideboard.

With a cry, she flung herself toward their guests. They took turns engulfing her in hugs.

"You came! You came!" She practically jumped up and down for joy. She was now so accustomed to her boots that most people barely noticed her limp when she wore them.

Jared drew her aside as Tabitha and Noble greeted their Cherokee visitors. He growled an affectionate rebuke into her ear. "You're not supposed to be up. You promised to let Tabitha prepare the meal."

With a brief, concerned glance their way, Tabitha plucked Micah from his blanket by the fireplace and presented him to Ahyoka. The chubby ten-month-old teethed on one of his blocks and chortled as she tickled his tummy.

"Oh, I haven't done much. Tabitha would hardly let me out of my chair." Esther waved a dismissive hand, her attention on the others. "Dinner is just now ready to be served." When his frown remained in place, she added, "I promise to sit and talk with White Owl and Ahyoka the rest of the evening, all right?"

"I will hold you to that." He chafed her hand with his. "You scared me, Esther."

"I know. I'm sorry. But all is well now." Her bright smile reassured him.

Still, it could have all ended so differently. Jared shuddered at the bleak and horrible picture of an alternative Christmas he could well be having alone.

Ahyoka turned back to Esther, pointing at Jared. "He tell us...a surprise?" She raised her hands in a questioning gesture, then looked around.

"Oh yes. There is a surprise." Sucking in a quick breath, Esther hastened to their bedroom. Everyone stood frozen until she returned with a blanketed bundle in her arms.

Ahyoka's mouth fell open. "Real baby? Not holy baby? This why you tell us come?"

Laughter echoed around the room as Esther came forward

and placed their first child in her stepmother's arms. "Meet Elias Lockridge, who wasn't supposed to be here yet."

"He come early?" Ahyoka's eyes flashed to Esther's for confirmation and a nod, then quickly lowered again to their tiny red-faced son. She eased her way over to the table and sat.

Esther followed, taking a place on the bench next to her. "A whole month early, just like his cousin over there. It must be a Lockridge male tradition. Jared said he and Noble were both born early as well."

Jared had no idea how much the Cherokees took her meaning, but they grunted and nodded.

Noble laughed and pumped his arm. "We lusty men are born ready for this world."

At the joke, Jared's chest swelled. They were indeed blessed beyond measure, both he and his brother.

White Owl hovered over his nephew until Ahyoka finally looked up and offered him the child. With tender care, the tall brave bent to take Elias into his arms. His angular face softened almost to a smile, but still he sought Esther's face.

"He is strong?"

She nodded and rose. "He is strong." She sensed what he sought to know. It was the same thing Jared had sought the minute Mrs. White and Tabitha had let him into the bedroom to see his new son. Esther gently turned back the blanket, revealing two perfect legs and feet.

A smile did break over White Owl's face then. He spoke in his native tongue. "I am happy for you, sister." He met Jared's eyes. "And for you, brother."

"Thank you." He held out his arms. "While he is still content, why don't I put him back in his cradle so we can eat dinner?" He still couldn't believe he had a healthy son. His chest squeezed with pure joy every time he looked at him.

"Yes, please." Esther giggled. She had joked with him that

she barely got her bodice buttoned before Elias wanted to nurse again, and her own appetite was ravenous.

Caspius trotted after Jared into the bedroom, already assuming his duty as protector of this newest member of their family. Once the infant was settled in his bed, the dog laid his wrinkled black muzzle on the edge. Jared patted the soft head but aimed Caspius's jowls away from the baby's face.

He chuckled. "We don't need your drool waking him up. Although you really must love him if you're willing to miss your meaty bone." The pup responded by licking his lips. "Don't worry. I'll bring it to you."

He found everyone seated at the table and Noble ready to serve the venison roast. Jared took his spot at the head. "Let us give thanks." When Ahyoka and White Owl kept watching him even after the others bowed their heads, he added an explanation. "We thank God, the Great Spirit, for our blessings by closing our eyes and speaking to Him."

They graciously complied.

Jared cleared his throat. "Our Father, we thank You for giving us so much more than we deserve. Family. Friends. Food. Home. You have brought us through a year of war to a year of peace. You have made our circle around this table unbroken. We honor You and welcome You here this Christmas. Amen."

After the prayer, praise over the food, small talk, and the crackling of the fire filled the room. Jared took bones with generous portions of meat still attached to both dogs. Baby Micah sat in a high chair Jared had made, fingering and slobbering over bites of soft food. Ahyoka delighted them with the news that in the spring, she would welcome a new daughter-in-law when White Owl took a bride. The girl had already begun to train with her to learn the healing arts. Esther expressed her pleasure that Ahyoka would have someone to help her and congratulated White Owl on the start of his family.

He nodded but made an unexpected, grim statement. "There is one who does not start a family."

"Who is that?" Jared frowned.

Everyone else had fallen silent, puzzling out White Owl's meaning.

He answered in Cherokee, with Esther translating. "The one who went west last spring, looking for his bride."

Ahyoka provided further clarity. "The one who call himself Shaw."

"Shaw Ethridge?" Esther gasped. "You've seen him again?"

White Owl nodded. "He came back this fall. To Suwanee Old Town."

Jared's mouth fell open. "He did not come by here."

Again Esther translated for her half brother. "He had women with him. And the old man who went with him to search. He was very eager to get home."

Tabitha gave a little cry and reached for Noble's hand.

"He found them?" His throat constricting so tight he could scarcely breathe, Jared refrained from standing up. The Caldwells had been in his prayers every day. Every missive he'd received, he'd hoped it had come from them. But they'd heard nothing. It had been the one piece of his life left unresolved. In low moments, guilt still whispered of failure.

White Owl thinned his lips. "He found them."

Esther laid her hand on his arm. "Were they with the Creeks?"

"Yes. Far into their land."

Ahyoka leaned forward. "Shaw write letter. Tell story." She inclined her head toward her son, and he reached into his tunic and drew out a paper sealed with red wax.

Jared reached across the table, palm open.

White Owl looked at him a moment before he gave it over —almost a warning look—*make sure you want to know what this says.*

A COUNTERFEIT BETROTHAL

Tabitha made a little choking sound and raised her napkin to her lips. "Please. Read it. Quickly."

He moved to the Windsor chair closer to the fire and tilted the letter toward the light. Shaw's spidery script filled the page.

Jared's heart thudded. Finally, he held answers in his hand. Strangely enough, the date was the same this year as the one he'd met Esther last year. Probably also a year removed from Keturah's abduction. Clearing his throat, he read aloud.

To Jared Lockridge.

I write to you to provide information about the abduction and current well-being of your former betrothed, Keturah Caldwell, so that you may close this chapter of your life just as I do. After crossing the Chattahoochee River, we hired a former militia scout, who escorted us to a series of frontier forts in what had been Creek Territory, mostly empty at the cessation of the war. At these, we interviewed officers about the location of enemy villages and Red Stick prisoners about white captives among their people. Though the war with the British continued elsewhere, the treaty ending this conflict with their Creek allies was signed on August the ninth. Since the Creeks lost most of their land in these parts, many will head west, or perhaps south to Florida, where it is said the remaining Red Sticks fled.

Before the treaty was signed, we were able to learn of several white women at a village on the Tallapoosa River, not far from where the Battle of Horseshoe Bend occurred. We rode there under military guard and located Mrs. Caldwell and her two daughters. Both Mrs. Caldwell and Keturah had been made wives of members of the tribe.

The page shook in Jared's hand, and he had to pause to swallow back emotion. His heart ached for the bright, spirited girl he'd known and once thought he'd loved who'd undergone so much. How changed she must be now. Was she broken, her spirit crushed? How she must regret ever coming to the frontier to seek him out.

Esther came to stand behind him and rested her hand on his shoulder.

He had to steady his voice and lift it above the sound of Tabitha's soft crying as he continued.

The younger daughter, Becky, had not yet been wed. She and her mother wept much and clung to us. Keturah, however, professes to have fallen in love with her new husband. It brought me some reassurance that he was also a white captive now known by the Indians as Wildcat for his fierce, fighting nature. However, he seems to treat Keturah with tenderness. It is my belief that his own boyhood captivity allowed him to offer Keturah comfort and advice when she first arrived in the village. She says he was her salvation. No amount of reasoning could convince her to leave him or him to leave with her. They said they will stay and farm in the manner in which they are accustomed to. Part of their reason for this may have been that Keturah was with child.

"Oh!" The exclamation slipped from Tabitha's lips, and Jared paused to glance at her. She blotted her eyes with her napkin. "So she must be happy, mustn't she? To have a husband she loved so much she would not leave, and a baby on the way?"

Jared nodded. "I believe Shaw wanted us to understand that, however unexpected it might be."

"Yes. Shaw has always known she and I were once very close. He would not want me to remain in fear for her." Tabitha folded her napkin. "It is not what we dreamed of, growing up, but sometimes happiness comes in unexpected ways." She gave Esther a meaningful glance. "So then, we must be happy for her." She tightened her lips to still their trembling. "Go on."

Jared continued.

Once we ascertained that Keturah was determined to stay, though it grieved our hearts terribly, we left her behind and set out for home with Mrs. Caldwell and Becky. Along the way, they have begun to share their story. They say that shortly after leaving Hog Mountain, they were set upon by white outlaws, just as you surmised, Jared. Their carriage was diverted. Their goods were stolen, and they were bound and taken across the border, where they were sold to a Red Stick war party. This was the most terrifying part of their ordeal, and when Mr. Caldwell resisted, he was killed.

By the by, with their help, we were able to locate his remains on our trip home so that we can return him to Augusta for a proper burial.

Blinded by grief for their husband and father, the women had been driven with all speed deep into enemy territory until they lost all hope of returning to civilization. Only when they heard that Jackson's forces approached this spring did they begin to think of possible rescue.

It will take a long time for Mrs. Caldwell and Becky to regain who they were. I should say, they will never be the same, but with God's mercy, stronger. Mr. Thompson and I are determined to provide them with the safe, secure, and familiar environment where this can happen. They are to stay at his home and sell their own so that they will retain a reliable income. I believe Becky may make a full recovery. I will call on her often. She relies on me in such a way that it gives me hope for a different future than the one I left Augusta expecting.

Yours truly, Shaw Ethridge

As Jared folded the letter, silence descended except for Baby Micah's babble, Duchess's bone-licking, and the fire's crackling.

Finally, Esther squeezed his shoulder. "Are you all right, my dear? That was a lot to take in."

He tried to piece together the fragments of information and

strange pictures the letter had created in his mind. "Yes. I'm just...absorbing it all."

Esther nodded. "It sounds as if Shaw got resolution...and so did you."

Tabitha drew in a breath. "I hope he does have a future with Becky Caldwell. I can't imagine how he felt, actually finding Ketruah, but her not only wed to another, but expecting his child. To have gone so far for her, the poor man must really have loved her."

"Indeed. He deserves happiness at the end of this." Jared rose and placed the letter behind the clock on the mantel, then he came to stand behind Esther, resting his hands on her shoulders. "As we have all found. We pray God's plan for each of the Caldwells may be worked out just as it was for us. Thank you, White Owl, for bringing this important information to us. We can now move forward unencumbered with questions and doubts." He nodded at Esther's half brother, who returned the gesture with his usual solemnity.

Esther's hand slipped back to cover his, and as she looked up at him with love in her eyes, a load lifted from Jared's shoulders.

Noble cleared his throat. "Shall we finish our meal?"

Jared took his seat again, and talk flowed around the table, this time about plans for the future. Elias fussed from the bedroom, and with a shy smile, Esther excused herself to go nurse him. She returned half an hour later to lower the babe onto Jared's lap and help Tabitha clean up.

Finally, they all gathered around the fire. Esther took Elias back into her arms as Noble unwrapped the family Bible that he'd brought from his cabin. With a smile, he handed it to Jared. "You are the head of this household, so tonight, you can read."

"Thank you, brother." Jared smoothed the pages as Noble lit his pipe. In the front of the precious book, Esther's name was now written, along with Micah's and Elias's. How many more children's names would fill the page—would fill their cabins and the land they now hoped to buy across the river? His chest swelled, and he looked at Esther. "Will you help me translate as we go?"

"Of course." Her face glowed as she smiled at Ahyoka and White Owl. "This is the story of the baby Jesus I wanted you to hear—the story of the first Christmas that changed the world. Just like last Christmas changed my life."

White Owl frowned and, crossing his arms, sat back against the table. "Because this story brought you much good, we will hear it, my sister."

His heart full, after glancing around at those gathered, Jared began to read. In a single Christmas, they'd come so far. From war to peace. From mistrust to harmony. From separation to the heart of family. A family with a legacy hacked from this frontier that could thrive for many generations.

Did you enjoy this book? We hope so!
Would you take a quick minute to leave a review where you purchased the book?
It doesn't have to be long. Just a sentence or two telling what you liked about the story!

Receive a FREE ebook and get updates when new Wild Heart books release: https://wildheartbooks.org/newsletter

Don't miss the next book in The Scouts of the Georgia Frontier Series!

A Courageous Betrothal

Chapter 1

January 1, 1779

Scarcely after midnight, Jenny had just settled into a slumber as decent as the cold loft allowed when a pounding on the cabin door made her sit bolt upright. Beside her, Hester levered to a similar right angle. On the floor beneath them, from the one-legged bed, their mother gasped, "Asa, get the gun!"

Gabriel scrambled down the ladder, and their parents scuffled around below, loading the musket and igniting a stick of fatwood in the banked embers of the hearth. Hester's small-boned, chilly hand slid over to tangle with Jenny's. "Well, it cannot be Indians," Hester whispered. "Else they would have already tomahawked the door down."

"No, but perchance someone fleeing them."

They counted their June escape a miracle. Settlers puzzled over the strange markings that appeared on the "fork tree" at the Whites' the morning after the incident, conjecturing that Jenny's bravery had earned the Indians' protection. To her chagrin, she had become something of a local legend. That fall, word came that Creek Indians destroyed two county forts, McNabb's and Nail's. Now people scurried for the safety of Fort White's walls at the slightest provocation.

"Who goes there?" their father's voice boomed.

The cheer of the reply belied the scolding words. "Yer fellow hatchet man, freezin' his rear off. Will ye not admit me and me friends from this cold?"

"It cannot be!"

The musket's stock thumped softly on the floorboards installed only a month ago. They both lunged for the edge of the loft as their father slid up the bolt. In the low light of the burning brand, he offered a back-thumping embrace to a large, tall form, while several other shapes stood silhouetted in the moonlight behind.

"Happy Hogmanay!" the newcomer exclaimed.

"Whist, man, where did you come from? You cannot have been lurking about the wilderness for the sole purpose of crossing my threshold first on your silly Scottish holiday!"

"From Fort Martin, and the wilds beyond." The tall man swept his arm behind him. "But I do admit to using the moonlight to my advantage to claim 'first foot.'"

"Do you bring good luck or bad?" Father questioned as he took a step back inside, but Jenny could hear the grin in his voice.

"A mixture, I warrant. On such a dire mission, I lack the traditional gifts, but I do have a packet of salt on my horse." He drew out a silver flask that winked in the pale light. "And this, in hopes you will share your hearth."

Jenny's mother shuffled about said aperture, removing the curfew from the coals and spreading them with her poker, while Gabriel lingered nearby in the awkward waiting stance of youth.

"Dire?" Father's voice lowered, dropping the teasing edge. He waved the men in. "Come in, Caylan, and all your friends. Welcome. Tell us your mission and how we can help."

Hester pinched Jenny's arm, demanding her attention. "He called him *Caylan*. Jenny, I think he be the McIntosh."

"The McIntosh?" In the noise of the travelers divesting themselves of guns and accoutrements and settling onto benches around the smooth-drawn boards Gabriel brought from the wall and laid over the trestles, Jenny fumbled for her wool over-petticoat. "Even if he is the Caylan McIntosh Father speaks so highly of, he would hardly be '*the* McIntosh.' I durst say that honor would be due to his grandfather or great uncle or one of the other older and more important heads of that clan near Savannah."

"What are you doing?"

"Getting dressed. They are bound to be hungry." She grabbed her apron from its peg and tied the laces.

Hester's exasperated look said Jenny always demanded to be in the middle of any action. Jenny did not wait for her scolding but pushed aside the bearskin that separated her brother's corner of the loft from theirs and wiggled down the ladder. She landed with a thud just as Father introduced his friend to Gabriel, causing the man's head to swivel in her direction.

His look of surprise was nothing new to Jenny. She towered over most men, intimidating and alarming them with her bright-red hair and sturdy frame, but not this one. No, this one was over six feet himself, and the look he gave her…could it be admiration? At the notion, embarrassment licked its way from her toes to her scalp, making her cheeks heat.

Father gave a sigh. "This is my eldest, Jenny." As the buckskin-clad arrival reached for her hand and gave a slight bow, he added, "Meet Caylan McIntosh, Jenny, the crazy Scot I told you about."

In the firelight Mother had managed to resurrect, Caylan's hair, clubbed with twine, glowed like the rich mahogany of a wealthy merchant's sideboard Jenny admired once in Augusta. When he spoke, his voice was teasing. "And what, pray, did he tell you of me?"

He still held her hand. She pulled back. "He said that you led the charge at the Battle of Alligator Bridge and broke your horse's leg trying to leap the last ditch separating you from the British regulars."

267

The light left those amber-tinged brown eyes. "Dinna think that was my choosing, lass. He was a good horse. When I realized the ditch was purposely dug too wide, 'twas too late. I have never wished to make mince-feet of anyone so bad as I did those red-coated macaronis that day."

Father shook his head. "And yet Clark called the retreat."

"He had little choice." Caylan lifted one of his thick shoulders. "They had us hemmed in, and Clark himself was wounded."

"I was never so glad as to get my husband back from that campaign." With a clatter, Mother replaced the poker in its holder and brushed off her hands, turning toward them with her eyes glinting. "And I hope he never has to repair to the tangled swamps of Florida again."

"Well, ma'am, 'tis not to Florida I would take him, but Savannah."

"Savannah?" she asked. "Why?"

"The city has fallen."

A feminine gasp from the loft caused Caylan to look upward. A dark shape moved out of the light, and he continued.

"General Howe, uncertain where the British would land once their ships were sighted, spread out his troops. When a slave led part of the landing party through the swamp to flank him, he lost eighty-three killed and eleven wounded."

"Oh no," Mother murmured. She knew what this meant, that she would lose her husband again, prematurely, before spring even greened the trees.

Distress written on his gently lined features, Father turned to Jenny. "You should go back upstairs to bed."

"I came down to help Mother," Jenny protested, moving to her mother's side. Besides, nothing could prevent her from hearing the rest of Caylan's news now. They would have to drag her back up the ladder, and she doubted any of them were strong enough to do so, save Caylan himself. While her father

SNEAK PEEK: A COURAGEOUS BETROTHAL

was built sturdy, the three-month stints of militia service over the last few years had left him worn, shadowed.

"Oh, ma'am, we's not expectin' victuals at this hour," one of the men protested.

His burlier companion elbowed him. "Speak for yerself. I ain't et since we left Cherokee Corner."

"My Elizabeth will see that all are satisfied." Their father shot their mother a warm glance.

She nodded, then whispered to Jenny as she nudged her toward the sideboard. "We can heat yesterday's cornmeal mush." Under her mobcap and silvering corkscrew curls, her eyes told Jenny both of her gratefulness for her daughter's assistance and her concern over what the family themselves would now have to break their fast.

Jenny sought the butter bowl as Mother placed her short-legged iron spider over the heat.

The men settled around the table. "Is Clark at Woburn now?" her father asked.

He referred to their neighbor's plantation, now fortified and known as Clark's Station, about eight miles east on Red Lick Creek, another fork of Long Creek. After recovering from his Florida campaign wound at Sunbury, south of Savannah, Clark had returned to the care of his wife, Hannah. But the lieutenant colonel had likely already mobilized in the face of this new aggression.

Caylan confirmed it. "Clark's regiment musters across the river at Fort Charlotte. He sent me and several other scouts into the backcountry to gather new recruits and those on leave. You have met the Morris brothers here from across the Oconee. Philip Dunst of Scull Shoals is stabling the horses. He'll be in in a few minutes. Others will come. I thought to stay until dawn to set out for Clark Station, then on to South Carolina."

"By all means," Father agreed. "And the enemy?"

Jenny listened intently to the men's now-low voices as she

269

fried the mush over the fire. Though she knew better than to give any man a second glance, Caylan McIntosh commanded the room. Scout or no, he clearly hailed from warrior stock.

"The Georgia banks of the Savannah River are controlled by a Loyalist force under Colonel Daniel McGirth. We expect Campbell in Savannah to be reinforced and make Augusta his next conquest. The lobsters think to find their own recruits in these parts, to turn the war against us."

Father's arm thumped on the table. "So we take the fight to them."

"Aye. Can we count on ye, Asa White?"

"You know I am always there for Clark. And even his Sawny neighbor on the Broad."

Surprised to hear her normally straight-laced parent—since her youth in North Carolina a convert to the New Light Baptist persuasion—use a slang term for a Scotsman, Jenny glanced up as her father sat back from the table with a wink and a half smirk. Somehow, this McIntosh brought out his youthful, mischievous side. The same, however, could not be said of her mother. No one but Jenny saw the grimace that twisted her dainty features at her husband's military commitment. It vanished by the time the stout, short German, Dunst, entered, seated himself at the table, and accepted his hostess's offer of cider.

He swiveled around to acknowledge her. "Thank you, ma'am. I am plumb chapt."

Mother offered a stiff smile as she reached for the wooden trenchers on the shelf. After slicing a portion of salted fish onto each, she came to kneel by Jenny. "Almost ready, daughter?"

Wrapping the iron spider's handle with a rag, Jenny moved it forward. "Yes."

Mother passed her the plates as Jenny served with a spatula.

Gabriel's voice came, pitched almost as low as his elders'. "Father, I wish to go with you."

Mother's head jerked around, and Jenny steadied the plate she held out.

"Nae, son, you are too young," Father replied.

"How old are ye, boy?" Caylan studied him with narrowed eyes.

Gabriel raised his chin, as yet untouched by any hint of a beard. "Fourteen."

Caylan gave a slow nod. "There are some in the regiment of that age."

Mother stood and scowled. "Not my son. Who would protect us at Fort White?"

Gabriel's gaze turned their way as Jenny rose from the hearth and brushed off her skirts. "Jenny."

At the guffaw that issued from one of the Morris brothers, telltale color heated her cheeks again. Gabriel did not help by continuing, "You all know she shoots better than I do, can hoe a straighter row, and even knows how to tan hides. She is no stranger to hard work—"

Father's command cut off his son's sentence. "Gabriel, that will be enough."

"Mayhap we ought to enlist the sister, Lieutenant," the older, taller Morris observed, leaning a shoulder into Caylan's.

Father continued as if he had not spoken, his gaze on Gabriel. "I could not do my duty knowing I left my womenfolk alone in the wilderness. You will remain and man this fort house."

Her brother hung his head and released a quiet breath of frustration.

"Many civilians are fleeing to safety in the Carolinas," the German told them.

Jenny put her hands on her hips and spoke without hesitation. "We shan't flee."

When her father nodded, she moved toward the table with two plates. As she slid them onto the board, Caylan's hand shot out, his strong, warm fingers curling around her arm. She darted a look at his face, her heart skittering to her stockinged toes as their gazes tangled. "Lass. Something tells me you must be *Wahatchee*."

"*What?*" Jenny had not forgotten the word the warrior in the forest had bellowed across the creek. She had just never thought to hear it again.

"The carved letters on the trunk of the tree that stands at the river's fork. They spell '*Wahatchee.*' And there is also a sign instructing travelers to pass by the land in peace."

She placed a hand over her galloping heart. "There is?"

Caylan nodded. Jenny felt the others watching. She could not look away from the Scotsman.

"What does *Wahatchee* mean?"

A slow grin creased the corners of his mouth. "War Woman."

AUTHOR'S NOTE AND ACKNOWLEDGEMENTS

The idea for *A Counterfeit Betrothal* struck with the discovery that a War of 1812 fort existed near where I grew up. Fort Daniel sat at the westernmost tip of white settlement—then Jackson County, now Gwinnett. For some of you who live in areas rich with history stretching back to the 1700s and beyond, the fort's date might not seem like anything noteworthy. But most of my home state of Georgia was still frontier—and the land of the Cherokee and Creek Indians—in the early 1800s. Land grants and bounty lands following the American Revolution, some illegal, had just begun to open up what is now mid- and western Georgia.

My 2021 novel, *Bent Tree Bride*, follows the Red Stick War in Creek Indian Territory, modern-day Alabama. Stirred up by the Shawnee leader, Tecumseh, and his brother, The Prophet, the Red Stick Creeks allied with the British during the War of 1812. The Cherokee Regiment fought alongside General Andrew Jackson's troops to help quell the insurgence. As I learned of the existence of Fort Daniel, attended a living history there (*thank you* to the living historians, Fort Daniel Foundation expert James D'Angelo, and author Mark Warren with his valuable resource, *Secrets of the Forest*), and began receiving the county's archeological newsletter, it quickly became clear that the stockade was constructed and utilized during exactly the same timeframe as my *Bent Tree Bride* story occurred. I thought how neat would it be to set a parallel tale between fall of 1813 and spring of 1814 on the Georgia frontier, right here in my own backyard?

On October 4, 1813, Indian Agent Benjamin Hawkins wrote to General John Floyd, commander of the Georgia militia, of a reliable report he'd received that the Red Sticks planned to sweep east and north, harassing the frontier all the way up to the new settlement of Hog Mountain. Governor David Mitchell wrote to Major General Allen Daniel that he did not believe the Indians would cross the Chattahoochee River but that spies or scouts should be used rather than a military detachment to keep an eye on the frontier without inciting the enemy. A divisional order from General Daniel on October 21, 1813, instructed the rebuilding of "the fort which is poorly constructed of dry timbers" at Hog Mountain, indicating an earlier structure must have existed on or near the site. Some theorize the original fort was built around 1805. A number of militia units and scouts were recorded as having served at Fort Daniel, but I chose to have Jared Lockridge be a local citizen who volunteered before troops were brought in from outside the settlement. Benjamin Reynolds was just such an actual local scout identified as working out of the fort (though I made a guess on his age), just as the men named as supplying meal and meat to the militia and helping build Atlanta's now-famous Peachtree Road actually did so.

An attack by Creek Indians indeed occurred on the frontier as noted in the story, south of the Jackson Line and Clark (now Clarke) County in Morgan County. On November 6, 1813, a party of warriors entered Georgia at the High Shoals on the Apalachee River and attacked settlers in the area of what is now

AUTHOR'S NOTE AND ACKNOWLEDGEMENTS

Hard Labor Creek State Park, estimated to have killed nine. The parallel attack on the Snow settlement was fictional, a plot point that would bring the action closer to Jackson County. Given the Morgan County attack and the fact that the reminisces of Thomas Woodward of Alabama state that the entire year of 1813 was fraught with white women in western Georgia being taken hostage by the Creeks, this seemed entirely plausible. My Snow family was also fictional, although a Snow's Mill did exist in this general area.

The Hog Mountain trading posts and hotel and the individuals who populated them were fictionalized but inspired by historical fact. The real Hog Mountain House was constructed by Shadrack Bogan around 1815, although a document from a notable citizen references an "old" Hog Mountain House. Therefore, I took a liberty for my story of having the Footes construct a new hotel in 1813. There was indeed a trading post run by the firm of former Connecticut residents Moore and Maltbie, which began operating several years before Bogan came to open his inn and another store. Moore died on a purchasing trip to New York in 1814, after which his young partner, William Maltbie, came to Hog Mountain to take over the business and married the thirteen-year-old daughter of Elisha Winn (whose fine house is mentioned early in the story). Winn became a Jackson County and then a Gwinnett County justice of inferior court, state senator, and state representative. Therefore, I depict an older Mr. Moore doing business in 1813, though it was hard to find much detail on these early citizens—including Moore's first name. Records before the Civil War are sparse at best, especially for this part of Jackson County, which became Gwinnett in 1818. The story about Indians cutting a hole in the storeroom of a frontier trading post and taking back their furs was another one I came across in my research.

Readers may wonder about the seat of Jackson County being identified as Jeffersonton in this time period. According

275

to a website of the Jackson County government, Jefferson, as the town is known today, was incorporated in 1806, but settlers called the town Jeffersonville from 1805-1810 and Jeffersonton from 1810-1824. Interestingly enough, one of my first jobs in high school was working for the probate judge at the Jackson County courthouse in Jefferson ... where I got to bury myself in the vault to answer research requests. Apparently, my penchant for searching out obscure historical details continues to this day.

Local legends have also always captured my attention. One of an abandoned carriage insisted on appearing in *A Counterfeit Betrothal*. *The History of Gwinnett County, Georgia, 1818-1960* by J. C. Flanigan tells of a family who stayed one night at the Hog Mountain House, then disappeared and were never found even after relatives arrived to search for them. Years later, their abandoned carriage was discovered on a distant hill. Chilling, right? I couldn't resist weaving that bit of lore into Keturah's misfortune. I knew readers would want to know what had become of her, so I provided some conjectured answers in the epilogue.

If *Bent Tree Bride* is more a story of the actual Red Stick War, *A Counterfeit Betrothal* is a story of frontier life, capturing not just man vs. man struggles but also the man vs. nature situations the early settlers faced. *The Early History of Jackson County, Georgia*, first published in 1914, was—even allowing for caution due to its folklore style—a treasure trove of information. The flocks of pigeons so massive that they darkened the sky and broke branches when they roosted to eat chestnuts and acorns, a canebrake in the county from which panthers prowled in cold weather, and the necessity of burning pine knots in the yard of a winter's night were all taken from descriptions of local frontier life. Even the existence of the Wog was recorded as early as 1809 near Jug Tavern, present-day Winder. I found that especially fascinating, as I grew up still hearing stories of the Wog in 1970s and 1980s Jackson County.

AUTHOR'S NOTE AND ACKNOWLEDGEMENTS

And the hair-raising panther attack? Such an encounter occurred almost exactly as I described to a Missouri woman left alone with her newborn in 1835. According to naturalist and botanist William Bartram, settlers in the Southern states during this period called the panthers *tygers*. He described them as much larger than a dog, yellowish-brown or clay-colored, with a long tail. I can't imagine the fortitude daily survival required for these settlers pitted so closely against nature.

I sincerely hope you have enjoyed journeying with me through these amazing times and that the story of a downtrodden woman who came into her own through the love of Christ and a good man warmed your heart and reaffirmed your worth as a child of God. As a merciful and loving Father, He is waiting to redeem life's pain and to make beauty from our ashes.

Special thanks to Misty Beller and her amazing staff at Wild Heart Books for bringing this story and series to my readers. Much appreciation to my skilled and perceptive editor, Robin Patchen. And to my ever-so-helpful beta readers, Gretchen Elm, Adrian Harris, and Johnnie Steinberg.

If you enjoyed *A Counterfeit Betrothal*, your reviews let publishers know my stories are worth continuing to publish. I notice and treasure each one.

ABOUT THE AUTHOR

North Georgia native Denise Weimer has authored over a dozen traditionally published novels and a number of novellas —historical and contemporary romance, romantic suspense, and time slip. As a freelance editor and Acquisitions & Editorial Liaison for Wild Heart Books, she's helped other authors reach their publishing dreams. A wife and mother of two daughters, Denise always pauses for coffee, chocolate, and old houses.

You can visit Denise at https://www.deniseweimerbooks.com, and connect with her on social media.

Monthly e-mail list: http://eepurl.com/dFfSfn
https://www.facebook.com/denise.weimer1
https://twitter.com/denise_weimer
https://www.bookbub.com/profile/denise-weimer

WANT MORE?

If you love historical romance, check out the other Wild Heart books!

Marisol ~ Spanish Rose by Elva Cobb Martin

Escaping to the New World is her only option...Rescuing her will wrap the chains of the Inquisition around his neck.

Marisol Valentin flees Spain after murdering the nobleman who molested her. She ends up for sale on the indentured servants' block at Charles Town harbor—dirty, angry, and with child. Her hopes are shattered, but she must find a refuge for herself and the child she carries. Can this new land offer her the grace, love, and security she craves? Or must she escape again to her only living relative in Cartagena?

Captain Ethan Becket, once a Charles Town minister, now sails the seas as a privateer, grieving his deceased wife. But when he takes captive a ship full of indentured servants, he's intrigued by the woman whose manners seem much more refined than the average Spanish serving girl. Perfect to become governess for his young son. But when he sets out on a quest to find his captured sister, said to be in Cartagena, little does he expect his new Spanish governess to stow away on his ship with her six-month-old son. Yet her offer of help to free his sister is too tempting to pass up. And her beauty, both inside and out, is too attractive for his heart to protect itself against—until he learns she is a wanted murderess.

As their paths intertwine on a journey filled with danger, intrigue, and romance, only love and the grace of God can overcome the past and ignite a new beginning for Marisol and Ethan.

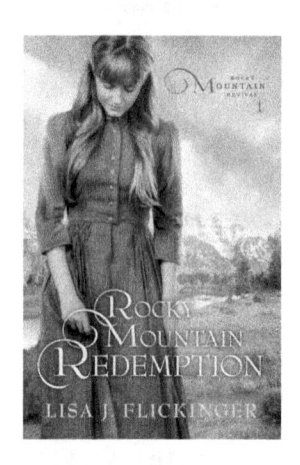

Rocky Mountain Redemption by Lisa J. Flickinger

A Rocky Mountain logging camp may be just the place to find herself.

To escape the devastation caused by the breaking of her wedding engagement, Isabelle Franklin joins her aunt in the Rocky Mountains to feed a camp of lumberjacks cutting on the slopes of Cougar Ridge. If only she could out run the lingering nightmares.

Charles Bailey, camp foreman and Stony Creek's itinerant pastor, develops a reputation to match his new nickname — Preach. However, an inner battle ensues when the details of his rough history threaten to overcome the beliefs of his young faith.

Amid the hazards of camp life, the unlikely friendship growing between the two surprises Isabelle. She's drawn to Preach's brute strength and gentle nature as he leads the ragtag crew toiling for Pollitt's Lumber. But when the ghosts from her past return to haunt her, the choices she will make change the course of her life forever—and that of the man she's come to love.

~

Lone Star Ranger by Renae Brumbaugh Green

Elizabeth Covington will get her man.

And she has just a week to prove her brother isn't the murderer Texas Ranger Rett Smith accuses him of being. She'll show the good-looking lawman he's wrong, even if it means setting out on a risky race across Texas to catch the real killer.

Rett doesn't want to convict an innocent man. But he can't let the Boston beauty sway his senses to set a guilty man free. When Elizabeth follows him on a dangerous trek, the Ranger vows to keep her safe. But who will protect him from the woman whose conviction and courage leave him doubting everything—even his heart?